GHOSTS of MANHATTAN

GEORGE MANN

TITAN BOOKS

GHOSTS OF MANHATTAN

Print edition ISBN: 9781783294084
E-book edition ISBN: 9781783294138

Published by Titan Books
A division of Titan Publishing Group Ltd.
144 Southwark Street, London SE1 0UP

First Titan edition September 2014

1 3 5 7 9 10 8 6 4 2

What did you think of this book? We love to hear from our readers. Please
email us at: readerfeedback@titanemail.com, or write to us at the above
address.

To receive advance information, news, competitions, and exclusive offers
online, please sign up for the Titan newsletter on our website:
WWW.TITANBOOKS.COM

To Lou Anders, for boundless passion,
enthusiasm, and friendship.

PROLOGUE

He had watched cities rise and fall, had seen civilizations crumble. He had led armies across the wastes of old empires and sat in state as the world steadily reshaped itself around him. He had lived entire lives while those around him withered and died. He had been forgotten and reinvented, had been present at the founding of nations. He had held the darkest magick and the brightest technology in the palm of his hand, and stood shoulder to shoulder with kings and paupers alike.

Now, he had come to the New World, to the glittering city where even the very buildings reached for the sky, cathedrals raised in the worship of profit. It lay before him like a shining jewel, fresh for the taking. New York City. The thriving metropolis, the symbol of a new age.

The people, these "Americans," thought themselves immortal, the future theirs for the taking. They'd survived the Great War, and they knew themselves to be unstoppable.

He, of course, knew better. They were nothing but a fledgling race, fresh upon the planet—upstarts who had yet to trip and fall. He had watched from afar as they'd grown in confidence, and now he had come to teach them the true meaning of power.

A new epoch was dawning. This was the time of the Roman.

ONE

DOWNTOWN MANHATTAN, NOVEMBER 1927

Something stirred in the shadows.

"Fat Ollie" Day flicked the stub of his cigarette toward the gutter, watching it spiral through the air like a tumbling star. It landed in a puddle of brackish rainwater and fizzed out with a gentle hiss. Nervously, he rested his sweaty palm on the butt of his pistol and edged forward, trying to see what had made the noise. It was too dark to discern anything other than the heaps of trash piled up against the walls of the alleyway, illuminated by the silvery beams of the car's headlamps. The air was damp. Ollie thought it was going to rain.

Behind him, the car engine purred with a low growl. He'd left it running, ready for a quick getaway. Ollie had stoked it himself a few minutes earlier, shoveling black coal from the hopper into the small furnace at the rear of the vehicle, superheating the fluid in the water tank to build up a head of steam. It was a sleek model—one of the newer types—and Ollie couldn't help grinning every time he ran his hands over its sweeping curves. Who said crime didn't pay?

Now his smart gray suit was covered in coal dust and soot, but he knew after they'd finished with the job they were doing, he could buy himself another. Heck, he could buy himself a whole wardrobe full if he had the inclination. The boss would see him right. The Roman knew how to look after his guys.

Inside the tall bank building to his left, the four men he'd ferried downtown in the motorcar were carrying out a heist—their third in a week—and once again he'd been left outside to guard the doors. It suited Ollie just fine; he'd never had a stomach for the dirty stuff. Being on the periphery didn't worry him—as long as he still got his share of the proceeds.

There was another scuffing sound from up ahead, like a booted foot crunching on stone. Ollie felt the hairs on the back of his neck prickle with anxiety. The pressure valve on the vehicle gave an expectant whistle, as if in empathy, calling out a shrill warning to its driver. Ollie glanced back, but the car was just as he'd left it, the side doors hanging open like clamshells, waiting for the others to finish the job inside.

"Who's there?" He slid his pistol from its holster, easing it into his palm. "I'm warning you. Don't you mess with Ollie Day."

There was a sudden, jerky movement as a nearby heap of trash was disturbed, causing cardboard boxes to tumble noisily to the ground. Ollie swung his pistol round in a wide arc. His hand was shaking. He couldn't see anything in the gloom. Then more movement, to his right. Something crossed the beam of the headlamps. He spun on the spot, his finger almost squeezing the trigger of his pistol...

...and saw a black cat dart across the alleyway, scuttling away from the pile of boxes. Ollie let out a long, wheezing sigh of relief. "Hey, cat. You got Ollie all jumpy for a minute there." He slipped his pistol back into its holster, grinning to himself. "Man, I gotta learn to take it easy." He looked up.

Two pinpricks of red light had appeared, thirty feet further down the alleyway, hovering in the air at head height. Ollie stood silent for a moment, trying to figure out what was going on. For a minute he thought he was seeing things, and made to rub his eyes, but then the lights began to move, sweeping toward him through the gloom.

Footsteps running. Ragged breath. Ollie fumbled for his weapon, but he was already too late.

The man sprang at him from nearly ten feet away, hurtling through the air toward him like a panther, body coiled for an attack. Ollie caught only glimpses of his assailant as the man was crisscrossed by the headlamp beams: dressed fully in black, a long cape or trench coat whipping up around him, a fedora on his head. And those glowing red eyes, piercing in the darkness. Ollie thought they might bore right into him, then and there.

He got the gun loose just as his attacker came down on him, hard, causing the weapon to fly from his hand and skitter across the ground toward the car. It clattered to a stop somewhere out of sight. The man was fast, and Ollie was hardly able to bring his hands up in defense before he was punched painfully in the gut and he doubled over, all of the air driven out of his lungs. The man grabbed a fistful of Ollie's collar and heaved him into the air. Ollie tried desperately to kick out, or to cry for help, but was able only to offer an ineffectual whimper.

Before he knew what was happening, Ollie felt himself being flung backward. He sailed through the air, his limbs wheeling, and slammed down across the bonnet of the car. He felt the thin metal give way beneath his bulk, but he had no time to lament the damage to his precious vehicle. Pain blossomed in his shoulder. He realized that his arm had been crushed and was hanging limply by his side. The back of his head, too, felt like it was on fire, and he could sense a warm liquid—blood?—running down the side of his face. He emitted a heartfelt wail, just in time to see the grim face of his attacker looming over him.

The man was unshaven and unkempt. His eyes—his real eyes—were obscured by a pair of glowing goggles, strange red lights shining bright behind the lenses, transfixing the mob driver as he struggled to inch backward on the car bonnet, to get away from this terrifying apparition. He had nowhere to go. He was going to die. He squeezed his eyes shut, waiting for the fatal blow. Seconds passed. Tentatively, he opened them again.

The man was still hovering over him. After a moment, he spoke. "In there?" He gestured toward the set of double doors that the others were planning to use as their escape route from the bank.

Ollie nodded. He knew he was likely signing his own death warrant by giving them away, but all he could think about was getting free from this maniac, this… *vigilante*. He could taste blood. If the car would still drive…

The stranger grabbed the front of Ollie's jacket with both fists and hauled him into the air again. "Oh no. No, no, no…"

Turning, the man charged at the double doors, swinging Ollie in front of himself like a battering ram. Ollie's shoulder connected painfully with the heavy wooden doors as they burst through, causing the hinges to splinter and the doors to cave inward with a huge crash.

Stars bloomed in his field of vision. His head spun. He couldn't remember what it was like not to feel numb with pain. He felt as if he was going to die, and realized that he probably was.

They were standing in the main lobby of the bank. The scene inside was one of utter chaos. Around thirty or forty civilians were scattered over the polished marble floor, laying prone on their bellies, their hands behind their heads, their distraught faces pressed to the ground. Another of the Roman's men was standing over them with a gun, keeping guard. Two further men were standing by the bank tellers as they stuffed cloth bags full of paper bills, and a fourth was up in the gallery overhead, surveying the scene below, a tommy gun clutched tightly in his hands.

A huge holographic statue of Pegasus dominated the lobby space, flickering ghostly blue as it reared up on its hind legs, its immense wings unfurled over the swathe of terrified civilians below. Above that, an enormous chandelier shimmered in the bright light.

Silence spread through the lobby as everyone turned at once to see who had burst through the doors in such violent fashion. A woman screamed. The four mobsters offered Ollie and the other man a silent appraisal before raising their weapons.

Ollie was struggling to catch his breath. He couldn't feel his left arm anymore, and he didn't know if this was troubling or a blessed relief. He didn't have time to consider it any further before he found himself unceremoniously dumped against the wall.

"Stay there."

The man in black stepped forward, glancing from side to side. Ollie could see now that his billowing trench coat concealed a number of small contraptions, including what looked like the long barrel of a weapon under his right arm. Dazed, he watched the chaos erupt again before his eyes.

His attacker spread his arms wide, facing the rest of the Roman's men. "Time's up, gentlemen."

One of the mobsters opened fire. There was a series of loud reports as he emptied his chamber, yelling at the others to take the newcomer down. The man in black seemed unconcerned by the spray of bullets, however, simply stepping aside as they thundered into the wall behind him. He didn't even flinch.

Ollie watched in dismayed awe as the man gave a discreet flick of his right arm, causing the long brass barrel of the concealed weapon to spin up on a ratchet and click into place along the length of his forearm. It made a sound like a steel chain being dragged across a metal drum.

The man swung his arm around toward the crook who had fired on him and squeezed something in his palm. There was a quiet hiss of escaping air, and then he gave his reply. A storm of tiny steel fléchettes burst from the end of the strange weapon, a rain of silver death, hailing down on the crook and shredding him as they impacted, bursting organs and flensing flesh from bone. It was over in a matter of seconds. The ruined body crumpled to the floor, gore and fragments of human matter pattering down around it in a wide arc. The teller who'd been standing beside the felon dropped in a dead faint, the pile of cash in his hands billowing out to scatter all around him as he fell.

The vigilante didn't wait for the stutter of another gun. He dropped and rolled forward and left, moving with ease. He came up beside the holographic statue, his weapon at the ready.

Another hail of fléchettes dropped the man in the gallery above, sending him tumbling over the rail, his face a mess of blood and broken bone. He crashed to the marble with a sickening crunch, his limbs splayed at awkward angles.

The mobster guarding the civilians—who Ollie knew as Bobby Hendriks—wasn't taking any chances. He leapt forward, grappling with one of the women on the floor and dragging her to her feet. Looking panicked, the heavily set man pressed a knife to her throat, which glinted in the bright electric light as he turned the blade back and forth, threatening to pull it across her soft, exposed flesh. The woman—a pretty blonde in a blue dress—looked terrified and froze rigid, trying not to move in case she somehow made the situation worse.

"I'll kill her! I'll kill her!" Hendriks's voice was a gravelly bark.

The man in black flicked a glance at Hendriks, and then back at the other mobster guarding the tellers, who were still furiously emptying the cash drawers. He took a step toward Hendriks and the hostage.

Hendriks stepped back, mirroring the movement. He pressed the blade firmly against the woman's throat, drawing a tiny bead of blood. She wailed in terror, trying to pull away.

A shot went off. The vigilante flinched as a bullet stroked his upper arm, tearing a rent in his clothing and drawing a line of bright blood on his skin. He turned on the gunman, but Ollie realized he wasn't able to draw a clear bead due to the tellers. Instead, the man reached inside his trench coat and gave a sharp tug on a hidden cord.

There was a roaring sound, like the rumble of a distant

explosion. Bright yellow flames shot out of two metal canisters strapped to the backs of the man's boots, scorching the floor. Ollie stared on, bewildered, as the stranger lifted entirely into the air, propelled by the bizarre jets, and shot across the lobby at speed, flitting over the prone civilians and swinging out over the mobster's head. He didn't even need to fire his weapon. Bringing his feet around in a sweeping movement, he introduced the searing flames to the gunman's face, who gave a gut-wrenching wail as his flesh bubbled and peeled in the intense heat. He dropped on the spot, still clutching his gun, hungry flames licking around his ears and collar.

The man in black reached inside his coat and pulled another cord. The flames spat and guttered out. He crashed to the floor, landing on one knee. All eyes were on him. He climbed slowly to his feet and stood, regarding the last of the felons.

"I'll kill her! I'll kill her!" Hendriks was swinging the girl around as he looked for an escape route, edging away from this terrifying man who had come out of nowhere and murdered his companions. "I'll kill her! I'll kill her!"

When he spoke, the vigilante's voice was drenched in sorrow. "You already have."

Hendriks looked down at the girl in his arms. Sudden realization flashed on his face. His knife was half buried in the woman's throat, blood seeping down to drench the front of her dress, matting the fine hairs on his forearm. Shocked, he stumbled backward, allowing the dead woman to slide to the floor, the knife still buried in her flesh. "Oh crap. Oh crap. I didn't mean to do it. Hey, mister, I didn't *mean* it! I just—"

There was a quiet *snick*. Something bright and metallic

flashed through the air. Hendriks's head toppled from his shoulders, the stump spouting blood in a dark crimson fountain. The body pitched forward, dropping to the floor. The head rolled off to one side. Ollie glanced round to see a metal disk buried in the wall behind the body. He started to scramble to his feet.

All around, people were screaming, getting up off the floor and rushing toward the exits. The massacre was over. Or at least Ollie hoped it was over. He needed to get to his car, fast. Wincing, he scrabbled to his feet.

The man in black stooped low over the body of the dead hostage. He seemed to be whispering an apology, but Ollie wasn't quite able to hear over the noise of the crowd.

Ollie backed up, edging toward the burst double doors. His arm was hanging limp and useless by his side, he was sure his ribs had been shattered, and he was still bleeding from the wound in the back of his head. Even if he made it out of there alive, he'd never be the same again.

He saw the stranger's red eyes lift and fix on him from across the lobby. He didn't know what to do; didn't dare turn and run or take his eyes off the stranger for a second. The man watched him for a moment, unmoving. Then in three or four graceful strides, he was on top of him. He grasped Ollie by the collar. The fat man whimpered as the vigilante leaned in close. He could feel the hot breath on his face, smell the coffee and whisky it carried. Ollie's heart was hammering hard in his chest. Was this how it was going to end?

"Today, you get to live."

Ollie nearly fainted with relief. "I... I—"

"But you take a message to the Roman for me."

Ollie nodded enthusiastically, and nearly swooned from the movement.

"You tell him he's not welcome in this town anymore."

The stranger dropped Ollie in a heap on the ground and then stepped over him, making slowly for the exit, his boots clicking loudly on the marble floor.

Ollie's mouth was gritty with blood. He called after the mysterious figure. "Who... who are you?"

The man shrugged and kept on walking. "Death," he said, without bothering to look back.

TWO

"Eggs! I need eggs, Henry. Two of them. With a side of toast."
Gabriel Cross dropped the morning paper onto the breakfast
table and leaned back in his armchair, stretching his weary
limbs. He was a thin, wiry man in his mid-thirties, clean-shaven,
with hair the color of Saharan sand. He was dressed in an
impeccable black suit of the expensive variety, but wore his
collar splayed open, betraying his innate sense of informality.
Some, he knew, would call him louche for such behavior, but he
preferred to consider himself freethinking, unbound by the
stuffy conventions of the age. In truth, he was simply unbound
by the conventions of money; he had about him the casual air of
the exceptionally rich.

Yawning, Gabriel surveyed the aftermath of the prior
evening's entertainment. His eyelids were heavy with lack of
sleep. All around him, devastation reigned. The drawing room
was cluttered with discharged glasses, a few still holding the
remnants of their former owners' drinks. Accompanying these
were the pungent stubs of fat brown cigars and pale cigarettes;
even a woman's red silk scarf and a man's topcoat, abandoned
there in the early hours by drunken lovers, carefree and
searching for intoxication of a different kind.

Gabriel had a love/hate relationship with New York society:

it loved him—or rather, it loved his wealth and status—and he hated it. He disliked "society" as a concept. To him it was a metaphor for the socially inept, the "upper" classes, a means of filling one's head with notions of self-import and grandeur. Yet he adored people. He needed people. He surrounded himself with them, night and day. He was an observer, a man who watched life. An artist without a canvas, a writer without a page. He lived to amuse himself, to attempt to fill the vacant space where a real life should have been.

Gabriel Cross was a nothing. A man defined by his inheritance, characterized by his former life. He'd heard people whispering in hushed tones at the party, huddled in small groups under the canopy on the veranda, or leaning up against the doorjambs in the drawing room, drinks in hand. "Yes, it's true! He used to be a soldier. I heard he fought in the war." Or, "A pilot, I heard. But now he just throws parties. Parties! Who needs parties?"

Gabriel knew they were right. Yet they swarmed to his Long Island parties like honeybees in search of pollen, intent on finding something there that would make their own lives that little bit easier to bear. He had no idea what it was. If he did, he would administer it to himself in liberal doses.

Gabriel rubbed a hand over his bristly chin. "Better send a Bloody Mary with those eggs, Henry. God knows, it's going to be one of those days." He turned and looked out of the window at the sound of a motorcar hissing onto the driveway in the watery morning sun. Its wheels stirred the gravel track, whilst black smoke belched from its rear funnel. He recognized the sleek curves of its black bodywork, as well as those of its owner, who sat in the driving seat, her head and shoulders exposed to the stiff breeze. It ruffled her shock of bright auburn hair as she turned toward the house and saw him watching. Smiling, she raised her hand and offered him a brief wave. Gabriel smiled and raised his own hand in reply. He watched her climb out of the side door, swinging her shapely legs down from the cab. Gabriel felt his heart beat a little faster in his breast. Celeste. Celeste Parker.

He'd missed her at the party. Missed the opportunity to peel away with her to a quiet spot and blot out the presence of everyone else. But he was also pleased, in a sense, that she hadn't come. She didn't need the party, not like everyone else needed the party. And for that reason, if no other, he was very much in love with her.

Gabriel listened to the sound of her heels crunching on the gravel, a soft rap on the front door with a gloved fist, Henry's footsteps as he crossed the hallway to let her in. Smiling, Gabriel retrieved the newspaper from the breakfast table and rustled it noisily, as if intent on continuing with an article he had earlier abandoned. He attempted to exude his most nonchalant air. He knew Celeste would see through this ruse, but then, such was the game they played.

A moment later the drawing room door creaked open. Gabriel didn't look up from the newspaper to watch Celeste enter the room. She hovered for a moment at the threshold, silent save for her soft inhalation, awaiting his acknowledgement. The moment stretched. Gabriel turned the page and pretended to scan the headlines.

Finally, the visitor broke the silence. "You look terrible,

Gabriel. I see the party was up to its usual... standards." Her voice was soft and melodious; it had broken many hearts.

Gabriel folded the left page of his *New York Times* and peered inquisitively over the crease, as if he'd only just realized she was there. Framed in the doorway, the soft light of the morning streaming in from the hallway, she seemed to him like an angel; surrounded by a wintery halo, beautiful, ethereal. She dressed with the confidence of a woman who knew she would turn heads: a black, knee-length dress, stockings, high-heeled shoes, and a black jacket. Her auburn hair was like a shock of lightning, bright and electrifying, her lips a slash of glossy red.

"You didn't come." It was a statement, not a question.

"Of course I didn't come. Did you expect me to come?"

"You were missed."

Celeste laughed. She stepped further into the room, placing her handbag on the sideboard beside the door. Gabriel crumpled the newspaper and tossed it on the breakfast table, where it disturbed the ashtray, sending a plume of gray dust into the air. Henry had yet to tidy away the last vestiges of the party. The house was in a dreadful state. Gabriel wrinkled his nose. "Yes, it does rather make a terrible mess of one's house." He paused, as if thoughtful. "I think next time we'll stay outside. We'll all have to wear beach clothes. A bathing party, out by the pool."

Celeste looked confused, despite herself. She offered him a wan smile. "In November? Whatever are you talking about?"

Gabriel grinned profusely. He leaned forward in his chair. "Yes! Why not! There's that place down in Jersey selling some newfangled contraption. A thing that heats your pool. The Johnson and Arkwright Filament, they call it. Just imagine. It would be a showstopper! I'll order one next week. A pool party in November! Oh, do say you'll come?" He knew she wouldn't come. But he had a role to play, and so did she.

"I'm busy."

He glanced out of the window. His voice was quiet. "Yes. Of course."

"Oh really, Gabriel. You need a drink. And I need a cigarette."

Gabriel smiled. He reached for the small silver cigarette case he kept in his jacket pocket. It was engraved with his initials: GC. "Do you want eggs? Henry's making eggs. Sit down."

She sat. "No. Not eggs." She reached over and took one of his proffered cigarettes. He noticed her fingernails matched the color of her hair. She crossed her legs and leaned forward, pulling the tab on the end of her smoke so that it sparked and ignited. A blue wreath encircled her head.

"Are you singing tonight?"

"Yes. At Joe's. Will you come?"

"I'm busy."

"Yes. Of course." Her lips parted in a knowing smile.

Gabriel grinned. Celeste was a jazz singer at a club in downtown Manhattan. That was where Gabriel had met her, six months earlier. He'd taken a pretty girl named Ariadne, a perfectly lovely young thing, all lipstick and short skirts and oozing sexuality. But Celeste had stolen his attention. It had nothing to do with romance; it was dark and harsh and exotic, an attraction of a different kind. When she'd parted her lips at the microphone the entire world had ceased spinning. Her voice carried truth. It spoke to him—not to Gabriel Cross, but to the real man who hid behind that name. It carried knowledge of the world, and poor Ariadne hadn't stood a chance.

He'd driven Ariadne home in silence; abandoned her on the front steps of her house. She'd been sanguine yet desperate, resigned yet somehow wanting more. She still came to his parties sometimes, floating around ethereally in her sequined dresses, catching his eye as he showered platitudes and cigarettes on his other guests. She needed a reason, an understanding of what had passed between them. She needed to know what she had done wrong, what fatal act of sabotage she had committed. But Gabriel couldn't bear to tell her the truth, couldn't bear to strip away civilities and reveal to her the hollow reality of the matter: that poor Ariadne was just another girl in just another city. That her life filled with parties and laughing and booze didn't *mean* anything. That she could never compare to a woman like Celeste. She couldn't see the world for what it was.

Ghosts. New York was full of people like that. So were his parties. People who drifted through life as if it didn't matter, as if it were simply something that they had to do. Get up in the morning, pass time, sleep, fuck, die. Even Gabriel Cross was a member of that illustrious set, as much as he hated to admit it. But Celeste was not, and her allure had been unavoidable, her effect on Gabriel predetermined from the outset. He had been ensnared, and for the rest of that night he had lain awake in the stifling summer heat, drunk on whisky and desire, replaying the sound of Celeste's voice over and over in his mind.

The next night Gabriel had returned to the club by himself in search of the jazz singer. He'd found her haunting the bar, drinking orange juice laced with cheap illegal gin. He'd bought her drinks, offered her cigarettes, watched her as she brushed aside the other men who each lined up to make a play for her attention. At first she'd seemed amused by his presence—the confident interloper—intrigued by the fact that he had returned to the club so soon after his previous visit, this time without the pretty embellishment on his arm. But Gabriel had seen where the other men had tried and failed. He wouldn't make the same mistakes. Not this time. So, instead, he had simply offered her a final cigarette for the evening, before retiring. He didn't leave his name or his number. He didn't need to.

A week later he had found her playing cards in his breakfast room with three other girls whose names he could never remember. His party was in full swing; it was dark outside, but drunken men strutted loudly on the lawn by the light of the moon, and women laughed gaily as though being treated to the height of theatrical endeavor. All around them the house was full of bustle, of noise and tension and sex and booze. Of people looking for a way to force some feeling into their lives, or else to numb the pain. But when Celeste had turned to smile at him, he'd wanted nothing more than for them all to disappear. He'd wanted the world to stand still again, like it had a week before, the night he'd first watched her open her mouth to sing.

He'd fucked her that night at the party, hot and fast and urgent. And in the morning, as the sunlight streamed in through the window to dapple the pillow where she had lain, he knew then that he was in love with her.

He looked up. She was watching him now while she gently rolled the end of her cigarette around the rim of the cut-glass ashtray. He turned to meet her gaze. "Have you read the papers?"

Celeste shrugged. "It's not news, you know, Gabriel. Not real news. It's just hearsay and opinion. It's what people tell each other to make the time go by."

Gabriel smiled. "But what about this 'Ghost'? Did you hear about that? The crazy vigilante who burst in on that bank job and killed all the crooks? Now *that's* news."

Celeste shrugged, pursing her lips. "Yes, I suppose it is. But I don't know why it's so surprising. It was only ever a matter of time before someone tried to take the law into their own hands. Crooks and vigilantes, they're just different sides of the same coin. He's as bad as the rest of them."

Gabriel nodded. "Perhaps you're right. The papers certainly share your opinion. But I can't help wondering if the guy is actually a hero. He saved people's lives."

"And took others. He caused that woman's death. The hostage."

Gabriel fingered his cigarette case before turning it over, flicking the catch, and withdrawing a cigarette. He pulled the tab, and met Celeste's penetrating gaze through a brief wall of smoke. "Perhaps... but I'd still be inclined to blame that on the crook who put the knife in her throat, rather than the guy who tried to save her."

Celeste looked as if she was about to speak, but then she turned to watch Henry, the valet, enter the room through another door. On a tray he bore a plate of toast and eggs, with a Bloody Mary on the side. He smiled genially when he saw her looking. "Will Miss Parker be taking breakfast this morning?" He'd made her breakfast before, on more than one occasion.

Celeste folded the stub of her cigarette into the ashtray.

"Not today, Henry. I have rehearsals. And I think Mr. Cross could use some more sleep."

Henry nodded politely and placed the silver tray on the table beside the crumpled newspaper. He straightened his back, glancing at his employer. "Will that be all, sir?"

Gabriel nodded. "Yes, that'll be all, Henry." He glanced at the eggs. His stomach growled. "I'll be taking a trip into town later. I intend to watch Miss Parker's show this evening. Could you ask Graves to prepare one of the cars?"

"Very good, sir."

Celeste flashed Gabriel a wry smile. Gabriel offered her an abundant grin.

"I'll leave you to your breakfast." She regarded him with something approximating satisfaction, and then stood, collecting her handbag from where she'd left it on the sideboard. "Until this evening, then."

Gabriel dropped his still-smoldering cigarette into the ashtray and pushed himself up out of his easy chair, riffles of blue smoke billowing from his nostrils. "I'll walk you out." He took her arm and led her into the hall.

"What about your eggs?"

"Never mind the eggs." He stopped her at the foot of the stairs and took her face in his hands, pulling her near, kissing her deeply on the lips. Once again he felt his heart hammering in his chest. He wondered if she could feel it too.

They stood for a moment, staring into one another's eyes. Then Celeste broke away, moving toward the door. She pushed it open and Gabriel felt a cold breeze sweep into the hallway. He shivered involuntarily.

Celeste crossed to her motorcar, the gravel crunching noisily with every step. Gabriel followed to open the door for her, watching as she smoothly lowered herself into the driver's seat. A moment later the engine roared, a shot of black smoke belched out from the exhaust pipe, and the vehicle hissed away. Celeste didn't look back.

Gabriel watched the car slide off into the distance, steam rising from the rear funnels to leave long vapor trails in the crisp morning air. As he turned back to the house, already lamenting the fact that she'd had to leave so soon, he noticed a small, dark bundle on the ground, resting on the driveway at the bottom of the step. He crouched so that he could get a better look. It was a dead bird, its black feathers ruffling in the breeze. It looked as if it had been mangled somehow, caught and abandoned by a predator, perhaps, its head twisted awkwardly to one side, its wings broken out of shape. He'd seen a man like that once, lying in a ditch in France. His neck had been broken, too, blood caked ominously around his ear, eyes glazed and milky-white. If it hadn't been for the startled look of terror frozen on the dead man's face, Gabriel could almost have imagined he was resting, his head on a soft pillow of mud, watching the plumes of distant explosions as innumerable airships drifted lazily above, relentlessly bombarding the landscape below.

Sighing, he stood. He wished his mind wasn't full of such memories. He'd have Henry come and clear the remains of the bird away later. Now, he needed eggs. And he needed to clear his head. The Bloody Mary would help.

THREE

F elix Donovan was having a terrible day.

He'd been dragged from his bed at five-thirty by the buzzing of the holotube, only to find his sergeant on the line, nervously informing him there'd been a homicide. From the look of the flickering blue image that appeared in the mirrored cavity in his holotube terminal, he'd been able to tell that Mullins was calling from a private booth in a hotel or bar, and that he very much considered himself out of his depth.

Nevertheless, for a moment Donovan had actually considered going back to bed. It wasn't as if murders were anything new or unusual in downtown Manhattan. Another dead body on another apartment floor. He was sure it could wait until a reasonable hour of the morning, at least until he'd showered and eaten his breakfast. But then Mullins had told him who had been murdered, and suddenly everything had changed.

Now, at a quarter after eleven, his head was still thick with lack of sleep, and he was desperately in need of a coffee.

"Inspector?"

Donovan turned to see Mullins standing sheepishly behind him. The sergeant was a portly man who sported a short, clipped moustache and appeared to Donovan to have a permanently ruddy complexion. He was currently dressed in a long gray overcoat, which covered his disordered blue suit: a symptom of being roused from his bed at such an ungodly hour of the morning. The inspector could forgive him that. Donovan himself, however, was dressed immaculately, as usual; his black suit and crisp white collar were pressed and pristine, and he had taken the time to freshen up before driving out to the scene of the crime. It was a small, fruitless rebellion, but it made him feel better just the same. After all, he was alive and the victim was dead, and the dead man wasn't going anywhere in a hurry. Regardless, the man had been an odious toad. Politicians, Donovan found, were very rarely anything else.

He regarded Mullins with an impatient eye. "What is it, Sergeant? Have you finally managed to search out some coffee?"

Mullins wouldn't meet his eye. "No, sir. Not coffee. But there's a gathering crowd of reporters out front, and they're calling for a statement. Are you planning to say anything?"

Donovan looked round at the tall revolving doors of the lobby. Beyond, through the glass panes, he could see a gaggle of reporters and photographers being shepherded back from the sidewalk by a couple of uniformed men. Flashbulbs blinked, reflecting in the glass and causing miniature shimmering coronas to burst momentarily to life.

He and Mullins were standing in the lobby of the Gramercy Park Hotel, all plush modernity and chandeliers. It was a bit rich for Donovan's decidedly down-to-earth palate. He gritted his teeth. "No. They can wait." He looked back at Mullins. "They can wait like everyone else. We haven't even informed his wife yet, for God's sake." He was muttering now, as if to himself more than his sergeant. "How the hell are we going to break it to his wife?" A sigh. "And then there's the matter of the scandal. The Commissioner might want to keep the details out of the press." He gestured at Mullins. "Tell them to get back to the gutter."

Mullins sucked in his breath. For a moment Donovan thought he looked even redder in the face than usual. He hadn't thought that was possible. "They're asking, sir, if it's the work of the Roman."

"Well, yes. I'd very much imagine they are." Donovan gave another plaintive sigh. His voice was tinged with weariness. "Look, Mullins. Find that coffee. And let's have another look at the crime scene. Then the ambulance crew can take the bodies to the morgue. After that—we'll see about facing those reporters."

"Yes, sir." Mullins nodded and shot off in the direction of the kitchens.

The murder of James Landsworth Senior had taken place in the early hours of the morning on the top floor of the Gramercy Park Hotel. It was a sordid affair, and Donovan, standing on the threshold of the room with a cigarette dangling from his lips, didn't quite know what to make of it.

The dead man was a senator—and a well-respected one at that—and this whole affair, Donovan had concluded, had been set up to discredit him. There was no doubt the scene inside the hotel room had been posed; a grisly diorama intended to embarrass the government.

Landsworth was—or had been, Donovan corrected himself—a middle-aged man of about fifty, with a full head of graying hair and a significant paunch, and he had built his career on a foundation of right-wing policies and conservative opinions. He supported prohibition. He had a healthy hatred for the British Empire and he campaigned against "progress," claiming that science was "dehumanizing" the American people. He sold himself as a family man, and was often seen around town with his wife and two young children. He never attended parties or large social gatherings, and the newspapers had a dog of a time digging up anything about the man that could even be considered controversial.

But nevertheless, here he was, his pants round his ankles, chained to a bedpost, wearing rouge, with a half-drunk bottle of illegal whisky on the bedside table. His chest was covered in cigarette burns and there was lipstick all over his prick. His mouth was hanging slack-jawed and two small Roman coins had been placed over his eyelids. They glinted in the lamplight as if they had been freshly minted.

Across the room, a dead whore lay on the floor, her skirt pulled up around her hips, stockings torn, her face bruised and split where she had been viciously beaten. Donovan couldn't even tell what she had looked like before the beating, except for the fact that the lipstick smeared across her lower face matched the color of that now found on Landsworth's corpse. Mullins had told him she'd been asphyxiated, but Donovan hadn't yet brought himself to take a proper look. He'd needed a coffee and a cigarette before even contemplating that.

Donovan looked from one body to the other, and shuddered. The reporters were right to be asking. This was clearly the Roman's handiwork. It was the third murder in as many weeks, and each victim had been a man of standing: a councilor, a surgeon, and now a senator. Each of them had also been found with identical Roman coins resting on their eyelids: a calling card, of sorts, from the mob boss responsible for their deaths. Donovan had had the coins analyzed, assuming them to be recent copies that he could somehow trace through the city's dealers, but had been startled to discover they were actual Roman coins, dating from the reign of Vespasian. They looked as fresh and new as if they had been pressed the day before, not nearly two thousand years in the past. He didn't know what to make of that, either.

The Roman had seemingly come from nowhere, but had quickly risen to become one of the most powerful mob bosses in the city. His network of heavies, informants, and petty criminals was unparalleled, and he managed to inspire an unflinching dedication in his men. Donovan suspected it was a reign of terror, but so far he hadn't managed to get close enough to find out.

No one had ever seen the Roman. That was the most bizarre factor in the whole matter. It was supposed he was Italian—thus the moniker—but the truth of the matter was that the police had been unable to establish any information regarding who he really was, or even where he could be found. Whoever he was, the only certainty was that he had somehow managed to bring the city to its knees. And it was Donovan's job to find a means to stop him.

He took another draw on his cigarette and then stubbed it out on the doorframe, ignoring the appalled look this inspired from his sergeant. As if in response, he nonchalantly handed the butt to Mullins, who accepted it with a surprised expression, and then, seeing no obvious place to discard it, slipped it into the pocket of his overcoat without a word.

Donovan crossed to the bed, screwing his face up in disgust. Landsworth was a mess. He couldn't let the papers get hold of the details, of that much he was certain. He might not be able to put right what the Roman had done, but he could prevent him gaining any satisfaction from it. He turned to Mullins. "Do you think he was already here, with the good-time girl, before the Roman's men... interrupted things?"

Mullins shook his head. "No. I think he was killed elsewhere and brought here later. The girl was killed here, though. There're signs of a struggle." He indicated for Donovan to follow him across the hotel suite. "Watch you don't step on the bloodstains, sir."

Donovan swallowed. The girl had been viciously brutalized. He couldn't be sure, but she must only have been nineteen, twenty years old.

Mullins lowered his voice, as if trying to mask his horror. "What a waste of life."

Donovan didn't know whether he meant the fact that she'd been murdered, or the fact that such a young girl had been forced into whoring herself to unscrupulous politicians and gangsters. Either way, the sergeant was right.

Donovan glanced around. An overturned table, a smashed lamp, a rug all ruffled up at one end. Yes, there'd been a struggle here. She'd been a spirited girl. "She probably thought she had a good paying gig here, at this hotel, before all this." He shook his head and glanced at the uniformed officer who was still lurking in the doorway. "Cover her up," he said, with a resigned gesture. He wondered what they'd made her do before they killed her. It didn't bear thinking about.

"Is there anything here, Mullins, that might give us any clues? Anything different about this one? Different from the others?"

Mullins shook his head but remained silent. Just like Landsworth's corpse, splayed out on the bed, unable to tell Donovan what the hell he should tell the Commissioner when he got back to the station. Unable, too, to bring him any closer to understanding who the Roman was, or how on earth he was going to set about bringing him to justice for his crimes.

FOUR

The man looked out, surveying the scene across the city. Electric lights glowed like pinpricks in the darkness, causing apartment blocks to take on the appearance of jewel-encrusted towers. Police dirigibles drifted lazily overhead, their searchlights punctuating the gloaming with long, brilliant columns of white. Above them, a full moon hung low over the city like the smoldering tip of a cigarette, shrouded in wispy clouds.

He'd heard it said that New York was a city that never slept, but his own experience told him that wasn't entirely true; Manhattan spent its days in a state of bleary-eyed lethargy, only truly coming alive after nightfall. That was the city that most people didn't see, the city full of urgency and emotion and life, the city he had grown to know and to need, and that—more than ever—needed someone like him in return. The police operated with one hand tied constantly behind their backs. They could never do what was necessary, bound as they were by law and convention. Yet the city was falling to crime and corruption, the government and politicians giving way to an endless series of crime lords. It was a war, and it called for brutal measures. The wound needed to be cauterized before the festering grew worse.

The man the newspapers were calling "the Ghost" shifted

slightly, reaching inside his long coat to produce a packet of cigarettes. He popped the lid and extracted one of the thin white sticks. With his gloved fingers he pulled the tab on the end of it and watched it flare, briefly under-lighting his face, before bringing the cigarette to his lips and taking a long, deep draw. The nicotine flooded his lungs, giving him a light-headed rush. He left the cigarette drooping from his bottom lip as he once again surveyed the city streets below.

From his vantage point atop the roof terrace on Fifth Avenue—above his city apartment—the Ghost watched the comings and goings of the people down below. Coal-powered cars hissed along the road, whilst lonely pedestrians drifted along the sidewalks, solitary specters in the wan light thrown down from the surrounding buildings. If it hadn't been for—

He stopped, suddenly, snapping his head to the right. He'd caught a sound, carried to him on the stiff breeze that rumpled the tails of his long coat. The sound of a man calling out in pain, from somewhere far below. Leaving his position at the front of the building, he rushed over to the other side of the terrace. He scanned the streets below. Nothing.

Reaching up, the Ghost felt under the brim of his hat until his fingers located the rim of his goggles. He tugged them down over his eyes, turning the lenses slowly away from the bridge of his nose. Everything took on a red sheen. Targeting circles floated, disembodied, before his vision. He cranked the lenses once again, tiny cogs whirring inside the device, and the view suddenly magnified, becoming sharp and bright. He could see the sidewalk five stories below as if he were only a few feet away.

The sound came to him again, a stifled cry. The Ghost

tracked along the sidewalk toward where he thought it had originated. There, by the mouth of an alleyway, was a large armored car, thick iron plates cladding its sides to form a tank-like vehicle, the windshield just a slit in the otherwise impenetrable metal sheeting. The engine was running, and the exhaust chimney was belching oily black smoke as it burned coal at a furious rate. Behind this, in the alleyway itself, he sensed movement. He decided to investigate.

The Ghost flicked a switch on the side of his goggles and the lenses snapped back into place, returning his vision to normal. He glanced along the edge of the building, looking for the quickest route down to street level. Just a few feet away, a steel fire-escape ladder was fixed to the outside of the building. Shrugging his shoulders, the Ghost pulled himself up onto the stone lip of the building, ran sure-footed but carefully along the top of it and dropped easily onto the metal platform below. His heavy boots rang out into the quiet night. Then, gripping the railings with his gloved fists, he used his weight to slide down from platform to platform, hitting the sidewalk a matter of moments later.

The alleyway was only a hundred or so yards away. At street level, the sound of the car engine was a constant background growl. He'd use that to his advantage, muffling his footsteps as he crept closer to the mouth of the alleyway. He liked having the element of surprise on his side; it usually meant he avoided getting shot.

The Ghost drew opposite the parked vehicle, trying to ascertain whether there was anybody inside. He guessed the driver would be waiting behind the wheel, keeping the engine running, ready for the others to make their getaway when they were done.

Whatever was going down, he knew it involved the mob. Only the Roman's men could afford an armored car like the one across the street from him, and only the Roman's men would ever have a use for it. The thought rankled him. Dealing with the Roman's lackeys was like dealing with the symptoms of an infection. Sooner or later, he'd need to root out the cause of the infection itself. For now, though, it sounded like someone needed his help.

The Ghost crossed silently toward the car, as graceful as a cat sneaking up on a bird. Careful to avoid any of the viewing slots that had been cut into the armor plating, he peered over the roof of the vehicle at the scene unfolding on the other side.

A middle-aged man in a shopkeeper's apron was on the ground. He twitched unconsciously as two men in black suits carried on with their indiscriminate assault, kicking him viciously in the face, chest, and stomach. Their victim had long since lost the will to defend himself and now his arms and legs were splayed out on the damp flagstones as he silently accepted each blow. The two men in black suits were laughing with each other as they went about their business. It was clear to the Ghost almost immediately what was happening. He'd heard from others that the Roman had started a protection racket, and either this man had bravely refused to pay up, or else he couldn't afford to meet his payment.

Whatever the case, he didn't deserve the kind of treatment he was receiving at the hands of the two goons.

He stood back from the car, flexing his gloved fingers and

stretching his neck muscles. He could feel the tension in his shoulders as he prepared himself for a fight. *In and out.* He didn't plan to linger. He'd take down the two stooges and then be gone with the unconscious shopkeeper before the driver had chance to even consider pulling a pistol.

He glanced at the weapon that was folded away beneath his right arm. The long brass barrel gleamed in the moonlight. For a moment he considered shooting the two men from a distance, safe behind the cover of the car. Then, almost imperceptibly, he shook his head. He couldn't kill in cold blood. He had to let them shoot first. That was his code, the thing that separated him from them. If they shot first, they died. For now, his fists would have to do the talking.

The Ghost glanced around him to make sure there was no one else nearby. Then, without further ado, he heaved himself up onto the roof of the car, his black trench coat billowing around him in a sudden gust. Almost simultaneously, the two mobsters turned to look at the interloper. Their kicking ceased.

"Hey, Mickey, it's that freak who shot up the guys at the bank." This from the goon on the left. The man's hand went inside his coat, searching for a pistol. "Let's plug him."

The other man, wide-eyed, looked less convinced by this course of action and remained standing, rooted to the spot, staring up at the imposing figure of the vigilante atop the armored car.

"Mickey!" The stooge's pistol barked loudly as he roared at his companion, just as the Ghost dived forward, swinging his arm out to catch the gunman beneath the chin. The man went down, heavily, his weapon skittering away across the sidewalk.

He groaned and rolled to the side, clutching at his throat. The Ghost didn't have time to worry about what the gunman was going to do next, however, as the report of the gun had somehow stirred the other man—Mickey—back to life. He swung at the Ghost, his fist glancing painfully off the vigilante's jaw as he turned quickly to face his new opponent. The Ghost was ready for it, however, and simply shook his head, steadying himself for the next attack.

Mickey was clearly a boxer. The Ghost could tell from the way he handled himself, from his stance and the power and accuracy of his blows. But the Ghost had boxed during his army years and knew what was coming. A swift jab with the left, a hook with the right, and the mobster was reeling. The Ghost brought him down with a sweeping kick that took his legs out from under him, sending him crashing into the garbage bins heaped in the alleyway beside the store.

The Ghost glanced back at the first goon, the gunman, but he was still on his knees, clutching at his throat and gasping for breath. The shopkeeper was still out cold, and blood was pooling around his head from a number of nasty-looking wounds. His nose was clearly broken, smeared halfway across his face, and a cursory glance suggested his cheekbone had been cracked, his face swollen and sagging. The Ghost knew that there would be internal injuries too; the man would be lucky to pull through after the beating the Roman's men had given him.

From behind him, the Ghost heard the sound of the car door creaking open. The driver. He hadn't been quick enough. He swept round, bringing his arms up in defense but expecting the impact of a bullet at any second. But the sight that greeted him was not at all what he was expecting.

If there was a driver, he was still seated in the front of the armored car, and his door remained closed. Rather, the two doors at the rear of the vehicle had sprung open, and two enormous figures had emerged. They were huge, both at least seven feet tall, and dressed in long overcoats and trilby hats. Their faces were lost in shadow. They walked with a shambling gait that did not look entirely natural.

The Ghost stepped back, swinging his right arm in a circle so that the long barrel of his fléchette gun ratcheted up into place along his forearm. His breath steamed before his face in the cold night air. The two men were slowly shambling toward him, menacingly, but so far their arms remained limp at their sides. They showed no sign of bearing any weapons.

The Ghost wasn't about to let himself get pinned in the alleyway by these giants, especially as the two goons were stirring. The odds were suddenly not in his favor. He decided his best recourse was to take them by surprise: charge them and try to smash his way through to the street beyond. At least then he'd be out in the open and he'd have more chance of getting away if he needed to bolt. But then there was the shopkeeper...

He had to act. He'd fight the men, but he needed to change the odds. Steeling himself, he charged, aiming squarely for the space between the two giants, hoping to knock them aside as he rushed past. He'd then fling himself over the armored car and duck for cover while he worked out his next move.

The Ghost dipped his head and presented his shoulders to the two men. Too late he saw them close ranks, and he was unable to stop his forward momentum. He crashed into the mobsters at full speed, hopeful that his weight would carry him between them. But instead he rebounded painfully, his head and shoulders smarting as if he had charged into a solid wall. He fell to the ground, shaking his head groggily, his nostrils filled with the scent of damp earth.

Regaining his senses just in time, he rolled to the left as a powerful fist came slamming down, narrowly missing his head. He hit the alley wall and sprang to his feet, using the brickwork to steady himself. Who were these men? He'd barely had time to ask himself the question when another fist came flying at him, and he had to duck to one side to avoid its crushing impact. It crashed into the wall where he'd been standing with enough force to shatter all of the bones in its owner's hand, but the man seemed hardly to notice, simply wheeling around in an ungainly fashion to take another swing at the vigilante. He didn't even grunt with the pain or the exertion.

The Ghost kicked out, catching one of the giants in the midriff. The mobster didn't react, didn't even acknowledge the blow, whilst the Ghost came away with a sharp pain in his leg, as if his booted foot had just encountered solid iron. He could hear one of the goons laughing in the background somewhere. "Hey, Mickey, looks like the Roman was right about these things, eh?"

Trapped against the wall, the two giants closing in on him, the Ghost decided that the only thing he could do was shoot his way out. He flicked his right wrist and the pneumatic trigger for the fléchette gun slid into his palm. He squeezed, showering first one of the lumbering figures, then the other, in a hail of tiny steel blades. He heard the fléchettes strike home, embedding themselves in the giants' torsos with a rapid series of dull thuds. But again, his efforts appeared to have no effect on the men, and they continued their assault regardless. He had no idea what the things were, but it was becoming clear to him that they weren't human. There was no way a human being could have withstood a spray of steel blades like that and carried on walking.

Unsure what else he could do, the Ghost tried to duck away again, but one of the giants' fists struck home, powering deep into his stomach. He doubled over, clutching at his belly, unable to stop himself from slumping to the ground. All of the wind had been driven out of his lungs by the impact of the blow. Gasping, he glanced up, realizing with horror that, beneath their hats, these giants—these *monsters*—had no faces.

The creature loomed over him. The Ghost thrashed out in desperation, clawing at its throat. His fingers sunk into something soft and pliable and he tore at it, gouging a handful of the stuff in an effort to stop the giant in its tracks. With dismay he realized the monster was entirely unaffected by the action. He glanced down at his hand. His fist was filled with soft moss and crumbling earth. He was filled with a sudden sense of creeping terror. The things were formed from clods of clay; golems in the shape of men, somehow animated to create deadly foot soldiers, dressed in coats and hats for disguise.

He raised his arm in defense as the golem reared up again, ready to strike another blow, and he saw that he'd exposed a strut of gleaming brass where its throat should have been, a metal skeleton buried deep beneath its earthy flesh.

He knew then it was over. There was nothing he could do to stop these things. None of his weapons would work. He could see no way out. He waited for the killing blow, baubles of light dancing before his eyes as he tried to suck oxygen back into his lungs.

"That's enough." It was the voice of the goon who had shot at him earlier. The Ghost looked up, still gasping for breath, to see the two golems retreating to make way for the crook. "I want the pleasure of finishing this one myself."

The man came into view, a snide expression on his thin, pale face. He brandished his gun in front of him. The Ghost realized the goon must have retrieved it whilst he was engaged with the moss men. "So, you're the guy who took out Bobby Hendriks, eh? Don't look too much to me." He laughed, glancing over at Mickey.

That was his fatal mistake. The Ghost took his chance. He swung his arm around, squeezing the trigger in his fist and loosing a storm of silver blades in the direction of the gangster's head. The fléchettes struck home, ripping into the man's face, flensing flesh from bone as the relentless stream of razor-sharp metal turned the man's head into a bloody pulp. He was dead in seconds. The Ghost didn't wait to see how the others would react. Still crouching, he reached inside his trench coat and pulled the cord that ignited the canisters strapped to the backs of his boots. There was a flash of bright yellow light, and then the Ghost shot into the air, up the side of the wall toward a windowsill. He howled in agony as he realized, too late, that the canisters weren't adjusted properly. The hungry flames scorched his ankles through the tough hide of his boots. He could feel his skin bubbling and blistering under the intense heat. Anything, though, was better than death.

Bullets ricocheted off the wall behind him. Mickey had found his automatic, and his confidence. But it had come too late. Using the wall to spin himself around, the Ghost kicked his legs out and propelled himself through the second-story window, covering his head with his arms so that the splintering glass wouldn't lacerate his face. He shot into the dark room beyond, striking his head hard against the ceiling. Dazed, he reached inside his jacket, pulled the cord, and fell, with a loud, painful bump, to the floor. By the remains of the window, tiny flames were licking at the edges of the curtains like mischievous imps. He lay there on his back for a moment, breathing hard. The room was dark and devoid of life. The backs of his legs were agony, and he had a deep pain in his stomach where the moss man had struck him the blow. He closed his eyes and let out a long sigh.

Then, rolling onto his side, he scrambled to his feet, using the back of a sofa as leverage, and began to hobble—painfully— toward the door. He had to get out of there before Mickey sent the moss golems after him. He was in no fit state to continue the fight. He presumed the apartment must belong to the shopkeeper, and felt a momentary surge of guilt. He'd failed. He'd been unable to help the man. But it wasn't over yet. He'd be back, and the Roman's men would know vengeance. For now, though, he had to find his way back to his apartment before any of the Roman's other goons discovered he was hurt. He was already sure the mob boss had half of the city looking for him, and he didn't want to get caught out in the open unprepared.

A moment later he had crossed the room, opened the internal door, and slipped out into the dark passage beyond, heading for the rooftops, and home.

FIVE

Donovan quit the restaurant with a heavy heart. It was late, and he knew Flora must have been in bed for hours. He'd thought about calling her from the holo-booth in the back of La Campagna—the Commissioner's favorite eatery—but even then he knew he'd left it too late. Still, he sighed to himself, he supposed she was used to it. Such was the life of a woman married to a police officer. That was the advice the Commissioner's wife, Patricia Montague, was regularly heard passing out to the wives of the junior officers: get used to the eccentric hours, the lack of calls, the fact he'll probably forget your birthday—or leave now. There was a strange irony in that, of course: the Commissioner hardly kept unusual hours, and Mrs. Montague, with her flashing red talons, eyeliner, and short skirts, had a reputation for being one of the biggest flirts in town. It was hardly a model relationship.

The Commissioner had invited Donovan to dinner to talk over the situation with the Roman, or rather, to apply another liberal dose of pressure to the inspector while the older, portly man took his fill of pasta. As if that was what Donovan needed right now, to be reminded that he had to do a better job whilst watching the Commissioner eat.

Commissioner Montague had explained that he was anxious to bring the situation to a head. He wanted to break the Roman's hold on the city, and to put an end to the recent spate of murders attributed to the Italian's mob. "And Felix," the Commissioner had said, leaning over the table with a cigar in his hand, his bushy gray moustache twitching as he spoke, "what's it with all these funny names, hmmm? 'The Roman.' 'The Ghost.' You go ahead and tell them that I'm 'the Commissioner,' won't you, and that I won't hear any more of it, hmmm? Not one bit of it!"

And with that he had rocked back in his chair, grinning wolfishly at his young wife, his smoldering cigar clamped firmly between his teeth. That outburst, apparently, was going to help Donovan to solve the case and smash the mob. It was all he could do not to throw his drink at the man and storm out of the place.

Instead, he had nodded appreciatively, assured the Commissioner that he was doing everything in his power to close the net on the Roman, and that he would redouble his efforts in the morning. As far as this "Ghost" was concerned, he would keep his ear to the ground and try to anticipate any further activity. What he didn't add was that, in his opinion, this "Ghost" had actually done them a favor, and that he wished the Commissioner would grant the police a little more leeway to do the same.

He'd had to sit through coffee, listening to anecdotes he'd heard a thousand times before and feeling embarrassed by the attention that Mrs. Montague was lavishing on the handsome young waiter. Then, finally, it was over, and he'd been set free to go about his business.

"Remember to tell them what I said, won't you, Felix?"

He'd bunched his fists in his coat pockets so hard that he

was sure he'd probably drawn blood.

Now it was a quarter after eleven and he knew that by the time he was home, he'd only catch a few hours' sleep before morning. Poor Mullins would have to suffer another day of tired imprecations.

Donovan turned the corner and stopped to draw a cigarette. He pulled the ignition tab but it didn't spark. Cursing, he discarded the useless white stick and took another from the packet. It was dark on 43rd Street. People had retired for the night, and the roads were still and empty. Dark shapes hulked in the shadows: garbage cans; railings; an old easy chair, abandoned in the middle of the sidewalk. Above, in the distance, searchlights reflected off the underside of pregnant clouds and the moon was hazy and lost behind a thick screen of mist.

The deafening roar of a rocket firing overhead momentarily punctuated the silence, causing Donovan to look up. A biplane had just taken off from the roof of one of the nearby buildings, its rocket launcher burning with brilliant light as it surged away into the sky on a great plume, leaving a shimmering trail in its wake. Donovan watched it as it banked to the left and disappeared around a skyscraper, its rocket booster fading to a dull glow as the propellers engaged. A moment later, the sky was clear once more.

Donovan shook his head. The world was changing. Already, the airships of his youth were becoming outmoded, archaic, a thing of the past. They still used them, of course. They were faster than steamships, and the new airplanes were only reliable over short distances. But he knew it wouldn't be long before something else came along to replace them. The Cold War would see to that. With the British to spy on, technology was being driven forward at an incredible rate.

Still, for all this technology, the criminals remained the same. They never changed. They were always after power and money. No matter what tools they had at their disposal, what new schemes they cooked up, a crook was a crook, plain and simple. The Roman was the same. Just another guy who thought the world owed him an existence, and who'd decided to take it regardless, no matter how many people put themselves in his way.

The Ghost... He was different, although Donovan had yet to put his finger on the guy's motivation. What was it that inspired someone to don a black suit and head out into the night to stop a bank job? He could see why it made the Commissioner nervous. It showed the police force up for what it really was: a bureaucratic bunch of peacekeepers who didn't truly have the power or the means to put a stop to the organized crime that was infecting the city. He needed to find out who this "Ghost" character was. Then he'd have to decide whether to shake him by the hand or lock him in a cell and throw away the key. If only he co—

Donovan pulled up short, his previous thought dissolving as he stared, fascinated, at the strange sight before him. There, on the sidewalk, were three dead birds. They were pigeons, he thought, although he couldn't be certain in this light, as their bodies were so contorted and mangled. They could have been rooks. This was the third time he'd encountered a similar sight in different locations around the city, and he looked up inquisitively, trying to ascertain whether they had fallen from the sky this way, or whether they had been caught by some sort of predator and then later abandoned. There was no way of telling.

Donovan grimaced. His cigarette was burning low, wreathing him in pale blue smoke. He was feeling edgy. He needed to get home.

He turned to see a long, sleek-looking car purr up to the sidewalk a few feet from where he was standing. It was a new, expensive model; black and pristine, its headlamps gleamed in the darkness and steam curled from the tall exhaust funnels at the rear. The windows were black and glassy, and he couldn't see anyone inside. He eyed it warily, unsure of the significance of its appearance.

Presently, just as Donovan was considering heading on his way, the front passenger window rolled down and a fat, porcine face peered out. The man was wearing a wide-brimmed hat and a black jacket. He looked at Donovan with haughty amusement. "Hey, Donovan. There's a man here who'd like to speak with you." He nodded at someone unseen in the back seat and the rear door nearest the curb clicked open, swinging out toward him.

Donovan peered inside the vehicle, but all he could see were shadows. He cleared his throat. "I'm busy." He flicked his cigarette butt at the wall and started slowly on his way. He knew it was dangerous to turn his back on these people—he might easily end up with a bullet in it—but he knew also that getting inside that car was an even more reckless pursuit. The police did not parley with the mob.

Keeping his head down, Donovan picked up his pace. He did not look back at the car. He made it about fifty yards before he became aware of the slow hissing sound of the vehicle as it reversed along the curb, and a moment later it pulled alongside him, creeping slowly so as to keep pace with him as he walked.

Donovan glanced over. The rear door was still hanging open, with its sinister invitation to climb inside. He continued to walk.

"Inspector Donovan. I really think it would be in your best interest to take me up on my offer to talk." The voice was thin and reedy, high-pitched for a man, and all the more minacious because of it. It emanated from the rear of the vehicle.

Donovan could see that the crook hanging out of the passenger window was now brandishing a snub-nosed automatic and was waving it in his direction. His options looked pretty limited. If he went for his own weapon, he'd likely be dropped by the goon before he had chance to draw it. But who was the character in the back of the car, and what the hell did he want? Was it some sort of elaborate trap? Was he going to end up like that poor bastard Landsworth? He shuddered at the thought.

Donovan stopped walking and turned to regard the vehicle. The driver hit the brakes and the car swung in alongside the curb. Donovan felt his pulse quicken. The back of his neck was damp with perspiration, despite the chill. He held his arms out in front of him to show that he had no intention of making any sudden moves. But he did not approach the vehicle. "Why don't you come out here and talk?" He gave a wry smile. He knew he was walking close to the line. "I have difficulties with confined spaces."

The goon in the front waved his weapon more forcefully in Donovan's direction. "It doesn't do to refuse a direct invitation from Mr. Reece, policeman. I suggest you get into the car now."

Shrugging, Donovan approached the open door. If it was a choice between that and being riddled with bullets on the sidewalk, well, at least this way he had a fighting chance. Resting a hand on the roof of the vehicle, he peered inside. A thin, spidery man, silhouetted by the weak light thrown out by the burning end of his cigar, sat in the back of the car, one leg folded atop the other. He was dressed in an exquisite black evening suit. He turned to look at Donovan and offered him a wicked smile. "You see, Inspector, we're not going to bite." The man chuckled, and the sound was like ice water running down Donovan's spine. "Please, come in, take a seat. It's late. Allow me to escort you home."

Donovan cringed at the thought that these people—whoever they turned out to be—knew where he lived. Still, it was too late to make a run for it now.

Dipping his head, Donovan slid into the car beside the thin man, clicking the door shut behind him. It was dark, and it took a moment for his eyes to adjust to the gloom. The man in the back was like a pale specter, the glowing end of his cigar the only source of light in the whole vehicle. The front seats were separated from the rear compartment by a glass partition. Donovan wrinkled his nose. The vehicle was filled with the pungent stench of the cigar smoke.

Donovan leaned back against the firm leather seat as the car purred softly away from the curb. He was reassured by the weight of the automatic in his pocket, and the fact that the goon in the front no longer had a bead on him, although he was quite sure that any wrong move now would be swiftly and efficiently punished.

Reaching into his pocket he carefully withdrew his packet of cigarettes, placed one between his parted lips, and pulled the tab. Then, trying to maintain his nerve, he glanced at the man who had effectively taken him prisoner. "So... Mr. Reece?"

The man leaned forward and his face loomed out of the murk, stark and white. "Gideon Reece. I work for the Roman."

So that was what this was all about. The Roman. Donovan almost gave a sigh of relief. At least he had some idea of what he was dealing with. He took the cigarette from his lips and allowed a riffle of smoke to flood from his nostrils. "The Roman, eh? So tell me, is he an affable sort of boss?"

A smile curled at the edges of Gideon Reece's lips, and he turned his head as if listening for something that wasn't there. For the first time since getting into the vehicle, Donovan noticed that the other man was missing the uppermost half of his left ear. "Affable enough, Inspector, as long as one pays one's due respects. Are you a respectful man?"

"Respect has to be earned, Mr. Reece."

"Yes. I believe it does. But it can also be bought." The man reached inside his coat and produced a brown paper envelope. He rubbed his hand over it in a bizarrely ritualistic gesture, and then placed it ceremoniously on Donovan's knee. Donovan picked it up, unfolded the flap, and looked inside. The envelope was stuffed with used bills. There must have been a thousand dollars in there. He closed his eyes for a moment, took a long draw on his cigarette.

"The Roman would like to offer you a token of *his* respect. He understands that you've been finding things... difficult... of late, and would like to compensate you for your trouble. He's aware that you've been having problems sleeping, Inspector. Anyone in your position would. It's understandable. You've seen some terrible things. The state of poor Mr. Landsworth, for example. I'm sure you'd rather just blank the entire affair from your mind..."

Donovan grinned. So this was a payoff. Forget about the murder of an odious old politician and walk away with a cool thousand in dollar bills. Flora would be ecstatic with that. For a moment, he was almost tempted. But he was a better cop than that. He was a better *man* than that. And besides, he knew it would never stop there. Once he'd taken the Roman's paycheck, it would only be a matter of time before someone was leaning on him again. He knew how it worked; he'd seen it a hundred times before.

Sighing, he laid the envelope neatly on the seat beside him. "You can tell the Roman that, whilst I appreciate his offer, my memory is in good working order, and I'm sleeping just fine." He took another long draw on his cigarette, listening to the sound of the paper crackling as he pulled the nicotine into his lungs. There was silence for a few moments, save for the hissing sigh of the steam vents at the rear of the car as it slid along the road.

Finally, Gideon Reece spoke once more. "I'm not sure you fully understand what's being offered to you, Inspector Donovan. This is a gift. To refuse it would be to, well... to fail to show respect." He paused, sucking thoughtfully on the end of his cigar. "We've already discussed the importance of respect. Landsworth had no respect." Another pause. He turned to regard the inspector and his eyes flashed with menace. "I'm sure that makes things clearer for you?"

Donovan didn't answer. He understood only too well what was being intimated. He was being presented with an ultimatum: take the money and dine with the devil, or end up dead in a backstreet, or worse, with his pants around his ankles in a hotel suite like that poor bastard Landsworth. He knew it wasn't an idle threat. But somehow that only worked to strengthen his resolve. Now it was him or the Roman. And what was more, he knew they were getting nervous. Why else would they try to buy him off?

Donovan glanced out of the window. They were in his neighborhood. He met the other's penetrating stare with a steady gaze. "Can I think about it?"

Reece laughed again, a cruel, terrible laugh. He spread his hands in a placatory gesture. "Of course, Inspector. Of course." He waved his fat cigar beside his head, as if somehow plucking thoughts out of thin air. "But if I may, I'll leave you with some well-intentioned advice. Don't go against him. He's been at this game for a long time. A *very* long time. Longer than you could possibly imagine. He knows how to get what he wants." He smiled, leaning back in his seat. "I'll need your answer by midnight on Friday."

Donovan nodded. "Then you can let me out here, Mr. Reece. This is my neighborhood, and I'd be thankful for the walk."

Reece nodded and rapped on the glass. The vehicle swung toward the sidewalk and pulled to an abrupt stop.

Donovan glanced at the brown paper envelope, and then, without looking back at the other man, pushed the door open and stepped out onto the sidewalk. The cold air hit him like a rush.

He turned and clicked the door shut behind him, and a moment later the car swerved away into the road and growled off into the night. Donovan watched it go.

He had four days to get something concrete on the Roman. Four days to find his way out of this mess. He'd spent weeks on the case already and hadn't even got close. But now it was different. Now he finally had a lead: Gideon Reece.

Donovan pulled his overcoat tight around his shoulders and set off for home. He needed some sleep, and he wanted to see Flora. More than anything else in the world, he wanted to see his girl.

SIX

The Ghost flung his apartment door open and pushed his way inside, leaning heavily on the doorjamb. The drawing room was dark, the only light leaching in through the wide, panoramic windows that looked out across the city far below. Shafts of silver moonlight pooled on the soft carpet, casting everything in a strange, ethereal glow.

He was breathing heavily. His ankles were bloody and blistered and he was finding it painful to walk. He'd made his escape across the rooftops, crossing four or five buildings before he'd had to force open a fire escape and swing down the stairwell to street level, five stories below.

The Roman's men—or what was left of them—clearly hadn't chosen to give chase. In that he'd been lucky: the moss golems had been slow and lumbering but effectively unstoppable, at least with the weapons he'd had at his disposal. He wondered where they had come from, what was controlling them. He'd never seen anything like them before. Automata, yes – but these were something different, something dangerous and new. Twice during the encounter he'd thought he was finished, and if the fight had continued, he knew it would only have been a matter of time. Tiredness would have seen him off. Tiredness and ineffective weapons. He needed to do something about that.

He'd hobbled the rest of the way back to his apartment building, being careful to stick to the shadows. The streets weren't busy, but he knew that in this city there were prying eyes at every corner, behind every blacked-out window. At one point, half delirious with pain, he'd stumbled out in front of an oncoming car, its headlamps cutting wide channels in the gloom. The vehicle had skidded to a screeching halt, the driver leaning out to shout abuse at the strange shambling figure in the road. The man had probably assumed he was dealing with a drunken bum. In some respects, he wouldn't have been far off. He certainly intended to open a bottle of whisky, just as soon as he'd cleaned up his wounds. The entire evening had been a less than successful enterprise.

Pushing the door shut behind him, the Ghost limped across the room, pausing by the window. Outside, from this height, the night looked still and silent, but the city was still shimmering with bright electric lights. The distant trails of biplanes crisscrossed the sky. He glanced at the clock on the wall. It was early, only ten o'clock. He was meant to be somewhere else. But the stinging pain at the back of his legs and the tender flesh where he'd received blows from the moss men meant that any thoughts of other activity that evening had to be put aside.

He turned away from the window and stumbled toward the bathroom. He had blood on his hands. He laughed at the irony of that thought. There was no redemption for him now.

This time, however, it was his own blood, from a gash in his palm. He must have sliced it as he crashed through the window.

He grunted as he pushed the door open with his shoulder. The lights blinked on, triggered by an automatic sensor, flooding everything in harsh electric yellow. He winced at the sight of himself in the mirror. He was still wearing his long black coat and hat, but his face was smeared with blood, his bottom lip split and still bleeding. His chest ached as if he'd cracked a rib, and he didn't dare consider what state the backs of his legs would be in once he'd managed to strip away the ruination of his boots.

He swept his hat off his head, casting it through the open door into the drawing room, not bothering to note where it landed. Then, leaning heavily on the edge of the sink, he cranked the hot tap. Water spat into the basin, swirling around the plughole. He thrust his hands into it, watching the red stains mingle with the running water and disappear, leaving a long, puckered cut across his palm.

If only it was that easy.

He knew that not all blood could be washed away like that. He thought of the war, of what had happened to him out there, in France. Those events had come to define him, to forge the shape of his future life. The anger still burned deep inside him. He doubted it would ever be quelled. Time had not done it. Perhaps this, perhaps the fight would help. Perhaps it would be enough to still the maelstrom at the center of his being.

In truth, however, he doubted it. He'd never be able to scrub the stains of that time away. They were indelible now, a part of who he was: a burned-out old soldier with a grudge.

He looked up, meeting his own gaze in the mirror. For a moment he didn't even recognize himself. The eyes of the man looking back at him were haunted, and the face was pale and unfamiliar. He no longer knew who he really was. He wasn't "the

Ghost"—that construct of the reporters and their overzealous headlines, as useful as that moniker had proved to be—and he wasn't that other man, either. That character was just as much a construct, a proxy; he existed only in the same world as the Ghost. He only existed at all because of necessity.

The Ghost sighed. Only one person had seen to the core of him, and he couldn't even be himself with her. The irony was not lost on him.

He lowered his face to the sink and splashed water over himself. Then, gingerly, he set about stripping his clothes. He unbuckled the straps that tied his fléchette gun to his forearm and allowed the weapon to clang noisily to the floor, the barrel skittering away across the smooth ceramic tiles. He looked down at his feet. He was going to have to bandage his ankles. And, he laughed to himself, wincing as he began peeling away the scorched leather, he would need to invest in some new boots.

An hour later the Ghost lowered himself into an easy chair by the window and broke the seal on a bottle of illegal bourbon, sloshing a generous measure into a glass and downing it in one long motion. He shuddered as the alcohol did its work. He poured himself another glass, studying the amber liquid as he held it up to the moonlight. It would numb the pain. All of it.

On the table before him sat a large device. It was the size of a wireless receiver, but looked more like a miniature holotube terminal; three large glass valves were set into an old wooden case, arranged like a crown of glass teeth around a small mirrored chamber. A series of buttons and dials on the front of the device were unmarked. A wire trailed from the back of the unit, snaking away to disappear into the corner of the room, its destination lost in shadow.

The Ghost downed his second tumbler of whisky and placed the glass on the table with a clink. Then, turning to regard the strange device, he reached out and twisted one of the dials. The unit gave an electrical buzz and flickering blue energy crackled to life inside the three glass valves. The device began to hum as it warmed up. After a moment, the Ghost flicked another switch and a small holographic image shimmered into being inside the mirrored cavity. It was a woman. She was standing beside a microphone, her hair pinned to one side of her face, wearing a long, flowing dress. Her makeup accentuated her features, and the dress accentuated her hips. The backdrop was fuzzy and indistinct, but it appeared to be the inside of a nightclub.

The Ghost reached for the bottle of bourbon and moved to pour another measure into his glass. Then, changing his mind, he sat back with the bottle in his fist and took a long slug from it. He stared for a moment at the unwavering image of the woman. Then, like some sort of mysterious god, he twisted another dial on the machine and imbued the woman with life.

The Ghost fell back listlessly in his chair. The woman swayed slightly from side to side, clasping the microphone stand, and then the music started, the faint strains of a piano, tinny through the imperfect speakers of the improvised recording device.

The woman—Celeste Parker—parted her lips and sang, and her voice, even relayed through the fizzing static of the holograph machine, was a thing of beauty. The words were immaterial. The cadence of her voice carried all of the emotional significance, all of the necessary sentiment. It was a lament for lost love. It was raw, and it was true.

The Ghost stirred, taking another long pull on the whisky bottle. He knew those emotions, knew what it was like to lose someone. Knew what it was like to feel unrequited love for another.

He glanced at the holograph. What the hell did she see in that buffoon, Gabriel Cross? How could she stand to be around him? He only hoped that she could see something others could not, that her perception of the man was different from that of those hordes of partygoers who gathered at his Long Island home to pay homage to their debauched leader. He was a libertine, yes, but he was also a fool, an emotionless caricature of himself. The Ghost could not understand how Celeste could bring herself to endure the man's company, let alone his bed.

He watched her as she continued with her plaintive song. It was a private performance, just him and the machine, but all the while it felt to the Ghost as if there were more than one man in the audience.

Presently, the song ended and the holograph stuttered to a halt, the image frozen once again; a moment captured in time. He considered starting it over, then held the bottle of whisky up to the light. It was half empty. Enough.

Carefully, he swung his legs down from the footrest and tested them with his weight. It was painful, but he could walk. The bandages would hold. The burns had looked worse than they were—his boots had taken the brunt of the scorching. His ankles were badly blistered, but he'd be able to carry on. He pulled himself to his feet.

The bathroom light was still on, throwing a sheet of electric yellow into the room, creating bizarre shadows that seemed to come to life as he crossed the drawing room toward the rear of the apartment. He passed the bedroom door, which hung open, revealing a bed that had been slept in and not made, the sheets thrown back and abandoned. This he ignored, continuing on until he reached another door, almost hidden in the shadows at the far end of the apartment. It was the same as all the others, outwardly at least—four panels, painted with white gloss—save for the fact that nowhere on its surface was there any sign of a handle.

The Ghost approached the door and gave a series of sharp knocks, each one carefully placed and timed to perfection. He paused for a moment. Then, as if in conspiratorial acknowledgement of his secret code, there was a pneumatic hiss from beyond the wooden frame, accompanied by the grinding of gears, and the door eased back from the frame and slid to one side with a metallic clang.

Light flooded the apartment. The Ghost had to shield his eyes for a moment to protect them from the glare. The room beyond the door was bathed in the brilliant light of an arc lamp, which curved across the entire extent of the ceiling. There were no windows, but the walls were plastered with drawings and schematics, blueprints and technical diagrams. At the far end was an old wooden writing desk, pushed up against the wall. Its once smooth surface was now covered with a series of pockmarks and scars, and it was piled high with all manner of bizarre paraphernalia, from empty ammo casings to filament wire, steam valves to canisters of propulsion fuel. Likewise, a vast array of equipment and components lined the walls, or was otherwise heaped against them: a rack of long-barreled guns; a plastic bucket of fléchettes; two black trench coats; a spare pair of goggles.

He crossed the threshold, bathing himself in the bright light of the arc lamp. This was his workshop: the true home of the Ghost.

He'd been an engineer during the war, as well as a pilot, and this was his haven, the place where he was able to create. That he created mostly weapons designed to incapacitate or kill others was a fact that did not sit well with him, but he reconciled this knowledge with the understanding that he wielded those weapons for the right reasons... and that he always allowed the crooks to shoot first. Violence was the language of the enemy, and he had learned to speak it well.

The Ghost approached the desk and used his left arm to brush away the surface debris with a long, sweeping motion. Papers, batteries, and clockwork components scattered to the floor around his feet in a tinkling shower. Then, his eyes gleaming with the glassy patina of alcohol and enthusiasm, he searched the floor around the desk until he located the device he was looking for. It was almost identical to the fléchette launcher he'd been carrying earlier: a long, thin barrel attached to a ratchet mechanism that clipped to his forearm, with a small pneumatic trigger that trailed on a rubber cable, and a top-loading canister for the ammunition. Unlike the other weapon, however, the barrel of this device had been finely engraved with a thinly traced pattern of roses and thorns. He weighed it in his hands for a moment. Then, popping the lid free of the canister, he tipped the weapon over so that the fléchettes inside it spilled out over the desktop in a scatter of shimmering steel. He placed the weapon carefully back on the floor and lowered himself onto a stool, which he extracted from the chaotic mess beneath the desk.

Picking one of the small arrow-shaped blades from the heap, he turned it over in his fingers appraisingly. If they were going to prove effective against the moss golems, he'd have to rethink his approach. He grabbed a small blade from the nearby stack of tools and slipped it between the two metal plates that comprised the fléchette. Being careful not to shred his fingers on the razor-sharp rim, he prized the two pieces of metal apart with the blade, just enough so that he could see inside. There was a tiny cavity in the head of the wedge. He smiled with grim satisfaction. He knew what he could do with that.

He dropped the fléchette to the desk and stood, heading back into the darkness of the drawing room. When he returned a few moments later he was bearing the half-empty bottle of bourbon. He set it down beside the pile of ammunition and returned to his seat.

It was going to be a long night, and he had much work to do.

SEVEN

The antechamber was empty, save for a white marble bust of the Roman emperor Nero resting upon a mahogany plinth, and the uncomfortable high-backed chair in which he was sitting.

Gideon Reece interlaced his fingers upon his lap. He always experienced a certain degree of anxiety upon visiting the Roman. It wasn't that he had anything in particular to fear from his employer—at least not at the moment—it was more that the man's quiet, reflective indifference left Gideon feeling on edge, as if there was something unsaid, some subtext to the conversation that he was never made party to.

The Roman had always seemed genial—welcoming, even— but Gideon suspected that just below the surface lurked a terrifying fury. He had yet to see it unleashed, but when he did, he only hoped that he would not be the recipient. He had a suspicion that the mob boss would slit a man's throat just as soon as look at him.

Minutes passed. He could hear nothing through the adjoining door. Was there someone else in there with him, or was he simply making Gideon wait?

His answer came a moment later when the door opened and a tall, young man in a black suit stepped out. He was a swarthy-looking fellow, of European extraction, possibly Spanish or

Italian. The Roman's butler, Carlucci.

"He'll see you now," said Carlucci.

Gideon nodded in acknowledgement and got to his feet. The butler held the door open for him, and then slipped away as Gideon entered the Roman's office.

The room never failed to amaze him. Here was the accumulated wealth of generations, stacked within a single, oak-panelled room. Fine art lined the walls, from the brushes of such masters as Michelangelo, Rembrandt, Van Eyck and Monet. Bookcases bulged with venerable old tomes, bound in vellum by legions of long-dead monks. A marble statue of a beautiful woman stood in one corner, naked save for the impression of a silken drape to cover her modesty.

The Roman himself perched upon the edge of his desk, regarding Gideon with amusement. He was a handsome man in his mid-fifties, with a tanned face that was lined and weather-beaten like old, familiar leather. He looked as if he'd spent decades toiling in the fields, rather than holed up inside his estate, issuing orders and slowly accumulating wealth. He still had a full head of thick black hair that was only now going to gray around the temples, and he had a wiry, athletic build, suggesting a harsh regime of exercise. His olive eyes were hard and unyielding. He was dressed in a smart gray suit with a white shirt and open collar.

"Gideon," he said, with a soft Italian lilt. "Will you walk with me? I must check on the progress of Dr. Spectorius."

"Of course," said Gideon, wondering who on earth this Spectorius fellow might be. He knew enough not to ask. If he needed to know then he would be told.

The Roman stood and guided him back through the door. They crossed the antechamber and emerged into the hallway. "Through here," said the Roman, indicating a door on the left-hand side of the staircase.

"To the rooms below?" said Gideon, surprised. He knew that the Roman had long ago excavated a series of chambers in the bedrock beneath the mansion, but he had never been invited to visit them, and was not entirely clear of their purpose.

The Roman smiled. "Indeed." He paused with his hand on the doorknob. "You are to be trusted, aren't you, Gideon?"

Gideon swallowed. "Yes, sir. Without question." He knew the Roman well enough to appreciate the underlying threat.

"Then follow me." The Roman pushed open the door to reveal a flight of stone steps descending into the gloom. He went first and Gideon followed. There was no handrail, and the steps had been worn smooth with the passing of countless feet.

"Tell me, Gideon, what news of the policeman?" Gideon had been anticipating this. "Did he accept our gift?"

"The man is obstinate," said Gideon. "Principled. It may take some time, but there are means by which I can... *encourage* him."

The Roman chuckled. "You see, this is what I like about you, Gideon. You understand the role you have to play. You're not clever or Machiavellian. You know what has to be done, and are clear on the consequences of failure. I admire that."

Another warning, thought Gideon. One way or another, he needed to ensure that Felix Donovan was kept quiet.

The Roman had come to the bottom of the flight of stairs, and Gideon hurried along behind him. They entered a small cellar, like the basement beneath any normal house, lit by a naked electric bulb. The walls were bare brick, and there was a damp, musty odour of disuse. A few moldering boxes were heaped in the far corner, and there was another door, leading to what Gideon presumed to be the excavated chambers beneath the house.

"Through there," said the Roman. "This is where we'll find the doctor." He crossed the room, opened the door and beckoned Gideon through.

The chamber on the other side must have been forty foot long and half as wide again, with a low, vaulted ceiling, from which a string of electric bulbs had been hung at irregular intervals. Another door at the opposite end of the room appeared to lead even deeper into the basement.

There was a damp, earthy odor, caused, Gideon realized, by the carpet of thick moss that covered most of the walls and floor. It was utterly bizarre. The bare stone walls were exposed in erratic patches where hunks of the moss had been cut away. He could see in a few places where it was beginning to grow back, healing over like emerald scabs.

A tall man in a battered leather apron stood hunched over a workbench, peering myopically through thick spectacles at one of three large brass skeletons, which were laid out upon the benches like corpses on mortuary slabs. Inside one of the metal frames, sods of moss and soil had been heaped and compressed, packing it out to form a solid, bipedal structure. A cavity had been left open in the center of the chest.

The man looked up as they entered, and then, upon seeing the Roman, straightened up and offered a wary smile. "Good morning, sir," he said.

"I see you are making excellent progress, Dr. Spectorius," said the Roman. "Another three, almost ready for deployment."

"Indeed, sir," said Spectorius. "They will be ready before the day is out, provided…" he trailed off, looking at the Roman expectantly.

"Ah, yes," said the Roman. He reached into his pocket and carefully withdrew three small objects, which he held out in his palm for Spectorius to examine. Gideon shifted his position in order to see them more clearly.

They were small pyramidal structures formed from twigs and bound together with twine. They formed little cages, at the centre of which rested black shriveled objects that looked disturbingly like desiccated animal organs.

"May I?" said the Roman, inclining his head toward the near-complete figure on the table.

"Please, be my guest," replied Spectorius. The relationship between the two men was curiously formal.

The Roman walked around the workbench to stand over the moss man. He selected one of the objects from his left palm, and then inserted it carefully into the cavity in its chest. He handed the remaining two to Spectorius, who quietly slipped them into his pocket.

"What are they?" said Gideon, indicating the effigy with a wave of his hand.

The Roman looked over at him and smiled. "Impressive, aren't they?" he said. "They are golems. Men of the earth. Soldiers."

"*Golems*?" said Gideon, surprised. So now the Roman was toying with monsters of myth and legend.

The Roman laughed. "Show him, Doctor."

With a thin smile, Spectorius crossed to the door at the far end of the chamber, and opened it. He spoke in hushed tones to someone on the other side, out of Gideon's view, and then stood back, holding the door open, as a figure lumbered slowly through the opening.

To Gideon's utter astonishment, it was almost identical to the inanimate thing on the table: a bulky, man-shaped golem, clearly constructed from brass, soil and moss. It lumbered to a halt a few steps into the chamber. It was primitive—hulking and shambolic—but appeared to be moving under its own volition. Somehow, Spectorius had breathed life into these things.

"But how?" Gideon could barely credit it.

The Roman smiled. "An ancient pagan ritual from Britain," he said. "The druids of the Wychwood used to animate these men of moss to aid them in their wild hunts. Now, they shall aid me in mine."

"The girl," said Gideon.

"The girl," confirmed the Roman. "How does your search proceed?"

Gideon was grateful for the change of topic. He wasn't sure he *wanted* to know how the Roman had come across such arcane knowledge, or indeed, how he had actually got it to work. "The net is closing," he said. "The Sisterhood had hidden her well, but I have a strong lead." He saw a minute change in the set of the Roman's jaw.

"She *will* be found," he said.

"Of course, sir," said Gideon, shooting a look at Spectorius, who was watching him, an amused smile on his lips. "I shall not rest until she is in your custody."

The Roman appeared to relax a little. "You may take some of my golems to assist in your search," he said. "Spectorius can make more, can't you, Doctor?"

"As you wish," replied Spectorius, who, out of the Roman's line of sight, raised a cynical eyebrow at Gideon.

Gideon wasn't entirely sure that he liked the idea. He felt uncomfortable in the hulking presence of the thing, and worse, he couldn't help thinking that the golems might represent more of an escort than hired help. Nevertheless, there was little he could do to protest. "Thank you, sir," he said.

The Roman nodded. "Then for now," he said, his tone dismissive, "our business is complete."

Gideon hid his sigh of relief behind a polite cough. "I'll see myself out," he said. The Roman's attention had already returned to Spectorius and the earthen figures on the table.

Quietly, he slipped away. He would have to prioritize the girl. He'd heard about a jazz club somewhere downtown where she put on a show. That was where he'd start. The policeman would have to wait a while longer.

EIGHT

The holotube was buzzing. An incessant sound, like a fly caught in an overturned tumbler, trying futilely to escape. Gabriel rolled over and tried to ignore it. His head was throbbing. He had no idea what time it was, but sunlight was pouring in through the half-open window, and he flinched as he peeled back his eyelids to regard the infernal device on the other side of the bed. His eyes lingered for a moment on the wall clock. Two in the afternoon. He'd only been in bed for a few hours, and he was still wearing his rumpled black suit. He covered his eyes with the crook of his arm and willed the trilling device to stop. Miraculously, it did.

Surprised, but happy in light of this new development, Gabriel rolled over once again and buried his face in the downy pillow. He drifted for a while in a state of delirious coziness, stretching his weary limbs and allowing his heavy eyelids to droop. Then the holotube began ringing again, loudly, and he knew he was in for another long day. At least, whatever was left of the day.

Lifting his head, he glanced at the holotube receiver. Then, with a weary sigh, he swung up and round, pulling himself into a sitting position on the edge of the bed and smoothing his hair with his hands, attempting, ineffectually, to disguise the fact that he had just been woken by the call. He leaned over to the bedside table and flicked the steel lever on the holotube receiver to the "Accept Call" position.

The machine whirred to life. A blue light gradually bloomed into being, accompanied by a sharp electric whine as the receiver unit warmed up to capacity. A moment later, a shimmering monotone image appeared in the mirrored cavity, and Gabriel couldn't disguise the smile that appeared on his lips when he saw who was calling. Celeste. She was smirking, knowingly, and was dressed in a long, pale dress that traced the line of her figure from her neckline all the way down to her ankles. She was smoking a cigarette.

"I figured you must have been asleep."

"I was." Gabriel grinned. "And now I'm awake."

Celeste was silent for a moment. "You look a mess, Gabriel. Did you sleep in that suit?"

"I hardly slept at all." He looked around absently for his cigarette case, and then, patting his pockets, discovered that it was still inside his jacket. He slipped it out and withdrew a cigarette. "Have you realized quite how often you open a conversation by telling me how terrible I look?"

"Have you realized how often you look terrible?" was her swift retort. The singer leaned in closer to the transmitting terminal and the holographic image suddenly fractured, becoming nothing but a blur of light and motion, before resolving once again, this time to reveal a stunning close-up of her face, a portrait of pure light. She was wearing a concerned expression. Her eyes darted about as she tried to get a better look at him. Gabriel couldn't help but smile; she was never more attractive to him than when she showed her true self, revealed her emotions through her oft-impenetrable mask of lipstick and rouge. He wondered if others saw it; he knew they must. "Is that a bloody lip?"

Gabriel took a long draw on his cigarette. "I suppose you wouldn't believe me if I told you I'd been fighting for your honor?"

"No. I wouldn't."

He laughed. "To tell you the truth, it's all a bit hazy. I had a run-in with that 'Ghost' chap. You know, the one in all the papers."

Celeste offered him an incredulous look. "Now I know you're lying."

Gabriel gave his best impression of looking hurt. "Well, perhaps 'run-in' is a little strong. I nearly hit him with my car. I was on my way to Joe's and the damn fool ran straight out in front of me. I had to slam the brakes on. Managed to give my face a good knocking on the steering wheel. Bashed my hand, too."

Celeste leaned back from the transmitter, revealing a little more of the soft flesh around her throat. It was adorned with a string of pearls. Gabriel had bought them for her a few weeks earlier. She blinked. "What did he do?"

"He leaned on the bonnet and stared directly at me, right at my face, and then he just carried on, as if nothing had happened. To tell you the truth, it was terrifying. Shook me up." He puffed on his cigarette. "He looked like he'd been in a fight."

Celeste glanced at something—or someone—just out of sight of the holotube transmitter. "So you drove home instead of coming to the club." She seemed distracted.

Gabriel nodded. "That's about the long and the short of it.

Knocked back a couple of whiskies to numb the pain, and then called it a night."

Celeste watched him, silently.

"You know I would have been there if I'd felt up to it."

No response.

"Look, where are you? I can come back into town now. We could have lunch."

Celeste laughed. "It's two o'clock, Gabriel. I've had lunch. Besides, by the time you get here I'll be preparing for tonight's show."

Gabriel dropped the stub of his spent cigarette into the half-empty glass of water by the side of the holotube terminal. It fizzed for a moment and went out. He was glad it was out of sight of the blinking lens that reflected his image down the receiver. "Tonight. That's it, then. I'll come tonight. I'll attend to things here and come over."

Celeste gave a wry smile. "Be sure not to hit any wayward vigilantes on your drive."

Gabriel shrugged. "I'll take the train."

She laughed. "You know where to find me." The link went dead, leaving him with nothing but a low burr.

"I certainly do," he said aloud, before reaching for the whisky bottle he'd abandoned earlier that morning, pulling the stopper free and taking a long slug.

The train that ran from Long Island to Manhattan was a vast, gleaming masterpiece of modern engineering. Constructed around a shell of iron, it had a tip like a snub-nosed bullet capped with a carapace of shining white ceramic. The carriages snaked in a long procession, linked by joints of reinforced rubber, forming one continuous open space within. Unlike the more traditional locomotives that still crisscrossed most of the country, the Long Island train had abandoned its reliance on steam and coal. Instead, the engineers had adopted a powerful pneumatic engine, created during the war for transporting missiles along the coast, but now relegated to shuffling people back and forth to the city. The result was a powerful, reliable, high-speed means of traveling to Manhattan Island, and Gabriel hated every moment of it.

It wasn't the speed of the thing, nor the discomfort; a first-class ticket commanded a particularly high standard of travel, and Gabriel could easily afford it. It was simply the fact that he was too enamored by the sense of control he felt when sat behind the wheel of his own car to care for the relatively passive experience of being a passenger on the train. He couldn't abide the notion that he was placing his own destiny in the hands of other people, no matter how unreasonable he knew that notion to be. He felt affronted by it, as if it somehow eroded him, made him lesser in some tiny way. It was a hangover from the war, from the horrible things that had happened to him over there, in Europe. Those experiences had left him feeling impatient, unwilling to concede control. Perhaps that was why he had a tendency to sabotage his own happiness. Perhaps.

Like most of the lost generation, Gabriel Cross was damaged, irrevocably scarred. The difference was that he recognized the fact, and embraced it. It was this that had prevented him from going insane. But even that, he knew, was debatable.

Stifling a yawn, he disembarked onto the platform, stopping to button his overcoat against the brisk winter chill. Behind him the engine sighed majestically, as if weary after its long journey, and the platform suddenly swelled with jostling people as the carriage disgorged the remains of its charge.

He stood for a moment, watching the crowds of people as they swarmed toward the exit, one after another, just like a flock of birds. His hand dropped almost involuntarily into his pocket, fingers probing for the item he had secreted there earlier. He found it, and the cold, hard feel of it was reassuring. His service revolver. It was an old weapon now, basic compared to the more advanced designs of recent years, but it had never let him down, and he carried it with him whenever he came to the city. Or rather, whenever he came to Joe's.

Turning the collar of his coat up, he set off, following the herd of travelers as they scrambled up the steps toward the cold Manhattan night.

The sky was clear when he emerged, his breath fogging in the frigid November air. It was dark, and the city was lit up like a show hall; electric lights burned in every tower, crisp and bright and stark against the black fabric of the sky. He checked his watch. Nine-thirty. He had time to walk.

He set off, carrying himself with an insouciant air that he didn't feel. Cars hissed by on the road, their engines crackling with heat and steam. Pedestrians continued to spill from the station exit, flooding the sidewalks with their loose tongues and even looser morals. Drains exhaled columns of steam; the breath of the underworld rising unbidden into the physical realm. Gabriel marched on. It felt to him as if the city were somehow alive, as if it were watching him with impassionate eyes from every window, from every corner or shadowy doorway. The thought made him shudder. He wanted to stop for a cigarette, but instead he pressed on, turning a corner into a fierce breeze that rattled down the avenue, bringing a cold bite in off the ocean. He ducked his head and continued on his way.

Half an hour later, just as he was beginning to wish that he'd taken a taxi after all, Gabriel rounded the block and turned onto East 14th Street. He blew into his hands to stave off the chill. The Sensation Club, or Joe's, as the regulars knew it, was between Fifth Avenue and Broadway, down a short flight of steps in the basement of a tenement building and behind an unmarked red door. The police knew about the place—of course they did—and knew also that it was patronized by a small-time crook named Johnny Franco, but they were also aware that the club served a valuable purpose. It kept the city's rich clientele away from the bigger, uglier drinking dens, and it kept Johnny Franco out of trouble. So they steered clear of the place, and Johnny went about his business, serving illegal gin to the elite of the city, reveling in the perceived radiance of the company he kept. Poor Ariadne had failed to see the charm of it all, but Gabriel knew it for what it was—an extension of the perpetual party, a home from home. And besides, Celeste was there.

Gabriel rapped on the door, and presently the handle turned and a small crack appeared between the door and the jamb. He leaned closer. He could hear the distant strains of music, see a bright red light shining somewhere on the other side of the door. He turned his head. There was a scuffling sound from within, and then the door swung inward and a beaming man in a tuxedo was standing before him, waving him through to the mysterious club beyond. "Good evening, Mr. Cross. It's nice to see you again." The doorman, a wiry little fellow with a neatly trimmed beard and darting brown eyes, ushered him forward and swiftly closed the door behind him. "You're just in time. She'll be on in a moment."

Gabriel nodded and shrugged off his overcoat. He handed it to the doorman. "Thank you, Clive."

The doorman cocked his head. He looked concerned. "Have you hurt yourself, sir?"

Gabriel looked down at his bandaged hand. "Oh, it's nothing, Clive. I had an incident in the car yesterday and gave it a knock. It'll be fine in a few days."

"Glad to hear it, sir."

Gabriel watched as the other man disappeared into a small cloakroom just off the lobby. Then, feeling the need for a smoke, he reached into his pocket, withdrew his cigarette case, and tapped out one of the small white sticks. He pulled the tab, and a moment later the sweet aroma of smoldering tobacco mingled with the myriad other scents in the club: alcohol, sweat, and cologne.

Pausing just a moment longer to smooth his rumpled jacket, he passed along a corridor under the red glow of the lamps, turned a corner, and then descended a short flight of steps to the main amphitheater of the club. The staircase wound round in a tight spiral, and as he emerged into the dimly lit hall below, he had the sense of stepping into another world; a hidden world, a fantasia of light and sound and debauchery, simmering just beneath the regular layers of the city. People laughed and caroused, sitting together in small cliques at a series of tables arranged around a large stage area, upon which a young woman—a pretty girl he'd never seen before—was performing a popular jazz tune. To the left of the stage was a long bar, with a smattering of people seated on stools along its length, all watching the girl on the stage whilst idly toying with their drinks.

The place was busy. Gabriel scanned the crowd. All the usual faces were there: businessmen, politicians, sportsmen. Johnny Franco and his cronies had taken their usual table near the front. The man himself—tall, gangly, mid-forties, wearing a pinstriped suit—sat with his back to the room, nonchalantly exchanging conversation with a man Gabriel didn't recognize. But his men weren't so relaxed. There were at least five of them clustered around the table, each of them covering Johnny from a different angle, their hands nervously resting inside their jackets, just in case they needed to produce their weapons in a hurry. Gabriel thought they looked jumpy. He wondered if they were expecting something to go down.

Taking another draw on his cigarette, Gabriel wound his way through the tables toward the bar.

"Usual please, Joe."

"Coming right up, Mr. Cross."

Gabriel lowered himself onto a bar stool and watched the burly barman slosh a measure of bourbon into a tumbler. He slid it across the lacquered bar with a smile. Gabriel nodded his appreciation and dropped a handful of coins into the other man's hand. Then, snatching up the glass, he downed the whisky in one quick motion and dropped the empty vessel back on the bar with a *clink*.

On stage, the performance had come to an end and had been met with a general apathy from the audience. Most of them weren't there to see the women. They were there to drink and do business. For some of them, of course, women *were* their business, but that was another matter altogether, and not something that Gabriel liked to dwell on for very long. Celeste was up next, however. Celeste always turned heads. Celeste was the jewel in Joe's crown, and everyone there knew it.

The lights dimmed. A hush rippled across the gathered audience. Someone smashed a glass across the other side of the room, and Gabriel could hear the tinkling fragments as they scattered across the floor. Joe placed another shot of bourbon by his elbow.

There was a mechanical grinding, the sound of gears choking and a chain being wound tightly around a barrel. Three enormous panels rose up from the stage, forming a petal-like arrangement behind the microphone stand. They were disk-shaped, and comprised of delicate iron fretwork and colored glass. Music stirred, slow and soulful, echoing around the cavernous interior of the underground club, the musicians hidden behind the stage or else somehow out of sight, ghosts murmuring sadly to the living. The glass panels began to turn, slowly and inexorably, like enormous multicolored wheels; cogs in some vast, unusual machine. Lights blinked on behind them, flooding the stage with dancing rays in reds, blues, pinks, and greens. And then, as if seeping from the ground like an ethereal puff of smoke, Celeste appeared, rising up through the center of the stage on a small wooden platform. She stepped forward toward the microphone.

She was wearing a red dress that fell just above the knee and accentuated her shock of auburn hair. Her lips were bright with crimson gloss, and her hands and forearms were covered in long, sensuous silk gloves. She reached out and took the microphone, silhouetted against the bright lights, and brought it closer to her parted lips. And then she sang, and not one person in the club stirred from their seat.

Gabriel felt a surge of desire. He watched her as she swayed on the spot, moving slowly with the rise and fall of the music. He'd known her sway in different ways; longed for her to sway that way again. And her voice... It was sultry and pure, knowing and innocent, dark and forgiving; it was life, in all its manifest glory. The words meant nothing. She could have been singing about anything at all. But the sound of her voice was like a portal to her soul, and Gabriel knew that he would never, ever find another woman like her in this world.

He reached for his drink and gulped it down. All thoughts of the previous evening were lost, banished by the ache he felt for this woman and the sound of her voice. It was a curse, and he knew it. It would be his downfall. Celeste was his Achilles heel. He played a game with her; let her think that he was something he was not, feigned disinterest. But truthfully, he was so very much in love with her that he knew he would do whatever she wanted. Knew he would—

The loud report of a gun firing echoed around the enclosed space. A woman screamed. Gabriel spun around on his seat to see a group of figures standing at the foot of the stairs, half hidden in shadow. The music stopped abruptly.

Gabriel shifted nervously on his seat. Was this what Johnny Franco's goons had been expecting? He tried to weigh up the situation. There were five of the newcomers. Two of them were huge, wrapped in long black overcoats and wearing hats. They stood motionless at the back, near the bottom of the stairs, as if waiting for permission to move. Two more were smaller men, each clutching pistols in their fists. The one on the right brandished a smoking barrel: he had evidently fired the initial warning shot. Between these two stood a thin, gangly man in an immaculate evening suit. His hands were steepled before his chest and his head was slightly bowed, as if in thought or prayer. Everyone in the room—including Gabriel—seemed to be waiting for him to speak. Even Johnny Franco, who Gabriel imagined was bristling inside, had maintained his cool, and was evidently biding his time, waiting to see what move the intruders would make next.

The moment stretched. Then, finally, the figure came to life, stepping forward so that Gabriel could just make out his face in the still-shimmering lights from the stage. His expression was serene, as if he were enjoying the interlude he had created. Nevertheless, Gabriel felt his hackles rising. There was something about this man, about the manner in which he carried himself, that spoke of violence and danger.

The man turned his head to survey the crowd, and Gabriel noted that the uppermost half of his left ear was missing. He didn't know who the man was, or who he purported to work for, but he had a notion. The Roman. Only the Roman would have the audacity to pull a stunt like this.

When the mobster finally addressed the gathered audience, it was with a soft, deliberate voice that sent shivers coursing down Gabriel's spine. "I apologize for the disturbance, ladies and gentlemen." He paused, as if carefully weighing his next words. "We will not detain you for very long. We have simply come to escort the lady from the premises, and then we'll allow you all to carry on with your evening." Gabriel felt his jaw clench as he realized that the man was indicating the stage—and, therefore, Celeste. What could these mob men possibly want with her?

The two goons on either side of the speaker—the men with guns—stepped forward. That was enough for Johnny Franco. With a bellow of rage he leapt out of his seat, accompanied by his small army of bodyguards and fellow crooks, and swung around to face the newcomers, brandishing a handgun boldly before him. "Now, I don't know who the hell you guys think you are, but this is my club, and I'm gonna give you one chance to quit before it starts getting messy."

Gabriel took the opportunity to glance over at Celeste, who was still hanging on to the microphone stand, clearly distressed, unsure how things were going to play out. He wanted to go to her. He needed to get her out of there. But he didn't want to give the crooks any more reason to start a firefight in such a confined space. He needed to wait for his moment. His hand went to his pocket, clasped around the butt of his service revolver. He felt a spike of adrenaline. And then, just as suddenly, he felt himself jerked back into the war.

Explosions flared before his eyes, scattering the dead that lay heaped on the muddy banks of the abandoned trenches. He could hear the whistle of projectiles swarming down on their position; see his friend, Olsen, with a hole in his skull the size of a human fist, his tin helmet spinning on the ground like a dropped coin. He took a deep breath, squeezed his eyes shut. When he peeled them open again, the moment had passed. But Johnny Franco was lying on the ground, dead, a bullet through his heart, and everyone was screaming.

Gabriel leapt into action. He whipped his weapon out from his pocket and swung it round, drawing a bead on the nearest goon. Almost without thinking about it, he squeezed the trigger and let off a shot, which whistled with deadly accuracy, catching the mobster in the temple and spattering brain matter across the wall. The man's body slumped in a heap on the tiles, and Gabriel didn't wait to see how his comrades would react. He turned and ran for the stage, dimly aware of the *rat-a-tat-tat* of gunfire chewing up the bar in his wake. Celeste was staring at him in blunt shock. "You... you—"

Gabriel grabbed her by the shoulder. "Get down!" The command was uncompromising, and she did as he said, dropping to the stage just as the whole place ignited in a storm of bullets. Gabriel hit the wooden boards beside her and then rolled, keeping his weapon pointed at the intruders. He wasn't about to let them take Celeste, whatever the reason.

The thin man with the scarred ear had disappeared, and now the two hulking giants were lumbering forward, slapping people out of the way in an attempt to get through to Johnny Franco's guys, who were showering them with bullets, to little or no effect. Relentless, the looming figures stomped forward in the dimly lit bar, single-minded, resolute.

The other goon, the one who had originally fired the warning shot when they'd first stormed the club, was coming after Gabriel and Celeste. And behind him, Gabriel could see more of them flooding down the staircase, blindly firing their guns into the sea of seething shadows; the clientele of the club, desperately trying to escape. It was turning into a massacre.

Gabriel raised his head just enough to squeeze off a shot, but his aim was wide and he missed the goon. A moment later the mobster replied with a spray from a submachine gun, which he was wearing on a strap around his neck. The glass panels behind Gabriel and Celeste exploded in a hail of colored fragments, and Gabriel felt glass embed itself in his back. He gasped with pain. But it was better than a bullet. He glanced at Celeste and then rolled again, crunching broken glass as he moved to the other side of the stage, coming up on one elbow and letting off another shot from his revolver. This time he caught the man in the throat, and the goon's head snapped back as his larynx was ripped out in a gobbet of soft flesh. Blood fountained into the air as he went down, his finger still depressed on the trigger of the tommy gun, spraying the floor with hot lead.

Gabriel didn't waste any time. He scrambled to his feet and darted over to where Celeste was still lying on her belly, her hands covering her head. Blood was streaming down his face from cuts caused by the glass shards. He wiped it away from his eyes, looking back at the stairs. There was no chance they were getting out that way, and what was more, the second wave of goons had now divided, half of them rounding on Johnny Franco's men, who were still putting up an extraordinary fight, and half of them heading in Gabriel's direction. He had bullets, but he knew he'd never be able to hold off six or seven armed men. He turned to Celeste, raising his voice over the clamor of the blazing guns and the screaming. "Is there another way out of this place?"

Celeste looked at him, her eyes wide with shock.

"Celeste! Listen to me! Is there another way out of here?"

She nodded weakly. "Under the stage. We have to get under the stage!"

Gabriel gave a curt nod and then squeezed off another three shots, trying to buy them some time. One of them struck home, burying itself in the shoulder of one of the men, who cried out in pain as he dropped his weapon and fell to his knees, clutching at the wound. There was nothing between them and the advancing goons except for an overturned table. That would give them precious little cover. But why had the men stopped shooting at them? A thought dawned on him. Celeste!

He grabbed for her arm. "Do you trust me?"

"What?"

"Do you trust me?"

"Of course, but—"

"No time to explain." He grabbed her roughly by the shoulder and then, in one swift movement, leapt to his feet, hauling her round in front of him like a shield. His heart pounded in his chest; his palm felt sweaty and hot against the grip of his revolver. He was taking one hell of a gamble.

Celeste was screaming. "What? Gabriel, no!"

He whispered in her ear. "Be quiet and trust me!" He glanced over her shoulder. The advancing men had stopped, lowering their weapons. He was right, then. They were under orders to take her alive. Gabriel pulled her closer, so close that he could smell her perfume over the heady scents of damp earth and cordite that were otherwise overpowering in the confined atmosphere of the club. He glanced to the left. Franco's men had been decimated by the lumbering giants in the black overcoats. The army of bodyguards now lay sprawled and broken on the floor, limbs torn from torsos, shattered bodies still writhing in agony, but not long for the world. And all the while the strange shambling moss men seemed able to absorb any amount of gunfire that was thrown at them without even flinching.

One of them had lost its hat, and Gabriel caught flashes of a green, faceless mask; he knew then that he had to get away, that even if he could hold off the goons with his ancient revolver, it was only a matter of time before the monsters finished with the remnants of Franco's men and turned on him. He guessed the thin man in the evening suit was counting on it. They would tear Celeste away from him, and then pound him to oblivion.

He glanced at the assembled men. Five of them, each one armed. Slowly, tentatively, keeping his revolver trained on the nearest of the crooks, he backed up, practically dragging Celeste across the stage with him. She was clearly terrified, and she had no idea what he was up to. He stopped when he saw one of the other men take a step forward.

"Easy…" Gabriel waved his gun. "Just stay right where you are." There was a loud crash from over to the left, and he realized that signified another of Franco's men being flung across the room by the moss men. The crowds were thinning now, the revelers either dead or hiding. The scene was one of utter chaos and brutality.

Gabriel leaned in closer to Celeste, his lips practically brushing her right ear. "How the hell does that platform work?

The one that brings you up onto the stage?"

"There's a paddle. It's on the floor, connected to a cable. It controls the speed."

Gabriel cast around, looking for the paddle. It was just by his foot: a small black box with a lever on it. He gripped Celeste even more firmly around the waist. "Hold on tight." He moved his foot.

Suddenly, the ground gave way beneath them. Gabriel was vaguely aware of the sound of Celeste screaming, of howling voices from above, and then blackness overwhelmed him.

NINE

The sky was on fire.

Gabriel craned his neck to watch the light show. Black funnels of oily smoke rose like inky towers in the distance, far beyond the trees, and searing plumes of orange and red streaked crazily across the bright canopy of blue. Rockets. Bombs.

He was in France.

He shook his head, tried to get his bearings. He was on his side. His leg was hurting. God! It was hurting so much. He felt around with his hands. Grass and metal. Mud. He was still in the plane, or at least what was left of it. He strained against his seat straps. The nose was crumpled and the propeller had gone, lost as he'd struck the ground. He'd lost a wing, too—that much was obvious by virtue of the fact he was on his side—but the other was still intact, pointing up at the sky like an accusatory finger.

Forcing himself to breathe, Gabriel reached down and felt for the buckle that would release him. His fingers were numb with cold; he noticed his breath was fogging in the frigid air. He pulled the catch and slid out of the pilot's seat onto the damp loam, crying out as his injured leg caught on the rim of the cockpit.

Fumbling, he managed to extricate himself and struggle into a sitting position. The plane was buried in a long, deep furrow. The earth had been ploughed as the machine had hurtled out of the sky, as he'd struck the ground at such tremendous speed, out of control and hoping not to die. He was lucky to be alive.

Gabriel pulled himself up against the fuselage, testing his weight on his damaged leg. He could hardly stand. He needed help. He surveyed the surrounding area. A farm. He was in a farmer's field, and about two hundred yards away the farmhouse sat small and squat, a tumbledown building that had likely stood there, unchanged, for centuries. The battle was far off now, raging away under that canopy of fire, and he knew that no one would come looking for him. They'd all assume he was dead—struck by an enemy missile, dropped from the sky. People didn't walk away from disasters like that.

The farmhouse it was, then. He looked up at the old building, suddenly cast in shadow, with some trepidation. Something about the look of the place caused the hairs on the nape of his neck to stand on end. But it was the only shelter for miles, and he needed to take a look at his leg. If he could get help there—or even find some sort of provisions with which to bind his wound—he could start thinking about how he was going to get back to the front and join up with his squadron.

The trek seemed like miles, and each step caused him to whimper in pain, his feet sinking in the soft, sticky mud. He steadfastly refused to look at his injury. It would be of no use. There was nothing he could do until he got to the farmhouse. He kept telling himself that, over and over. Get to the farmhouse and everything will be okay. "Everything will be okay." He even spoke it aloud in his delirium.

It was only when he got closer that he realized the building was a partial ruin. There were gaps in the stonework and one of the windows was missing. The chimney had slumped to one side, too, opening the roof to the elements and scattering bricks to the ground. The place had been abandoned for some time, perhaps since the onset of war, perhaps even earlier. He felt his heart sink. At least it was somewhere safe, away from the crashed plane, away from the hail of bullets and rockets and death. At least in the farmhouse he'd be able to strap his leg and formulate some sort of plan.

Wincing, he shuffled toward the door and tried the handle. The old latch creaked as he turned the wooden doorknob, and he pushed the door open, stumbling inside. It was dark, lit only by the pale shafts of light that filtered down through the holes in the ceiling. The place was sparsely furnished, from what he could see in the half-light: a roughly hewn wooden table; two chairs, one upturned; an old dresser against one wall. He crossed to the table, leaned heavily against it to catch his breath.

And then he heard it move. Something there, in the darkness. Something large. He was suddenly alert, the pain in his leg forgotten. He backed away from the table, edging toward the door. What was it? What had he disturbed? A bear? Did they even have bears in France?

He caught sight of something then, in the thin light: a thick, glistening tentacle, curling slowly across the floor toward him. He stood transfixed in abject horror as another one, and then another one, crept forward, reaching out for him as though sniffing at the air. The thing must have been huge.

He turned and ran, all sense of pain in his leg gone. All he could think about was getting as far away from that farmhouse as humanly possible. All he could think about was—

Gabriel woke with a start.

His cheek was smarting. Celeste was on top of him, a look of desperation in her pretty eyes. "Wake up, dammit! Wake up, Gabriel!" She raised her hand to slap him again, but he parried the blow with his arm.

"I'm awake. I'm here." Groggily, he pulled himself up onto his elbows. He looked around. He was in some sort of cellar. The walls were redbrick and slick with mildew. The ground wasn't much better. He could smell the damp, too, stuffy and pungent in his nostrils.

He tried to get his bearings, tried to shake off the remnants of his dream, of his memories. The club! Joe's club. They'd dropped through the stage. Now they were in a small room, positioned directly beneath the stage. A naked electric bulb was clipped to a bracket on the far wall, casting a pale, watery light. A long cable snaked away into the darkness, and Gabriel realized the room was flanked by two tunnels, one heading east and one heading west. It was remarkable, a cellar beneath a cellar. It was little wonder Johnny Franco had chosen the place as his base of operations. Absently, he wondered what these walls had seen in their time.

Gabriel glanced at Celeste. His vision was limned with fuzziness; he must have banged his head in the fall. He became aware of a series of sharp pains in his back. Glass, tiny fragments of it, buried in his flesh. And then shouting, coming from somewhere above: a husky male voice barking commands.

Celeste, on her knees before him now, cupped his face in her hands. Her touch was soft and gentle, and it sent a shiver along his spine. "Gabriel. We have to *go*. They're coming for us."

Still a little dazed, Gabriel got to his feet. Then, realizing he must have dropped his gun in the fall, he began searching the ground where he'd been lying.

"Are you looking for this?"

He turned to see Celeste holding his service revolver. The weapon looked incongruous in her small, gloved hands. He nodded, and then took it from her, slipping it into his pocket. Then, giving her his hand, he allowed her to lead him along one of the passages at a run, their footsteps echoing in the empty space.

Minutes later, it became clear to Gabriel exactly where she was taking him. The tunnel terminated in a short flight of steps, leading up to the basement level of the next building. Johnny Franco must have bought the building next door to the club and kept the connecting tunnel as an escape route, should Joe's ever be raided and he needed to make a quick getaway. As he mounted the steps behind Celeste, Gabriel couldn't help thinking that Johnny could have done with an escape route that night. Not that he'd mourn the passing of another gangster. Crooks usually got what they deserved, one way or another.

Celeste hesitated at the top of the stairway, putting her ear against the plain wooden door, listening closely for any sounds from the other side. She glanced back at Gabriel and shrugged.

He met her gaze. They could hear voices in the tunnel behind them. They didn't have much choice. If they encountered someone on the other side of the door, they'd just have to deal with them.

Gabriel climbed the last few steps, brushing past Celeste in the tight space of the stairwell. He pulled his revolver from his pocket, cracked it open and slipped a couple of extra bullets into the chamber. Then, taking a deep breath, he grabbed the handle of the door, gave it a sharp twist, and flung it open, covering the dark space inside with his gun.

Everything was silent. He realized he was holding his breath. He waved Celeste inside and then rushed in after her, hoping there would be enough time to barricade the door behind them before the gangsters arrived.

The room on the other side was sparsely furnished, with only one exit in the shape of an open door that appeared to lead out into the basement proper. There was a roughly hewn set of wooden table and chairs, a mirror, a sink, and a pile of old newspapers. Gabriel guessed that this was where the showgirls prepared for their performances, preening themselves before the mirror and each other. It was hardly the most salubrious of dressing rooms.

Celeste made for the door. Gabriel called out, stopping her in her tracks. "No! Wait. Help me with this." He dropped his gun on the table and then grabbed the wooden lip, dragging the heavy piece of furniture toward the door, its legs squealing against the tiled floor in protest. Celeste rushed over to help him, and a moment later they had formed a rough blockade, propping the table beneath the door so that it jammed the handle. Next, Gabriel heaved a couple of the chairs on top of the table and piled the rest around it, trying to make the barricade as deep as possible. It wouldn't stop the mobsters for long—especially if they had managed to bring one or both of their green-faced monsters into the passageway with them—but it might just buy them enough time to get away.

Gabriel retrieved his weapon, and then indicated to Celeste to lead the way. She knew this building better than anyone. That was their only real advantage.

The basement beneath this adjoining house had clearly been put to more nefarious use than the club next door. Passing through the low archway that led from the small room, it opened out into a space roughly the same size as Joe's. But here the decor was far less plush and expensive, and it had about it the stink of old cigar smoke and whisky. Rats, too. Gabriel could always tell if there'd been rats. He hated the dirty animals. He'd seen them devouring the dead, in France. It still haunted his dreams.

He glanced around, trying to make sense of the shapes he could see hulking in the gloom. There were round tables, identical to the ones in Joe's. He crossed to the nearest of them. A deck of playing cards had been abandoned there; used, heaped haphazardly, along with half a dozen empty glasses and an ashtray, the stubs of fat brown cigars now cold and nestling amongst the ash. It took Gabriel only a moment to realize what this was. "Poker. A gambling den. So that's how Franco keeps his nose clean at Joe's."

There was a crash from the small room behind them. The goons were trying to break through the door. Celeste nearly jumped out of her skin. "Come *on*!"

Gabriel rushed to her side. "Okay. Which way?"

"Follow me."

They raced to the back of the room, narrowly avoiding all manner of obstacles as they wound their way toward the stairs that would lead them, hopefully, to safety. Wooden crates full of imported goods, barrels of cheap alcohol, boxes of cigarettes—Franco had been running quite an operation. Gabriel wondered who would be in line to take it over, now that the man himself was dead.

Celeste, even in her heels, cleared the short staircase in three bounds, and Gabriel followed close behind. He could hear muffled voices now, from down below, and realized that their pursuers had finally managed to smash their way through his temporary barricade.

Panting for breath, he called after Celeste. "We need a vehicle. A car. We need to get away from here."

Celeste stopped in the mouth of the doorway, hovering like some ghostly siren leading him on in a wild chase. Beyond her was the hallway, and beyond that, the relative safety of the Manhattan night. She turned toward him, a wild look in her eyes. "Where's *your* car?"

"I told you. I took the train."

She laughed, then, and Gabriel didn't know whether it was in desperation or hysteria. He realized there wasn't much difference at that point in the proceedings. "I didn't think you actually *meant* it!"

He grinned. "I know." The voices behind them were getting louder. He could hear footsteps on the stairs. "Looks like we'll just have to make it up as we go. Now *run!*"

He grabbed her and pushed her toward the exit, his breath ragged, his heart thumping in his breast. They crossed the hallway, and he was shocked by the relative comfort and modernity on display. Here, unlike the rest of the building he had seen so far, there was a thick, plush carpet, a hat stand, and a large painting adorning the wall. It was the entrance to somebody's apartment. Johnny Franco must have lived upstairs.

Gabriel had no time to ponder the matter further, though, as the crooks were gaining on them. Celeste flung herself at the door, and then fell away in dismay when she found it wouldn't budge. The door was locked, and there was no key. They were cornered.

"Stand back!" Gabriel practically shoved her out of the way as he brought his revolver up, pointing it at the lock. "Cover your ears." He squeezed the trigger; watched as the chamber revolved, loosing a shot into the wooden door and sending splinters showering into the air. He fired again and then grabbed hold of the handle and yanked the door open. Outside, the night was cool and dark. The moon was a shining disk in the sky. He turned to Celeste. "Go!"

She fled, her heels clicking on the paving slabs as she ran up the steps and out into the street. There was a grunting sound from the other end of the hallway, followed by the report of a shot being fired. Gabriel felt the bullet whistle past his thigh, felt the hot pain of it graze his skin as it only just missed its mark. He didn't wait for the next one. He practically dove out of the doorway, tumbling over a stone pot and falling against the steps that led up to the street. He scrambled up the first few steps, and then felt a hand grab him by the wrist, hauling him up to standing. Celeste. He offered her a grateful smile.

It was dark outside, but the streetlamps cast their warm, radial glow. The street itself was deserted. Gabriel knew it wouldn't stay that way for long. The police would be on their way by now, and soon they'd be flooding into the wreckage that was once Johnny Franco's Sensation Club. He wasn't about to hang around waiting, though, not with people taking shots at him. He needed to get Celeste to safety.

There were two identical cars parked outside the front of the club; black, sleek, and modern. Steam and smoke billowed out from the rear of one of them, and Gabriel knew he had no choice but to take it, with force if necessary. He rushed over to the driver's side and flung open the door. The driver—clearly a goon belonging to the same mob as the men pursuing them—looked up, startled. Then, just as he recovered himself and was about to reach for his weapon, Gabriel clubbed him across the temple, hard, with the butt of his revolver. The man crumpled into unconsciousness, and Gabriel grabbed his lifeless body by the collar and hauled him out of the vehicle, dropping him carelessly to the road. He glanced up to see Celeste standing by the car, unsure what to do. "Get in!" he screamed, and, startled, she leapt into the passenger seat, visibly shaking.

Gabriel released the handbrake and slammed his foot on the accelerator, tearing away down the road just as a hail of bullets shattered the rear windshield and pattered into the armored plates covering the back end of the vehicle.

The car careened down the road, swerving around other parked cars whilst Gabriel attempted to get it under control. He glanced in the rearview mirror, and then, sighing, tossed his revolver across to Celeste. "They're coming after us. Here. Fill this up with bullets. They're in my pocket. You'll have to find them while I drive."

Celeste was clearly in shock. She turned to stare at him, her eyes wide. "You shot that man! After they killed Johnny Franco. You just casually pulled this... gun... out of your pocket and shot him dead."

Gabriel took a deep breath. The circumstances had been... *different*. It wasn't that he'd killed in cold blood. He'd shot to protect the woman he loved. He knew what those people were capable of. When he spoke, his voice was low and serious. "Shoot first. That's what they taught us in France. Always shoot first. Take them by surprise and don't give away your advantage. I was trying to protect you."

"Protect *me*..." She seemed lost, as if the horrors she'd witnessed down there in the cellar bar had somehow caused her mind to disengage. Gabriel decided not to press the point; he didn't have time to consider the implications anyway. But later—later he would get to the bottom of why these men had gone to such terrible lengths to attempt to kidnap this woman he loved. What could they possibly want with a jazz singer?

"Celeste!"

She seemed shocked by his forcefulness.

"Fill the gun with bullets. We're going to need it..." He trailed off as he swung the car wide around a sharp corner, narrowly missing a pedestrian crossing the road, an old man in a gray overcoat who looked more surprised than angry as they shot off along the slick tarmac, black smoke erupting from the twin exhaust funnels at the rear.

The other car was gaining on them, and he could see two of the mobsters leaning out of the windows, tommy guns at the ready. He needed desperately to stay out of their range.

Celeste, woken from her momentary reverie, was now

fishing around in his pocket, attempting to grab hold of the stray bullets. And then, a moment later, she was screaming.

Gabriel, trying to keep one eye on the road, turned about in his seat to see what was happening. A man—a mobster—was in the back of the car, leaning through the gap between the front seats so that he could grapple with Celeste, attempting to wrestle the weapon out of her grip. He must have been in the vehicle all the while, lying low in the back, waiting for his opportunity to strike. Gabriel chanced a proper look. He was a big man with a bushy black moustache, and he was wearing a satisfied sneer as he twisted Celeste's wrist, causing her to cry out again in pain. To her credit, she still had a tight grip on the revolver, but the angle of the man's attack meant that it was pointing away from him, forced low, toward the dashboard.

Gabriel had to help her. But he had to keep moving, too. If he stopped the vehicle, the others would be upon them in seconds, and if he let go of the wheel, they'd likely end up as a burning wreck in the side of a building when the car veered off course. His choices were limited.

He glanced at Celeste. Her eyes were pleading. Keeping one hand on the wheel, he tried to hold the vehicle on a straight path as he twisted around in his seat and jabbed his right elbow back sharply into the other man's face. It connected hard, jarring the crook's neck, and the man howled in pain. Gabriel tried again, this time catching the man in the mouth and loosening a couple of teeth. Blood spattered over the seats. The man momentarily relaxed his grip on Celeste. That was all she needed. Gripping the gun, she twisted around in her seat and pulled the trigger, firing a shot into the man's chest at point-blank range.

The mobster gave a short, burbling cry, and then, blood trickling down his chin, slumped back into the rear seat, his eyes staring unseeing at the jazz singer, his hands folded across his lap, dark liquid oozing between his fingers. The smell of cordite filled the air.

Gabriel grasped the wheel with both hands. He was breathing hard. "Are you okay?"

Celeste was wearing a hard expression. "I'm okay." She resumed her search for the bullets in his pocket, feeding them into the chamber of the gun. Gabriel noticed that one of her gloves was scorched with residue from the gun. He glanced in the mirror again.

"They're gaining on us!" The incident with the man in the back had slowed them down; he'd taken his attention off the road. He pushed his foot flat to the floor, heard the engine roar in protest. The streets were getting busier here, and he had to dodge out of the way of an oncoming vehicle, another car, which sounded its horn expressively to signal its driver's distaste.

Rat-a-tat-tat. More gunfire. Gabriel found himself ducking instinctively as the projectiles hammered home. He heard the hiss of steam venting—a bullet had clearly punctured a valve. The vehicle slowed a little, losing some of its power.

"No! Don't slow down now!"

"I can't help it. They've hit a valve." Frustrated, Gabriel flung the vehicle around another corner, only to find them approaching Union Square. An immense holographic statue of Atlas stood proud over the city there, a true titan, towering over one hundred feet tall, supporting the celestial spheres on his broad, unyielding shoulders. The statue cast the surrounding streets and buildings in an eerie blue glow, washing everything as if it were being viewed through a filter, as if someone had painted the sky a different shade. The base of the statue, which housed the projection equipment, was at the center of a large park, around which the roads crisscrossed in a grid pattern.

Gabriel forced the car around another bend at speed, causing it to shake dramatically and almost lose its grip on the tarmac. The other vehicle swung around behind it, and the onslaught of bullets continued. He realized that they weren't trying to hit him; more that they were attempting to riddle the car with so many bullets that it was rendered useless. They didn't want to harm Celeste.

Gabriel watched her weigh the revolver in her hands. She looked across at him. "Do you love me?"

Gabriel tried to keep his voice even. "I love you."

"Good." She turned about in her seat, resting the barrel of the weapon on the seat back. Then, taking a deep breath, she squeezed the trigger. The shot was like an explosion in the confined space of the vehicle, and she flinched at the sound. But her aim was true, and the bullet caught the windshield of the other car, punching a hole in the glass and causing a spiderweb of fracture lines to spread out from the site of the impact. The other car swerved, and then the man in the passenger seat used the butt of his tommy gun to smash the broken glass out, sending shards of it skittering off the bonnet.

Celeste ducked back behind the seat as a retaliatory burst of fire sprayed the rear end of the vehicle again, a stray bullet *vipping* through the hole where the rear windshield had been, burying itself in the roof of the car not far from their heads.

Both cars swerved again, circling the enormous sculpture of light, driving around Atlas's massive feet.

Celeste took aim again, and this time she was ready for the noise. Gabriel watched her out of the corner of his eye, saw the look of intense concentration on her face. He tried to hold the car steady for a moment. She loosed a bullet.

For a moment, Gabriel thought that she'd missed, that her shot had gone wide or had no effect. But then he saw the driver of the other car collapse over the steering wheel, and the vehicle careened off the road at high speed, mounting the curb and hurtling directly for the park. He watched in the rearview mirror as it shot across the grass verge, *through* the flickering blue foot of Atlas, and over a wall, rolling onto its roof and sliding, with a loud *crunch*, into a large stone fountain. Hot coals spilled out across the plaza, and steam was gushing out of the engine housing in long, hissing jets. He had no doubt that the people inside were dead; there was no way anyone could have survived a crash like that.

Gabriel turned to Celeste. She'd collapsed back into her seat, the gun discarded in the footwell, and she was weeping uncontrollably. He felt his heart break, then and there. All he wanted to do was take her somewhere, anywhere, away from all of this, to hold her in his arms and tell her she was safe. But he knew she would never be the same again. He knew that she was different, now. He remembered how it had felt to take his first life, back in the war, and how you never, ever recover from the experience. He'd tried to shield her from that, to stop her from being damaged like him. He knew that there was nothing he could say, now. Nothing he could do to make it better.

GEORGE MANN

The car was losing power as they pulled into a nearby side street, rolling up to the curb. Black smoke was curling dramatically from the funnels at the rear of the vehicle. And Gabriel was smarting, from the glass fragments that were still embedded in his back, and from the gunshot wound that had scorched his leg.

He turned to Celeste, putting a gentle hand on her shoulder. "I love you, Celeste. Whatever else, you need to believe that."

She nodded, almost imperceptibly. Mascara was streaming down her cheeks and her hair had come loose, spilling down the side of her face. Gabriel thought she was still the most beautiful thing he had ever seen.

She wiped ineffectually at her eyes with the back of her gloved hand. Then, turning her head fractionally to look at him, she whispered the words: "I'm sorry."

He knew that they carried more weight, and more meaning, than he could possibly understand.

"Come on, we need to keep moving. We don't want to be here when the police arrive. I'm taking you back to Long Island. I'm not sure you'll be safe at your own place for the time being."

She didn't argue as he clambered out of the vehicle and circled round the front to help her out of the passenger seat. He stooped to collect the discarded weapon, too, slipping it safely into his pocket.

Then, moving as quickly as they could to get away from the scene of devastation, they set off to find a taxi driver prepared to take them out to Long Island at this hour of the night.

TEN

Celeste sat in the bay window as the sun came up over Long Island, spreading fingers of light inquisitively across the gardens. She'd been there for some time, statuesque in the gloom, unable to sleep. Her mind was racing, running over the events of the preceding hours: the men who had come after her at the Sensation Club, the shots she had fired, the lives she had ended. The thought of it lay heavily upon her, but also, she couldn't help questioning why.

She knew why the men had come for her, of course. It wasn't that. It was more that she questioned why it had to be *her, now*. The Sisterhood had agents in every major city the world over. It might have been any one of them, but instead, it had fallen to her. The Roman had chosen to come to New York.

As a child, during her indoctrination into the Order, she had longed for this, craved the opportunity, the glory. To those of her Order, this was the highest privilege, a chance to do what she had been born to do, to fulfill her purpose in a way that most people could never conceive of. She would give herself up for the greater good.

Time and distance, however, had a way of eroding such youthful zeal. During the intervening years, her will had wavered. She'd grown comfortable—happy, even. She felt guilty that a part of her had begun to hope that she would be given the chance to live a long and fruitful life without ever having to face this moment, like so many of her Sisters had before her, and so many would again.

But now it was here, and she had no choice. She recognized that. Circumstances had conspired against her.

She thought of Gabriel, still asleep on the bed upstairs, of what it would do to him. She was well aware that at first she had been nothing more than another conquest for the rich playboy, someone to brag about at his incessant parties.

Very quickly, though, it had become much more than that. They were drawn to one another, kindred spirits. They each understood that they were engaged in a game that could never last; yet they craved it, more and more of it, unwilling to acknowledge the truth. They clung to one another in fear of the future. They lost themselves in each other's company, and for a while, found the still point in the universe they had both sought for so long.

There was a tangible sadness in Gabriel, beneath his façade. There was strength, too—strength that she needed, that she borrowed. For him, she represented another lost soul, another person damaged by the world, who rose every morning to paint her face with powder, lipstick and a sultry smile. The masks they wore were different, but they were masks nonetheless.

Did he know more? Did he suspect the truth? She guessed after the events of the previous night he'd have questions. She wasn't yet sure how she would answer them, but she knew he would understand this was a trace of her secret life, somehow bleeding into their conjured world. Before that, though, she had other demons to face.

Celeste swung her legs down from the windowsill and stood. She could put it off no longer. She had to make the call before Henry was up and about, and the chance was lost.

She crossed to the door and closed it, quietly. Without pausing, she went directly to the holograph terminal on Gabriel's desk. She took a deep breath and moistened her lips. Her hand was trembling as she dialed the number she had hoped she would never have to dial.

The bell trilled at the other end and was answered almost immediately. It took a moment for the connection to be made, and then an image coalesced, displaying the head and shoulders of a thin, pretty woman, with long dark hair pinned up at the back of her head. Celeste didn't recognize her.

"Sister Parker?" said the woman, her voice crackling slightly over the long distance. "Speak."

"He's found me," said Celeste. "In New York City. I managed to get away, for now, to find a place to hide. He knows who I am. I don't have much time."

The woman nodded. "Do you know where he has established himself?"

"Not yet," replied Celeste. "I am only now becoming aware of his activities."

"The Roman mus ceremony," said the woman. "The timing is right."

"Then what I feared is true," said Celeste. "It is time."

"Do not be fearful," replied the woman. "The love of our Sisterhood is with you. Remember the sacrifice made by our grandmothers, and their grandmothers before that. The summoning cannot be allowed to go ahead. If the creature escapes into this world…"

"I understand," said Celeste, her voice level. "I know what I must do."

"Then go to it with pride. It is a great honor that is bestowed upon you, Sister Parker. For all of us, you must succeed. I only wish I could take your place."

As do I, thought Celeste, but did not give voice to such heresy.

"Your activities will be monitored," said the woman. "If you fall, another shall take your place."

"I shall not fall," replied Celeste. She terminated the call, and slumped back in Gabriel's chair. She closed her eyes and steadied her nerves. Her heart was racing.

She would go and wake him. It was early, but she needed his flippancy, his strength. She needed to forget all of this, for a few hours at least. More so, she needed to make use of the time she still had.

She rose from the chair and crossed to the door, her nightdress whispering around her. Outside, the birds had begun to sing. It was going to be a beautiful day.

ELEVEN

Night. That was his time. That was when the miscreants and crooks, the monsters and the nightmare things all spilled out into the open. That was when the city needed him most, and when he felt most alive. The city breathed that life into him at this hour; gave him energy, gave him freedom. And in turn he coursed through its network of arteries and veins, searching out the demons, purging the rotten elements like a wrathful flame. He was the spirit of vengeance.

The Ghost drifted lazily over the lip of a tall tenement building, firing his propulsion jets to give him enough lift to carry him over to another nearby roof terrace. Below, the city was stark in miniature; cars slid silently along the roads, their headlamps pooling on the black tarmac; revelers swarmed from restaurant to bar, and then back again, their voices lost on the wind.

His ankles were still smarting from the blisters they'd received a couple of nights earlier, and his other injuries—although minor—were a constant nagging reminder of his failure to take down the moss men. Now, though, he was ready for them. When he encountered them again, things would be different. He would make short shrift of their moss-covered bodies and brass frames. But for the time being he had a task to perform. He needed to speak with someone. He was looking for Jimmy the Greek.

Jimmy the Greek was one of the lowliest, sniveling life forms that the Ghost had ever encountered. He wasn't even Greek, but Cypriot, although that hadn't stopped the other felons he associated with from saddling him with the moniker by which he had become known. Jimmy was a minor crook, a pickpocket, a messenger boy for the mob. But more than that: he was also a snitch.

The Ghost despised everything that Jimmy stood for. The man didn't even have the decency to honor his own kind. He couldn't be trusted, not for a moment. He would just as soon turn his own mother in for a free pass, or else a hit of his favorite drug. But that fact, in itself, made him useful to the police, and even more so to the Ghost, who was prepared to go even further in his exploitation of the criminal if it meant he could get closer to the crooks that really mattered. The men he had vowed to bring down.

He'd already checked out most of Jimmy's usual haunts: the drinking place down on 12th, the whorehouse on 17th. Now, determined, the Ghost was heading over to the hovel that Jimmy called home, a small apartment in Greenwich Village. He'd been there once before, and the idea of spending any time there was repulsive to him, but he needed answers, and Jimmy was the most likely candidate to give them to him. He wanted information on the shoot-out that had gone down at the Sensation Club the previous evening: who was behind it, and what they wanted with the girl, Celeste.

He had his own ideas, of course. The presence of the moss men had to mean it was the Roman. But if he could find out who was actually there—the name of the thin man in the evening suit—it might be enough to put him on the trail of the Roman himself. But that still didn't answer the question about Celeste, and why the Roman felt the need to try to kidnap her. He couldn't believe for one minute that it was down to a sudden appreciation of her music. There was something rotten at the core of it, and he very much intended to find out what.

He touched down gently on the roof of the building, pulling the cord inside his trench coat to shut off the flames that roared from his propulsion canisters. He scanned the rooftop, the red lenses of his goggles flashing in the wan light. Just as he had expected, there was a fire escape on the roof. Jimmy the Greek kept his apartment on the third floor. It would only take a matter of moments to descend the emergency stairs down through the five intervening floors, and he knew there was less chance of being seen when coming in from the roof. He didn't want to alert Jimmy to his presence, didn't want to give him the opportunity to flee. That way, it would only get messy when he finally caught up with the snitch.

The Ghost crossed the rooftop at a swift pace and tested the door that led down into the apartment block. Locked. He thought about using his fléchette gun, but then reconsidered. It wouldn't do to make too much noise. Instead, he backed up a few paces and charged the door with his shoulder, slamming into the wooden panel with all of his weight behind it. The door didn't resist, bursting open on its hinges and bashing against the interior wall. The sound reverberated down the metal stairwell. The Ghost hesitated, waiting to see if the noise would attract any attention.

A few moments later, when he was sure that the way was

clear, he began his swift but cautious descent to the third floor, being careful not to miss his footing on the narrow, cramped stairwell in the darkness.

The building seemed almost deserted. He could hear the distant rumble of music coming from somewhere down below, but on many floors the lights were out and there was little or no evidence of habitation. He wondered what had driven people away, aside from the squalor. Most likely the mob. If they were operating their usual protection rackets in these parts, it was unlikely that the residents would have been able to maintain their payments. They might well have been terrorized out of their homes, or have fled to escape the beatings. Or worse.

Jimmy would have been looked after, of course. Jimmy had a hand in that sort of business, and that was exactly what made him useful.

The Ghost reached the third-floor landing. He crept forward, peering through the glass pane in the door. A light was on in the corridor, and he could see three other doors branching off from it and a stairwell at the other end. Garbage had been heaped up in front of one of the doors: discarded food wrappers, some old blankets, a child's toy. He guessed that the residents of that apartment had been gone for some time. Now it was most likely infested with rats. He shuddered at the thought. Across the hall was the door to apartment number nine. Jimmy's place.

Easing the fire escape door open, wincing as the hinges moaned, the Ghost slipped through into the corridor. Treading lightly, he paced along the hallway toward Jimmy's apartment. Then, when he was sure that there was no one else around, he rapped loudly on the wooden panel and waited for a response.

There was the sound of cursing from inside, followed by a cupboard door banging shut. What was he hiding from view? The Ghost knocked again, louder this time.

"I'm coming, I'm coming." The voice was muffled, but the Ghost smiled at the sound of it all the same. There was no mistaking Jimmy's weasel-like tones.

A moment later the door cracked open a fraction and Jimmy's thin face peered out. He looked pale and sweaty, and his eyes were tiny pinpricks in the half-light. He was either high on something, or coming down. He wasn't pleased to see the Ghost standing on his threshold. "Aww, shit." He tried to slam the door shut, but the Ghost was too quick and managed to get a booted foot between the door and the frame.

"That's not very polite, Jimmy."

The other man looked sheepish. "Now's not a good time. It's really not. You can't come in here."

The Ghost gave him an appraising look. "Are you going to stop me, Jimmy? Do you think that's wise?"

Jimmy backed away from the door, allowing it to swing open. "Well, if you put it like that..." He looked pained, as if he was scared that the Ghost might discover something, as if he'd been up to something nefarious that he didn't want anyone to see.

The Ghost stepped over the threshold and closed the door behind him with a deliberate *click*. "Very wise, Jimmy. Just what I would have done, if I were you." He glanced around. He couldn't see any signs that the man had been up to anything he shouldn't have been. And if he were honest with himself, he didn't much care. Jimmy was too small-time to be a real concern.

The Ghost wrinkled his nose. The place smelled like a

cesspit. It didn't look much better, either. He couldn't understand what led a man to want to live like this. Poverty was one thing, but Jimmy worked for the mob. Perhaps he just found it comforting in some sick, twisted way.

The man himself was skinny and unshaven, and was dressed only in a pair of brown felt trousers. His hair was long and unkempt, and fell about his shoulders. His rib cage was showing through his papery skin, and his hands were describing nervous gestures in the air as he tried to work out what this man—this bizarre, terrifying man—wanted in his apartment.

The Ghost decided to oblige him with an explanation. "I'm looking for some answers, Jimmy, and I think you're the man to help me out."

"Wh… wh… what makes you s… s… say that?"

"I know who your friends are." He rubbed a hand over his chin. "I know what company you like to keep."

Jimmy continued to twitch nervously. "My friends, they won't like it. They don't like what you did at the bank the other night. They think you're trouble."

"I *am* trouble, Jimmy. More trouble than you could ever imagine. What you need to decide is how much of that trouble do you want?"

The man was visibly shaking now. "I don't want any trouble. No trouble at all. But, mister, I'm telling you, if I spill to you, those friends of mine, they'll give me trouble of their own."

The Ghost sighed. "Now, they don't sound like the right sort of friends to me, Jimmy." He stepped forward, and the other man let out a whimper. The Ghost's voice was suddenly serious. "There was a raid last night, at a joint called the

Sensation Club. A lot of people ended up dead. All you need to do is tell me who was behind it."

Jimmy shook his head, frantically, from side to side. "I don't know what you're talking about. I have no idea. I don't know who was behind anything." He indicated the door. "I really think you should leave now."

"I'm not going anywhere, Jimmy, not until you give me what I need."

Jimmy took a step backward. "I really can't help you. I don't know what you're talking about."

The Ghost decided to try another approach. He glanced around the room, looking for a cupboard. The apartment was small, and the kitchen was next to the living room, separated by a tall, open archway. Cupboards lined the walls. He pushed his way past Jimmy into the small space. Then, grabbing hold of one of the cupboard doors, he flung it open. Inside was a stack of plates and other assorted china. They were covered in a thick layer of grime and dust. He turned to the snitch. "What were you doing in here, Jimmy? What were you up to when I arrived?" He opened another door. This time the cupboard was bare, save for a packet of crackers and half a loaf of bread.

Jimmy started forward. "No, look, I'd tell you if I knew anything. You know I would. There ain't nothing in those cupboards to worry you."

"How can I be sure about that? How can I be sure there isn't something in these cupboards about the Sensation Club and what happened last night? That proves you were there, and that you've got yourself all mixed up in someone else's business?" As he spoke, the Ghost continued to open the cupboard doors, one by one, working his way along the length of the small kitchen.

The crook looked appalled. "That business ain't got nothin' to do with me! I ain't never had a part in that sort of thing. I keep my hands clean."

The Ghost reached into the cupboard he had just opened, pulled out a small brown envelope. He tipped the contents onto the floor, watching the individual leaves of paper scatter like a multicolored waterfall. He glanced at the mess he had made. They were photographs. Images of the strange clockwork geisha girls that could be found—and bought—down in Chinatown; images of Jimmy doing things to them. They stared at the camera with their blank porcelain expressions, as the thin, gaunt body of the snitch paraded before them, or touched them, or worse. If they'd been real girls, the Ghost would have sworn he could see sadness in their eyes.

So that's what Jimmy had been up to when he'd arrived. Nothing but some cheap pornography. The Ghost had been suspecting something different. Something he could use as leverage. He couldn't care less what Jimmy got up to in his own time, what his proclivities were, or what sort of pictures he liked to look at.

Jimmy stepped back, his hands in the air. "I ain't never seen those pictures before. Seriously! You just planted those in my cupboard to make me look bad." His voice was a high-pitched whine. He looked terrified.

"Is this all, Jimmy? A few photographs. Is this why you're so scared? Wouldn't want your friends to know about it, though, would you? About your particular... tastes. They wouldn't be as open-minded as me, would they?" The Ghost stepped over the pool of photographs toward the snitch.

"You... you wouldn't. You wouldn't do that... would you?"

"No, Jimmy. I wouldn't. And there's the difference between you and me. But you better start talking, and fast."

Jimmy stuffed his hands in his pockets and then withdrew them again, folding them across his chest. He seemed somewhat relieved by the Ghost's reaction to the photographs. "I told you, I ain't got nothin' for you—"

The Ghost moved like lightning. One moment he was in the kitchen, staring at the sad, half-naked snitch, the next he had crossed to the living room and had his right hand around the other man's throat. He raised his left hand and brought it down hard across Jimmy's face. The crook gave a low moan, like a keening animal. "Still going to tell me you don't have anything for me?"

Jimmy blinked and gave a quick shake of his head.

"Good." The Ghost relaxed his grip and the thin man slumped to the ground, his back to the wall. "Now, I'm going to make this easy for you. Who was responsible for the raid on the Sensation Club last night?"

Jimmy swallowed. His response was barely a whisper. "The Roman."

"And who was the thin man in the evening suit? The guy in charge."

Jimmy looked up at him, panic behind his eyes. The Ghost had seen that look before, back during the war. The look of a condemned man, haunted by the knowledge that he was about to die. "G... G... Gideon R... Reece. Gideon Reece. He's the

Roman's right-hand man. He's trouble. Real bad trouble."

"What would Reece want with the jazz singer Celeste Parker? Why did they come after her?"

Jimmy stared up at him, his eyes pleading. "I don't know. I don't know why they wanted her. They do what the Roman tells them to do. That's all I know."

"You're doing well, Jimmy. Now, tell me where I can find them."

"You can't. You can't find them. No one knows. They find you. That's how they work. They always come to you."

The Ghost dropped into a crouch, bringing himself level with the snitch. His voice was forceful, full of menace. "Jimmy, where can I find Gideon Reece?"

The snitch wouldn't meet his gaze. His eyes flitted nervously from side to side. For a moment the Ghost thought the other man might piss himself.

"Jimmy, I'm going to count to five. One, two, three—"

"Okay! Okay! There's something going down tonight. Across town from here. I don't know the details, but they're doing over some doctor. Over on Suffolk Street. Reece will be there."

The Ghost stood. Suffolk Street. He could be there in ten, fifteen minutes. He glanced at his watch. A quarter after eleven. He hoped he wasn't already too late. He looked down at the sniveling wretch by his feet. "Clean yourself up, Jimmy. You owe it to yourself."

He stepped over the slumped figure, pulled open the door, and left. Behind him, Jimmy the Greek let out a long, whistling sigh of relief.

* * *

The Ghost dropped down onto the iron rungs of an external fire escape that clung, limpet-like, to the side of an apartment building. It was similar, in many ways, to the building from which he had just come, but this part of town was considerably more affluent than the neighborhood where Jimmy the Greek made his home, and the buildings and streets had been maintained to a far superior standard.

He'd come across the rooftops again, using his propulsion jets to help him make the leaps where needed. He didn't yet know what he was looking for. A doctor. He wished now that he'd pressed Jimmy for a name, but in truth he suspected that the snitch wouldn't have known the details of the hit; he wasn't high enough in the pecking order to be trusted with information like that. In fact, he'd probably only picked up the details he did have from another goon who didn't know how to keep his mouth shut.

The Ghost crouched on his haunches in the darkness, surveying the street for any signs of life. His goggles overlaid his vision with tiny blinking readouts and washed everything with a warm red glow. A couple of pedestrians passed beneath him, and he adjusted his lenses, focusing in on their faces. A man and a woman, out for a late-night stroll. Civilians. People in love. He felt a sudden stab of jealousy. Some days—*most* days—he wished he could lose himself in that same blissful ignorance in which most of the city's population breezed through their days, unaware of what was truly happening around them, of the lurking danger that bubbled just beneath the surface of their lives. To most of them, he was one of the monsters, a myth of the city, a creature that lived in other people's nightmares but would never touch their own. They thought of the mob in the same way. *Let it happen to other people. We'll be alright. It won't affect us.* He supposed that was for the best. Better that they lived their lives in ignorance than fear.

A car engine roared up ahead. The Ghost shifted his position so he could see. No headlamps. It could have been any one of the three parked vehicles across the street. He toyed with his goggles, trying to get a closer look. Too late—he saw the column of steam release from the rear of one of the cars, and then two men appeared from the doorway of one of the apartment blocks, crossed the sidewalk, and opened the rear doors of the vehicle. Both men were wrapped in heavy winter overcoats, but there was no mistaking one of them: Gideon Reece. He was tall, thin, and carried himself with an immaculate, graceful air. His hands were held in a thin steeple before his chest, and even from high up on the side of another building, the Ghost could see that the uppermost half of his left ear was missing. The other man was unfamiliar to him: a goon, or else another of the Roman's deputies.

The men ducked into the car, and the Ghost, leaping into action, swung down from the fire escape, taking the steps five, six at a time, dropping the last ten feet and crunching onto the graveled courtyard a few seconds later, his trench coat billowing out around him like long, unfurling petals.

He'd been too slow. The car was already speeding away from the curb, heading toward him, its headlamps still dimmed so as not to draw attention. He thought about trying to give chase, about leaping onto the bonnet as it sped past, but he knew it wouldn't get him anywhere, except perhaps a wooden box, six feet beneath the churchyard in his home town. He watched as the vehicle rushed by, sputtering as its furnace consumed coal from the hopper, superheating the water tank that fed steam to the paddles. And that was when he noticed the third exhaust funnel, rising out from the back of the vehicle like a finger, pointing at the stars. He smiled beneath the brim of his hat. A third funnel. He'd never seen a motorcar with a third funnel. It was clearly there to compensate for some modification that had been made to the engine, most likely to increase the capacity for extra torque and speed, to help Reece extract himself from any threatening situations as quickly as possible. But now he had a means of finding Gideon Reece again. It was a needle in a proverbial haystack, of course, but if he could find the car with three funnels, he could find Gideon Reece. And if he could find Gideon Reece, he was sure he could find the Roman.

The Ghost watched the vehicle recede into the distance, swallowed by the impenetrable night. Then, turning toward the building from which he'd seen Reece and his crony emerge, he crossed the street. He didn't know what he was likely to find inside, but if there was any chance he could save the doctor, he had to take it.

The lobby door was still hanging open where it had been forced by the mobsters, the lock smashed, the hinges partially wrenched from the frame. Inside, an electric bulb was swinging chaotically on its wire, causing the light to take on a bizarre stuttering effect, as if the room beyond was dipping in and out of existence, there one minute, gone the next.

The Ghost stepped through the opening, flicking the lenses up from his goggles so that his eyes could better adjust to the harsh electric light. The lobby was small; a mailbox, marked with the names and numbers for each apartment, a garbage bin, a door leading off to the first-floor apartments, and a staircase leading up to the floors above. The decor was plain and modern: magnolia walls and red tiles. But it was clean, and, he imagined, a rather expensive building to inhabit.

The Ghost approached the mailbox. It stood against the wall near the foot of the stairs, a series of small wooden cubbyholes, ready to receive the residents' mail. Some of the partitions were stuffed half full of unopened letters and packages of various shapes and sizes. Each one was labeled with the name of the occupant and the apartment number. He scanned the names on the top row, and then began working his way down the rows, one cubbyhole at a time. About halfway down, right in the middle of the third row, was a name that immediately stood out: Dr. Henry Sinclair, Apt. 11.

The Ghost quickly counted off the apartments. That would be on the third floor. He rushed to the stairs, taking them two at a time, and sprinted across the landing toward the doctor's apartment. He hadn't misjudged it: the door was open, light bleeding out onto the dimly lit landing. Cautiously, he edged inside.

If he'd had any hopes of getting there in time to save the doctor, those hopes were dashed by the sight that confronted him when he passed along the hallway of the apartment and into the living room. It was perhaps one of the most disturbing sights he had ever seen, certainly since the war. Surrounded by opulence—bright, colorful works of art, elaborate furniture dating back to the last century, a chandelier, a bookcase filled with fine bindings—was the doctor himself. He'd been stripped naked and positioned in a chair beside his desk. One hand rested on the arm of the chair, and his legs were crossed, his feet situated carefully on a blue and white rug. His head had been cleanly removed, leaving a bloody, oozing stump, and was now tucked beneath the other arm in a grotesque parody of a headless spirit, carrying its burden into the afterlife. The face was frozen in a rigid expression of terror, the lips curled back in a horrifying scream. Over the eyes had been placed two shining brass coins, as if in bizarre tribute to some demonic spirit.

The stench was foul; the iron tang of blood filled his nostrils and throat with its cloying scent, making it difficult for him to breathe. He stood for a minute, unable to take his eyes from the grisly diorama that faced him. After a moment, he realized what was wrong with the scene. The head had been removed, cleaved off with a clean blade, but there was no sign of any blood, other than that still seeping ponderously from the wound itself, dripping onto the milky-white flesh of the doctor's chest.

The Ghost decided to search the apartment. The murder must have been committed in another room, and then the body deliberately moved to its position in the living room, probably even cleaned up before being displayed. He repressed a shudder. He had the terrible sense that Gideon Reece had enjoyed his work that day, had sought and found some sort of appalling thrill in what he'd done to this Dr. Sinclair. He had to be stopped. Not simply because of his connection to the Roman, but because of his deadly sadistic streak, and because he wanted to lay his hands on Celeste.

After a few moments' pacing between rooms, he found what he'd been looking for. The bathroom was like a scene from an abattoir. The glistening white tiles had been decorated with a spray of dark, arterial blood that covered nearly every surface: the walls, floor, ceiling—even spattered over the mirror above the sink. The bathtub itself was cracked and splintered where it had received a series of blows from a sharp implement, suggesting the doctor's head had been hacked off over the side of the tub. Supporting that theory, the Ghost could see two tools had been dumped in the bottom of the tub: a bloody machete and a hacksaw. They rested in a long puddle of sticky blood. It seemed much of the gritty substance had been swilled down the plughole.

Bloodstained towels had been discarded haphazardly on the floor, and puddles of water marked where the body had been washed down after the event.

The Ghost felt bile rising in his gullet. He wondered what the doctor had done to warrant such a vicious, deliberate reprisal from the Roman. Turning away from the scene of the butchery, he made his way back to the living room, where the body of the late doctor was still waiting for him in silent vigil. Grimacing, he crossed to the blue and white rug and stooped to examine the body. He'd heard, from news of the other murders committed by the Roman's men, that the coins were a calling card, both an admission of guilt and a terrible warning to those who might consider opposing the mob boss. Or else they were some kind of ritualistic symbol, placed over the eyes to appease the gatekeeper that blocked the way to the afterlife; compensation, of a sort, that would enable the souls of the Roman's victims to buy passage into the spirit realm. The Ghost had heard talk that the coins were originals, too, real Roman currency, nearly two millennia old. But the coins in front of him didn't look like originals. They were far too pristine. All the Roman coins he'd seen displayed in the Metropolitan Museum of Art had darkened and oxidized over time, or else had been damaged by the years they had spent in the soil, turned over by plows, struck by spades. These, though, looked as if they had hardly been touched, as if they had only recently been minted. He reached out and gingerly prized one of them free, turning it over in his gloved fingers. It had to be a replica. If not—if they *were* real—they must have cost the Roman a fortune. He knew where he could find out. He'd ask Arthur. Arthur would know.

There was a shout from out in the hall, followed by the patter of footsteps coming into the apartment. The Ghost stiffened. He drew back from the corpse, just in time to see a man burst into the room.

The Ghost could tell immediately that the newcomer was a police officer. He had that look about him: haunted, exhausted, but like a dog on the trail of a fox, full of adrenaline and spoiling for a fight. The man was dressed in an immaculate black suit, with a crisp white collar and a black overcoat. He was wearing a porkpie hat, and had an automatic clasped in one hand, which he was pointing in the Ghost's direction. He looked as if he were trying to suppress the shock he was feeling at the sight of

Dr. Sinclair's naked, desecrated corpse.

"Hold it!" The man barked the command. The Ghost backed away, holding his hands out so the detective could see that he wasn't about to try anything. He wouldn't fire on a policeman, not even in self-defense. But neither could he allow himself to be captured. Given the circumstances, they'd probably link him to Sinclair's death and hit him with a murder charge, and if not for Sinclair, then for the goons in the bank. Either way, he needed to get away, and fast.

He glanced around the room. The detective was blocking the only exit. There was a window in the south wall, looking out onto the street below. The curtains were pulled back, but the window was shut. He wouldn't have time to open it. He was making a habit of this. Sighing inwardly, the Ghost steeled himself and then made a run for it, charging toward the window and leaping at the pane of glass, his arms tightly folded around his face to protect it from the shards.

He heard a gunshot reverberate in the small room just as he collided with the glass. He plowed through, the window exploding into a thousand tiny splinters as his weight carried him forward, into the abyss.

And then he was falling, tumbling over and over as he plummeted toward the concrete far below.

TWELVE

D onovan rushed to the window. The damn fool would be dashed across half the street after a drop from this height. He knew he'd missed him with the shot: the pockmark in the wall spoke for itself. But there was no way he could have survived a fall from this height.

Most of the glass had gone with him when he'd punched his way through, leaving only a few ragged teeth protruding from the frame. Gingerly, so as not to slash his face on the fragments, Donovan leaned out of the window, surveying the scene below. Where he expected to see the broken remains of the man who had dived out—the Ghost, he supposed, judging by the look of him—there was nothing but an empty stretch of road. Confused, he looked up and down the sidewalk, trying to see if the man had miraculously managed to get up again after his fall, and was now making good on his escape. Again, the road seemed quiet. What had happened to the man? He'd watched him leap through the window with his own eyes, but he seemed to have suddenly disappeared.

Just as he was about to give up on the matter and attend instead to the murder scene, he heard a grunting sound from somewhere above his head. He looked up. There, pulling himself over the lip of the building, was the Ghost, powerful jets of flame spurting from canisters attached to the backs of his legs, propelling him upward. Donovan was impressed, despite himself. He raised his automatic, took aim.

"Don't move. I don't want to have to shoot you."

There was a commotion behind him. He realized that Mullins had arrived with some uniformed men. One of them balked at the sight of the corpse. Donovan didn't take his eyes off his prey.

The Ghost, clutching onto the side of the building, continued to haul himself over the edge, heading for the roof. He looked back, just before he tumbled out of sight, meeting Donovan's gaze with an unreadable expression.

Donovan pulled himself back through the makeshift opening and turned to Mullins. "To the roof. NOW!"

Mullins looked startled and out of breath, but he wasn't about to start arguing with the detective. He waved for two of the uniformed men to follow him and set off at a run, bolting down the hallway toward the stairwell. Donovan followed behind them, still clutching his automatic in his fist. He couldn't let this chance slip out of his grip. Couldn't let the Ghost get away. There was too much riding on it. His life, for a start.

It had been two days since his encounter with Gideon Reece, two days since he'd been offered that ugliest of ultimatums: take the Roman's coin, or forfeit his own life. He'd heard nothing since then, for all the crushing anguish and insomnia he'd suffered. For all the fears he held for Flora's future. Nothing until today. And then today he'd received an anonymous tip-off, about half an hour earlier, that he might find "something of interest" at the home of Dr. Henry Sinclair.

The thought had filled him with dread. The caller hadn't revealed their identity—put through a voice-only call, in fact—but he'd recognized the sinister tones of Gideon Reece on the other end of the line, had imagined him smirking as he delivered his smug message. As the man had spoken, Donovan had felt the cold fingers of fear clutching at his belly, a tightening in his chest. He knew what he was going to find down on Suffolk Street, and even though he'd rushed over in his police car, he knew he wouldn't be in time to save the doctor from his grisly fate. The call hadn't been made for that reason. Reece had no intention of allowing Sinclair to live. It was simply a warning for Donovan, a reminder that if he didn't give Reece the answer he wanted in another two days' time, Donovan would likely end up the same way as the doctor before the weekend was out. It was a demonstration, an opportunity for Reece to show off. And it worked. Even now, Donovan was feeling dizzy with the horror of his situation. Then there was the Ghost. If he was tied up in this, then there was no way Donovan was letting him get away without a fight. Whatever his role, whatever part he was playing in this grisly pantomime, he was the only lead Donovan had, the only glimmer of a way out of his situation.

All of this ran through his mind as he charged up the stairs behind Mullins. The sergeant was puffing and panting as he hit the uppermost floor and stepped aside to let the uniformed men take care of the door. Then they were all out on the rooftop, and Donovan was swinging his weapon left and right, looking for the roaring glow of the Ghost's propulsion units.

It was nowhere to be seen. He ran across the rooftop, cursing, the cold wind whipping his hair across his face. He followed the lip of the building, all the way from the stairwell to the other end of the apartment block, his feet crunching on the loose chippings.

He was gone. The Ghost had disappeared, faded into the night like an apparition. Donovan shoved his weapon back into its holster with a sigh. He turned to Mullins, who was watching him from across the rooftop in the silvery-gray moonlight, waiting to see what the detective wanted him to do next.

"He's gone, Mullins. We were too late. Go and secure the crime scene. I'll follow you down in a moment." The sergeant motioned to the uniformed men.

"Oh, and Mullins?"

"Yes, sir?"

"Find some damn coffee whilst you're down there."

The portly man gave a brief nod and then disappeared into the brightly lit stairwell.

Donovan listened to the sound of their footsteps on the treads as they receded into the distance, muffled by the howling of the wind. Then, desperate to find some sort of release, however small, he withdrew his packet of cigarettes and took out a smoke. He put the filter to his lips and pulled the ignition tab, causing a brief flare of light—and then nearly fell backward as he caught sight of the Ghost's pale face in the stuttering glare, only a few feet away, staring at him with intense interest.

Donovan went to reach for his weapon, but the Ghost shot forward and caught him by the wrist. The man had a grip of iron. His voice was quiet and gravelly. "Let's not worry about shooting each other just yet."

Donovan let his arm relax, and the vigilante released his

grip. The detective took a long draw on his cigarette, and then regarded the other man with an appraising look. He was just as the descriptions had suggested: well built, mid-thirties, rugged. He was wearing a long black trench coat and a fedora. Goggles were strapped to his forehead beneath the brim of the hat, but the lenses had been lifted, revealing his quick, darting eyes. It was hard to make out what color they were in the darkness.

Donovan flicked ash from the end of his cigarette, watching it drift away lazily on the wind. His heart was hammering in his chest. "Did you kill him? Sinclair?"

The Ghost smiled. "No. I didn't kill him. But I know who did."

Donovan nodded. "Are you working for them?"

The Ghost's expression was hard. "I'm working for the city. For the people of New York."

"I thought that was my job."

The Ghost snorted. "Well, do it better, then. Where were you last night when the Sensation Club was getting all shot up? At the bank the other night? Or when Sinclair was being butchered in his own bathroom?"

Donovan shrugged. "Where were *you*?"

"I wasn't here." The Ghost paused. "I was looking for Gideon Reece."

That name. Perhaps the Ghost could help him, after all. Donovan scratched absently at his wrist. "Did you find him?"

"He was here. He killed Sinclair. Then he left."

Donovan nodded again. "Seems we're all looking for Gideon Reece."

The Ghost shook his head. "We're all looking for the

Roman. Reece is simply the means by which we reach him."

Donovan sighed. "I've got nothing on him."

"You've got a murder."

"With no evidence. I can't do anything without evidence."

The Ghost laughed. "And there's your answer, Inspector. That's why you need me."

Donovan's cigarette had burned down to a blunt stub in his fingers. He dropped it to the floor, crushed it beneath his boot. When he looked up, the Ghost had disappeared. He turned on the spot, trying to ascertain where the vigilante had gone. He caught sight of him again, standing on the ledge that ran around the top of the building, his arms spread wide as if he were trying to catch the wind beneath outstretched, invisible wings. He turned back to look at the detective. "Three funnels. Find the car with three funnels, and you'll have your man."

And then he jumped, throwing himself into the air, dropping below the lip of the apartment block before suddenly rising again on a plume of shimmering flame.

Donovan watched as the vigilante swept through the air toward another rooftop across the street, and then the plumes of fire extinguished once more and everything was dark, save for a few shafts of silvery moonlight, picking out the glinting aerials of holotube transmitters that pointed to the stars like so many upraised hands.

Donovan returned to the room with the corpse. His head was spinning. He still wasn't clear about what role the Ghost had played in proceedings here, but he was now sure of one thing—

the vigilante wasn't working for the Roman. Whatever his faults, however brutal his methods, the Ghost was right. Donovan needed him. He needed a blunt instrument, someone prepared to do what was right, to fight the criminals on their own terms, without one hand always tied behind their back. He wished he had the same freedom.

He turned things over in his mind. The car with three funnels. The Ghost must have been referring to the vehicle used by Gideon Reece, the sleek black modern thing that Donovan had sat inside the other night. So the Ghost had worked out how to find Reece. But finding a single car in a city full of them—surely that was like searching for a needle in a haystack? No matter what modifications had been made, how different it was from the similar models that purred constantly along the city streets, the city was a big place, and Donovan didn't know where to begin his search. Even if he found Reece, he knew he'd never be able to get him for Sinclair's murder. The man was too clever for that. And he was coming for Donovan, too. Time was running out. He almost laughed aloud at the irony. He realized he was hoping, hoping that the Ghost, that vigilante he had just encountered on the roof, was going to save him, was going to get to Reece first, and use whatever methods he deemed necessary to put an end to the man's reign of terror. He couldn't cross that line himself. But he could certainly turn a blind eye while the Ghost did.

Sighing, Donovan regarded the corpse. The poor bastard. It was clear to him that Reece's motive in dressing the scene in such a manner was to ridicule the dead man, to remove any last vestiges of his dignity. To defile him. It had been the same with Landsworth. The message was clear: oppose the Roman and he will not only take your life, but your reputation, too.

Donovan thought it was just crude. There was nothing subtle about removing a man's head and posing his corpse in a chair, or throttling a hooker and wiping her lipstick around a dead man's prick. It lacked finesse, for all its grotesque grandeur. It was barbaric, a punishment from another time.

He turned to see Mullins standing at his elbow, brandishing a mug of coffee. He took it with a grateful smile.

"Have you noted, sir, that the body only has one Roman coin on its eyes? Perhaps we disturbed him when he was placing them?"

Donovan shook his head. "No, Mullins. There were two coins here. That vigilante, the Ghost, wasn't placing the coins on Sinclair's eyes. He was removing one of them."

Mullins gave him a quizzical look. His top lip seemed to twitch in thought. "So, you don't think the Ghost committed the homicide?"

"No. I think the Ghost is as keen to find the Roman as we are. He took the coin as evidence. He's searching for clues."

Mullins frowned and brought his steaming coffee to his lips. Behind him, the uniformed officers were talking in the hallway, out of sight of the grisly corpse. "So what you're saying, sir, is that by following the Ghost, we might be able to find the Roman."

Donovan grinned. *Of course!* "Now that, Mullins, is one of the best ideas I've heard in days." He liked Mullins. The man had insight.

Mullins gave an embarrassed chuckle. "What I don't understand, sir, is what links the victims. They all seem to be upstanding members of society. Their deaths appear to be entirely random."

"Most likely they're just honest citizens who refused to take the Roman's bribes." Donovan knew he sounded weary. He took a long pull of his dark, oily coffee.

Mullins shook his head. "You've always told me, sir, to look for the link. The thing that binds the victims together. We need to find the common ground. There has to be something. We just can't see it yet."

Donovan shrugged. "I don't know, Mullins. I really don't know. A part of me suspects that's just wishful thinking, and a part of me desperately wants you to be right."

Mullins was stoic. "We'll find it, sir. The link is there. We just haven't looked in the right place yet."

Donovan glanced over at the screaming face of the dead doctor. "I hope you're right, Mullins. For all our sakes."

THIRTEEN

The Johnson & Arkwright Filament was a creation of miraculous proportions, or so Gabriel expounded to his guests as they lounged and splashed and caroused in the bubbling water, dressed in their swimwear even now, in the middle of November.

The filament itself was a huge cylindrical brass stove that sat on the edge of the swimming pool. It was covered with complex dials and switches, and had a hinged brass door in its belly that allowed access to the furnace. Henry, earlier, had rolled up his sleeves and shoveled in sack-loads of coal, enough to heat the pool for at least a day, if not longer. The device belched black, gritty smoke from a wide funnel in its roof and extended two long, brass fingers into the water, over the lip of the pool. These filaments reached almost to the bottom of the pool itself, and through them, superheated liquid was passed in a constant current, warming the surrounding water and causing steam to rise like a wispy veil from the surface, drifting away into the chill winter air.

It had cost Gabriel a small fortune, but he had been true to his word. He'd promised his entourage a November pool party, and that was what they were now enjoying.

Gabriel himself remained fully clothed. He was stretched

out on a sun lounger on the veranda, soaking up the hedonistic atmosphere. He watched the multitudes of people swarming about by the pool, or frolicking in the water, while sipping his bourbon and casually smoking a cigarette. He saw Ariadne—poor, beautiful Ariadne—skulking with her clutch of girlfriends, casting furtive looks at Gabriel and Celeste, the latter of whom was propped in a deckchair beside him, watching him with an amused gleam in her eye.

The whole thing was ludicrous, he knew. But then, that was the point of it. That was the nature of the perpetual party, the veil he drew over his own life to prevent others from seeing in. He found it fascinating that nobody should challenge him on such an outlandish idea. But no, the invitations had gone out and the people had swarmed; expectant, cheerful—some, perhaps, a little mystified. Yet they had accepted the notion without question, convincing themselves, and each other, that the masterful Gabriel Cross couldn't possibly *conceive* of having a bad idea. And so they had come, dressed in their bathing suits and carrying towels beneath their arms. It was a grand social experiment, and Gabriel knew that it proved something to Celeste about the nature of his parties: that she was right. All those guests were trying to escape from something, and they blinded themselves to the reality of it in exchange for a moment of blissful ignorance. They *wanted* Gabriel to tell them how to have fun because they couldn't work it out for themselves. He loved that she hadn't made a point of it.

Celeste had recovered well from the shock of the other night. But he knew she wasn't sleeping. She'd stayed with him since the incident, allowing herself to be cajoled into moving in, at least until things had blown over. Or, as Gabriel realized, at least until she was able to live with herself again. That was the crux of the matter, he was sure. She'd killed two men that night, snuffed out the lives of two other people, and she detested the feeling of assumed godhood that the weapon had given her. She didn't want to be able to decide who lived or died. That wasn't her role to take. In her worldview, that was the domain of higher beings. Higher than her, anyway.

She recognized, of course, that she had acted only in self-defense, but nevertheless those actions had changed her. Something inside of her had broken. It was something Gabriel would never be able to repair, no matter how hard he tried, no matter what he did or said. He knew that himself, all too well.

Celeste had told him all of this in the small hours of the night, when the only sound was the rustling of the trees through the window, and the only warmth the press of her body against his, the touch of her breath upon his face, the thump of her racing heart as she went over and over and over what had happened. He hadn't asked her why, and she hadn't volunteered an explanation, either. He still had no idea why those men—those mobsters—had been so desperate to take her away from him, so intent on their purpose that they had turned over the club and murdered all those people. Gabriel knew none of those victims were innocent, but neither did any of them deserve to die, not like that. Not at the hands of those terrible monsters rendered from soil and clay and death.

Whether Celeste suspected any reason for the Roman's attempted kidnap of her, he could only speculate. Yet he recognized within her a seed of discretion, a decision not to reveal that part of herself; not to him, not to the world. She was hiding something, withholding some secret that exposed her in some way, made her vulnerable, and she had chosen to bury it. She was tied up in something and she had chosen not to share it with him. He would have been a hypocrite if he'd expected anything else.

She turned to him, now, a wry smile on her lips. "You went to the city yesterday. I overheard you talking to Henry."

Gabriel accepted this as a statement of fact. He'd left her dozing on the sofa in the drawing room, resting at last, and had taken the car back to the city. He'd returned late that night. She'd been in bed, feigning sleep, as he'd slipped in quietly and curled up beside her. Later, when she'd woken, he'd been there to hold her as she wept.

Now, however, she had challenged him on his whereabouts, breaking the unspoken rule. He plumed smoke into the air, and turned to watch a couple by the side of the pool, holding hands as they jumped into the water together, crying out in delight like excited children. "Yes. I went into the city."

Celeste nodded, slowly. "You weren't—"

He swallowed the remains of his drink in one gulp. "I was."

She sat forward in her chair. She was both appalled and enamored. "Really? You went back. You brave, foolish, wonderful man!"

Gabriel waved his cigarette nonchalantly. "I didn't get very far. I asked a lot of questions. I discovered that the man we saw— the thin man in the evening suit—is called Gideon Reece. He works for the Roman, the mob boss that's been causing a stir. The police are looking into him, too. I met a nice inspector."

Celeste was just about to reply when a man Gabriel didn't recognize approached the veranda from across the garden. He wasn't wearing a bathing suit, but was dressed instead for the winter weather: a dark wool suit and a beige overcoat. He was wearing a brown hat. He beamed up at Gabriel and flashed Celeste a wide grin. "Quite a party you've got going on here, Mr. Cross. Unusual to see people in swimwear at this time of year."

Gabriel smirked. "Yes, indeed. Trying out my new acquisition. It's called the Johnson and Arkwright Filament. It heats the pool, you see—"

"Yes, I'd gathered as much." He looked down at his right hand, as if studying the palm, and then thrust it out in Gabriel's direction. "The name's Houseman, Jack Houseman. I'm with the *New York Times*."

Gabriel looked the man up and down appraisingly. There was an awkward moment while he made up his mind whether to take the man's hand or not. Then, remembering he had a role to play, he slid his glass tumbler onto the table beside him and leaned forward on the lounger, grasping the reporter's hand. "Good to meet you." He looked over the other man's shoulder. "You're welcome to join the party."

Houseman grinned. "Deadlines, Mr. Cross. I'm sure you understand."

"I'm sure he doesn't!" Celeste half whispered, a sweet smile on her lips.

Houseman laughed. "I understand there was an... incident the other night, downtown."

The smile suddenly faded from Celeste's face. She glanced

nervously at Gabriel to see how he was going to react.

"And what incident would that be, Mr. Houseman... Jack? I can call you Jack?"

Houseman nodded. "You can call me Jack. The incident with the vigilante. The Ghost." He raised his eyebrows in anticipation, as if what he really meant to say was, "How could I mean anything else?"

Gabriel laughed. "Oh, that. Yes. The incident." Celeste fell back in her chair, clearly relieved, and retrieved her gin and tonic, sipping at the straw, turning her attention to the revelers by the pool. Gabriel watched her for a moment. Then he turned to the reporter. "You want to know what happened?"

"Yes. I'm writing a piece about him."

"Well, I'll tell you. He's a menace. Make sure you get that. *A menace.* I was driving through town the other night, on my way to a party, when he simply ran out in front of my vehicle. I had to slam the brakes on and nearly knocked the guy across the street." Gabriel rubbed a hand across the back of his neck, as if unconsciously remembering the pain. "Jarred my neck, banged my hand. And all he did was lean on my bonnet and stare at me through the windshield. I think he must have been in a scrape, judging by the state of him." Houseman frowned, but Gabriel continued before he had chance to speak. "I mean, who does this guy think he is, anyway?" And then, "I'll tell you something. I'm going to find out. I'm going to discover the truth behind this so-called vigilante. I'll expose his true identity, and then everyone will know what a danger he is to the people of New York!"

He sat back, looking satisfied with himself. He knew this wasn't quite the true picture of how events had played out, but then, everyone was entitled to embellish things a little on occasion, and it suited him to add a touch of drama to proceedings.

Houseman looked rather taken aback by the outburst. "I can see you feel quite strongly about the matter, Mr. Cross. Can I ask: how do you plan to go about exposing this man?"

Gabriel sniffed. "Money, Jack. You can buy anything these days, for a price." He only wished this wasn't true. He glanced at Celeste out of the corner of his eye. Perhaps there *were* some things that money couldn't buy, after all.

Houseman nodded, as if he suddenly understood. "Very well. I think I have everything I need. Thank you for your time, Mr. Cross."

Gabriel nodded. "Are you sure you won't join the party?"

Houseman paused. "That's a merry-go-round I don't think I can afford to be a part of, I'm afraid." He turned and walked away across the lawn, heading for his parked car, back on the graveled driveway. Gabriel watched him drift away. A merry-go-round. Yes, that was a good description. Sometimes he wished he could jump off, too.

Celeste rubbed her arms, feeling the cold. "Can we go inside?" she said. Then, after a moment, "Can we go to bed? I want to be held."

Gabriel nodded, all of the bravado and flippancy suddenly gone. "Yes," he said, his voice quiet and serious. "Yes, we can go inside."

He dropped the end of his cigarette into the ashtray and stood, taking her by the hand. Together, they left the veranda, the party, the *New York Times*, and all of their fears, and Gabriel led her up to his bed.

* * *

Gabriel stirred and opened his eyes. He'd been asleep for some time. It was mid-afternoon and the sun was setting outside, the light becoming hazy, textured, as if seen through a filter of gauze.

Celeste was nearby, perched on the edge of the bed. He watched her for a while, choosing to feign sleep for a little longer. She had her back to him. If he'd been a religious man he might have seen God in the curve of that back. But Gabriel had abandoned God long ago. The war had done that to him. Now, he had faith only in money, and, perhaps, in the woman who sat on the edge of his bed, languorously smoking an unfiltered cigarette.

She turned to look at him, glancing back over her shoulder. Her painted lips were slightly parted, red and glossy. She blinked, and her long lashes stirred like brushes. She allowed a thin plume of smoke to escape from her nostrils. "When we do that… it's the only time I see you." Her voice was soft, subdued, as if she was aware of the weight of her words. She took another draw on her cigarette, the crisp sound of the smoldering paper the only noise in the room.

Gabriel let the moment pass. She was right. Of course she was right. It was the only time he let his guard drop. The only time he wasn't in control, wasn't Gabriel Cross. But he couldn't bring himself to give voice to that, to share that recognition with her. He couldn't admit that the man he saw in the mirror each morning was a reflection of somebody else. So instead he smiled and leaned back luxuriously on his pillow, reaching for his cigarette case on the bedside table.

"Then we should do it more often." He smiled, but the moment was gone.

She looked at him, confusion in her eyes. "What is it? What happened to you out there? What caused so much damage that you have to hide behind this preposterous facade?" She turned, crossing her legs on the bed so that she could face him. She traced her fingers over the scars on his chest, running her fingertips over the puckered skin. Some of those scars were fresh. Some of them were very old. Each one held a memory.

Gabriel looked away, watching the sunset through the window. "I... I saw *things* out there. Things you would never believe. Things that no man should ever have to see. I know what lurks in the shadows, Celeste. I know what's out there in the darkness."

Celeste lay down beside him, resting her head on his chest. Her auburn hair was like a splash of bright red blood against his pale flesh. Her voice was barely a whisper. "I know more than you think, Gabriel."

He closed his eyes, and wondered if she really knew. She couldn't. She couldn't have seen what he had seen. She couldn't even begin to imagine. If she knew... if she had any notion of what was waiting out there in the night...

Yet she clearly knew *something*. Something that meant she had to hide out here at Long Island, to shut out the world and pretend that nothing had happened back at Joe's. Something to do with Gideon Reece and the Roman, a secret life he knew nothing about. So what was she trying to tell him? What did she mean?

"Celeste... I..."

Celeste gave a long, tired sigh, and he realized she had finally fallen asleep. He smiled. The revelations would have to wait.

He stayed like that for a few minutes, stroking the back of her head, waiting until he was sure she had fallen into a deep slumber. Then, lifting her head gently so that he could slide out from beneath her, he arranged her carefully on the pillows and searched out his clothes.

Henry would have the car waiting for him round the front, and he had somewhere he needed to be.

FOURTEEN

Arthur Wolfe was an Englishman, which, given the current political climate in Manhattan, was perhaps not one of the most healthy provenances for a museum curator, or anyone else, for that matter. He'd lived in the city for over thirty years, since well before the outbreak of war, and long before the accession of Queen Alberta I. In those days he'd been welcomed as a kindred spirit, an expatriate from the motherland, an intelligent man in an intelligent city, a city full of metropolitan ideals and acceptance. Then the war had come, and whilst the British Empire had allied itself to its American cousin, the alliance had proved uneasy. When the British finally wheeled out the great weapon that won the war—the Behemoth Land Crawler—the Americans had grown concerned. The British were a superpower with a long history of invasion. They had once conquered half the globe, holding most of the known world in their sway. And now Alberta I was on the throne and had proved cold to her mother's former allies, referring to them in public as "those upstart colonists." She was a traditionalist, and believed that the British Empire needed to reclaim its former glories. The White House was worried, precisely because they believed she had the power to do it.

The result had been the dawning of a cold war between the

British Empire and the American Republic. And in turn that had led to a reassessment of the allegiances between former friends. It started first with strangers, visitors to the museum picking up on Arthur's unfamiliar accent, offering sly comments and sideways looks. But it soon spread to those Arthur had considered friends; the dinner invitations dried up, and he was no longer deemed a desirable person to have at a party. He'd continued working at the museum, tolerated because of his expertise in European history. But times were hard for Arthur Wolfe, and the Ghost, who'd never given much credence to the notion of racial responsibility, still considered the man to be a good friend. Indeed, he was the only person in the world to whom the Ghost had revealed his true identity, and to that end, he was one of the vigilante's most trusted companions.

Night was falling as the Ghost made his way across Central Park, his hat pulled down low over his face. He kept to the shadows, which pooled beneath the clumps of trees like inky puddles, careful not to be seen by any casual observers. In truth, the park was near deserted, but he knew there were uniformed police officers patrolling the area, and he was anxious not to run into any trouble. At least not yet. There'd be time for that later.

The Metropolitan Museum of Art was an immense, gothic structure that squatted like an ancient stone monolith beside Fifth Avenue. It was a repository of exotic treasures from all over the world, and Arthur Wolfe had spent years acquiring statues, artifacts, and trinkets for the Roman exhibition, turning it into one of the finest collections outside of Rome itself. During the day, people swarmed to see the vast forest of marble figures that filled the exhibition halls, or to admire the glass cases full of spear tips, arrowheads, and Roman coins.

It was for this reason that the Ghost had decided to pay a visit to his friend that evening, and had called ahead to ensure that Arthur would be able to meet with him. The man had seemed flustered on the holotube, yet cheerful in his peculiarly British way, and had relented when the Ghost explained the situation, agreeing to cancel his planned trip to the theater to meet with the vigilante at the museum. It wouldn't do for the Ghost to be seen taking the steps up to the main entrance, even at night, and so they had agreed to meet at the rear of the building so that Arthur could admit him by a back door.

As he hovered beneath a tree, waiting for his friend to show, the Ghost turned the Roman coin over and over between his knuckles, giving the illusion that it was trickling over his hand like a shining stream of bronze. It was a trick he'd learned as a boy, and he did it now, absently, as he reviewed in his mind the details of his meeting with the policeman the previous evening. He needed to find out more about the man. He could be useful. If he was also looking for Reece, there was a chance that, with the resources of the police department at his disposal, he could find him first. And that would lead the Ghost right to the Roman's door.

There was a sound from across the path. A door opened and a man appeared in the shadows, glancing from left to right. The Ghost recognized him immediately. "Are you there?" Arthur's voice echoed on the still November air. The curator had never been one for subtlety.

Sighing, the Ghost stepped out from beneath the tree and,

glancing up and down the path to ensure there were no passersby, darted across to greet the curator. "Yes, Arthur. I'm here."

The Englishman—tall, angular, with a crop of mousy hair, thin wire-framed glasses, and a crooked nose—regarded the Ghost with the haughty air of someone who had been very much caused to go out of their way. He peered down his nose at the vigilante. "It's late."

The Ghost nodded. "That's rather the point, Arthur."

The man seemed to think about this for a moment. Then, turning his body slightly but still keeping hold of the doorframe, he ushered the Ghost inside. "Well, I suppose you'd better come in, then."

The Ghost stepped through into the museum. The lights had been turned down, and the place had the eerie atmosphere of a mausoleum: funereal, silent, as if the weight of history was bearing down on them. The exhibits seemed to watch the two men as they made their way across the hall. Monolithic structures and blank faces loomed over them in the gloaming. Glass cases filled with unimaginable treasures covered every wall. They'd emerged in the rear of the American wing. Arthur had let him in through a fire escape.

The Englishman lowered his voice to a whisper, catching the Ghost by the elbow. "Come on, let's go to my office. There are still guards about. I don't want to have to answer any awkward questions."

The Ghost nodded but remained silent, partly in reverence to the ancient artifacts that surrounded him, partly to avoid drawing any unwelcome attention to his late-night visit. He followed Arthur as the curator wound his way through the exhibits, took the stairs to the next floor, and led the Ghost along a row of small offices to his room at the end of the corridor. "In there. We can talk without being interrupted."

Arthur's office always reminded the Ghost of his workshop. It was scattered with all manner of bizarre antiquities: the marble head of a statue, a broken amphora, a sheaf of old manuscripts, a stone casket, a map, and an assortment of clay tablets impressed with text in a variety of ancient languages. Many other peculiar items lined the shelves and surfaces, cramming the small space, filling the air with an old, musty scent. Then, incongruous amongst the dusty relics, there was the viewing machine that completely dominated an entire desk; a series of mirrored plates and long brass scopes, each one capped with a different lens, fixed to a rotating pillar. It was essentially an enormous microscope, but its power was beyond any similar device that the Ghost had ever encountered. He'd witnessed Arthur using it on more than one occasion, and it never failed to impress him with its results. He hoped the curator might use it now to investigate the brass coin he had come here to discuss.

An electric lamp was glowing on Arthur's main desk, and the curator pulled up a chair, dropping into it with a sigh. The Ghost remained standing by the door; a habit, he knew, that was now too deeply ingrained to shake. He had to stay close to the exits.

The Englishman looked at him expectantly. "You said it was important."

"It is. I need you to take a look at this." The Ghost flicked the coin through the air toward Arthur, who scrambled to catch it in his spindly fingers.

He scowled at the vigilante. "Show a little respect, man." He glanced down at the shiny object in his palm, turned it over gently with his finger. "Oh my," he said, all signs of irritation melting from his brow. "Now this really is something special." He raised his head to look again at the Ghost. "Where did you get this?"

The Ghost ignored the question. It wouldn't do to make Arthur jumpy. Not yet. "Is it real?"

Arthur nodded. "At least, I think so. Let me take a closer look." He stood, crossing to the viewing device on the other desk. He placed the coin—almost reverently—onto a glass slide and slid it carefully beneath the main shaft of the device. Then, standing back, he turned a wheel on the side of the main pillar. Cogs clicked and whirred, and the cluster of myriad eyepieces rotated until Arthur was satisfied. Then, stooping, he placed his eye to the lens.

Minutes passed. Pacing, the Ghost could feel himself growing more and more impatient with the Englishman, who was giving nothing away; not a remark left his lips, not even a sound to indicate what he might have been thinking.

Then, rubbing his lower back and easing himself upright once again, the curator turned to the Ghost with a wide grin on his face. "It's real. It's utterly remarkable, but it's most definitely real. Perhaps the best-preserved specimen of Roman currency that I have ever encountered. Tell me again where you got it from?"

The Ghost shrugged. He couldn't avoid the question again. "I retrieved it from a corpse. A murder victim."

Arthur let out a long sigh. He looked appalled. "This is what

I've been reading about in the newspapers, isn't it? The handiwork of that ridiculous criminal who calls himself 'the Roman.'"

The Ghost nodded.

"I heard he was leaving Roman coins on the eyelids of his victims. Is that what this is?" He reached under the microscope and retrieved the coin, turning it over in his hand.

"Yes. I wasn't sure that you'd want to know."

"I don't."

"Then tell me about the coin."

The curator nodded once and then crossed to his desk, returning to his seat. He placed the coin on the desktop. "It's rare. It's from the reign of the Emperor Vespasian and dates from between sixty-nine and seventy-nine AD." He paused, as if lost in thought. "It's never been in the ground, that much is certain. It's almost perfectly preserved." He glanced up at the Ghost. "Are there more?"

The Ghost shrugged. "At least one more the same—another one was left with the body, but I didn't have time for a proper look. There have been other victims, too. The people you read about in the newspapers."

"Yes. Quite." He scratched behind his ear, and then removed his spectacles, wiping them clean on the end of his tie. "I wonder where he's getting them from."

The Ghost rubbed a hand over his chin. "Is there anything significant about it, other than the condition and the age? Anything at all you can tell me?"

Arthur looked unsure. "I'm not sure what you're getting at."

"Symbolism. Does it signify anything?"

"Ah... Well, yes and no. I wouldn't read too much into the

coin itself. It's exceedingly rare, in any condition, but I don't think it symbolizes anything in the way you mean. Vespasian's was a short reign, and he didn't really do anything remarkable, other than begin the construction work on the Flavian Amphitheater—the Colosseum—or try to convince people that he had been granted a divine right to rule. The image on the other side of the coin is the goddess Fortuna, the capricious wielder of luck."

"The dead man, Dr. Sinclair, wasn't very lucky," said the Ghost, dryly.

"No, but that's the point. Fortuna was blindfolded and handed out her favors randomly. Not everyone could expect to be lucky. Not even her most faithful worshippers." Arthur looked around for his teacup, lifted it, and, seeing it was empty, waved it at the Ghost. "You want one?"

The Ghost shook his head. Arthur looked disappointed.

"I think the coin does tell us *something*, though."

"Go on."

"I think it tells us about the character of this 'Roman.' This is not a cheap trick, not a simple calling card. There's something else going on, something far deeper than we can see on the surface of it all. These coins weren't easy to come by. He clearly wants us—you, the police—to identify him with what he sees as his historical counterparts. But what is he trying to tell us by leaving them at the scenes of his murders?"

The Ghost sighed. "That's exactly what I'm trying to find out."

"Of course," the curator sat forward, filled with a sudden air of levity, "I could be completely wrong. I'm just a silly old

Englishman who works in a museum." He wrinkled his nose.

The Ghost smiled. "Yes. That's just what I was thinking." They laughed for a moment. "One last question for you, Arthur. Anything unusual been going on at the museum? Anyone taking their interest in Roman history a little too far?"

Arthur thought for a moment. "No. Only the regulars. Although... something a little odd did happen with Mr. Gardici the other day. He's been coming to the museum every week for over a year, a middle-aged chap with jet-black hair and olive eyes. He sits in the Roman exhibit and studies the statues. Says he likes to 'soak up the atmosphere' of his homeland." Arthur shrugged. "He's an Italian expatriate who's lived in New York for years. He still has a thick Italian accent."

"So what happened?"

"Two weeks ago he asked the guard if he could speak with me. Now, as you know, these days I tend to have a lot of time on my hands, so I was only too pleased to hold a conversation with someone who shares my passion for the esoteric. But I found Mr. Gardici in an... unusual mood. He wanted to buy one of the exhibits."

"To *buy* one?" The Ghost was incredulous.

"Yes, precisely." Arthur waved his hand dismissively. "Of course, I explained to him that none of the pieces on display were actually for sale, but he became quite forceful, insisting that he'd give a 'significant donation' to the museum on top of the asking price. When I refused, things became quite strained, and in the end the security guards were forced to escort him from the premises. He's quite a burly fellow so it took two of them to restrain him. He hasn't returned since, thankfully."

GEORGE MANN

The Ghost paced the floor, mulling over this new development. The likelihood was that it was nothing, unrelated to the Roman and the murders and the attempt to kidnap Celeste. But all the same... He stopped pacing. "What was the piece? The artifact that this Gardici man wanted to buy."

"That's just it. The piece isn't anything special, not really. It's a marble decoration, recovered from a villa in Pompeii. Parts of it are etched with ancient symbols, but we haven't been able to decipher the meaning of them all yet. Still, I have no idea why this particular piece should be of interest to a man like Mr. Gardici."

"Can you show me?"

Arthur looked puzzled. "Yes, of course. If you think it's relevant."

"*Anything* could be relevant."

Arthur placed his empty teacup on the desk with a sigh. "Come on, then. Back downstairs. I'll blame you if we run into any difficulties with the guards."

The Ghost smiled. He knew that Arthur's dourness was an affectation; that in truth he lived to discuss his work, and would grab any opportunity to do so, no matter what the circumstances. He understood the obsessive impulse; recognized a kindred spirit.

The two men made their way along the silent passages of the museum, and again, the Ghost was struck by the stillness of the place, the reverence he felt. It was a cathedral, dedicated to the study of the dead. The realization did not sit well with him.

Presently, Arthur led them to the wing that housed the Roman collection. Glancing from side to side to ensure they hadn't been seen, he waved the Ghost through. In the half-light, the sea of white statues, with their blank, staring eyes and missing limbs, gave the hall an oppressive feel. Arthur steered him to the left, past a row of glass cases containing fragments of pottery and items of long-spoiled jewelry, toward a gallery lined with stone plinths, fragments of buildings and broken columns, stone tablets and engravings. Arthur flicked a switch on the wall and the lights stuttered to life, blinking as the electrical charge gradually warmed the bulbs running the length of the ceiling. Then, about halfway along the gallery, the curator came to a stop before a large marble wheel.

"Here you are." His voice was a whisper. "This is what Mr. Gardici was so interested in acquiring."

The Ghost turned to admire the artifact beside him. It was perfectly circular, about as tall as a man. The center had been cut out to form a ring of glistening white stone, and the band around the opening was as wide as the span of his hand. It was mounted in a tall wooden frame.

The Ghost stepped closer, leaning in. The artifact was covered with an array of unusual symbols and pictograms that had been cut into the facing of the marble. They were unlike anything he had seen before, closer to medieval occult diagrams than anything Roman; circles with geometric shapes enclosed within them, a finger touching a six-pointed star, a crescent moon at the center of a starburst, a tower with an open eye at its base. "What are these?" He traced one of the pictograms with his finger.

"We don't really know. They must have some pagan significance. They're certainly not symbols that found general use across the Empire, or even elsewhere in Pompeii, as far as we know. These are the only known examples in existence. It makes the exhibit very valuable, but only as an academic piece; something for fusty old scholars like me to obsess over. Most historians simply write them off as 'ritualistic' and carry on with the more interesting stuff."

"Do you think Mr. Gardici knows something about them that you don't?"

Arthur raised an eyebrow. "Hardly. I think Mr. Gardici is enamored with the mystery of the piece, and has much more money than sense."

The Ghost nodded. "Thank you, Arthur. Will you call me if he comes back, or if anything else out of the ordinary occurs?"

"Of course I will." He paused. "Are you leaving, then?"

"Yes. Time I was elsewhere."

Arthur smiled. "One thing… What are you going to do with that coin? It's just that I…" He stopped as the Ghost flicked the coin through the air toward him, glinting as it caught the light. He scrambled to catch it.

"Keep it. I know where to find you if I need it again."

"Thank you, Gabriel." He clasped the coin tightly in his fist, as if afraid that he might open his hand, only to find that the precious object had disappeared.

The Ghost smiled. "Now, how the hell do I find my way out of this place?" He glanced in both directions.

"This way," Arthur said, as he led his friend away from the gallery. "I'll show you out the way you came."

Moments later the Ghost was standing in the chill darkness of the Manhattan night. His trench coat whipped up around his legs in the stiff breeze. He couldn't shake the feeling that what Arthur had told him about Gardici somehow fitted with the murders, and with Arthur's thoughts about the Roman. If the man really was trying to identify himself with the Romans of the past, could he be the one behind the attempt to buy the stone relic? Could Gardici be working for the Roman? Anything was possible. He needed to keep an open mind. Now, though, he needed to return to Long Island, to Celeste, to Gabriel Cross. Tomorrow, he would return to the city, to trail the policeman he had met on the roof at Suffolk Street.

Tomorrow, he would become the Ghost again.

FIFTEEN

Donovan heaved a heavy sigh and glanced up at the clock on the wall of his office. It was late. It would be dark outside, with just the play of the airship searchlights hanging over the city, picking out the buildings with their brilliant shafts of white.

He was alone in the office. Mullins and the others had all gone, back to their wives, their beds, their secret drinking dens. Back to the quiet monotony of their lives. Donovan envied them that. He wished for that monotony, cursed himself for years spent craving excitement and adventure. He had that now, in spades. Had it, and wished he didn't.

He glared at the hands of the clock as if trying, futilely, to prevent them from ticking. The room was silent save for that constant reminder, that ever-present *tick-tock*, *tick-tock*, counting down the seconds, minutes, and hours until his impending appointment with Gideon Reece.

He'd sent Flora away that morning, to her sister's place in Brooklyn. He'd told her it was a surprise, that he'd arranged everything with Maud, called her the day before to organize the trip. He'd stood over her while she threw some things in a bag, collected her shoes and her makeup. Then he'd driven her to the station, watched her board the train. She'd been bemused, excited, unsure what to make of this uncharacteristic gesture.

He'd kissed her hard and full on the lips, told her he would marry her all over again if he only could, and she had waved to him as the train hissed away from the platform, both charmed and—he could tell—concerned for him. He wondered if it was a form of weakness that had caused him to send her away, but decided it was, rather, a form of strength. He was protecting her, from Reece, from the Roman—and from what she might see when they finally got to him.

He had dealt with that eventuality. He'd arranged for Mullins to pick him up in the morning, just in case. He couldn't protect them all. Mullins would know what to do. Mullins would understand.

Donovan sighed for a second time. He'd spent the day searching for the car with three funnels. It had proved fruitless, a waste of time. And besides, he knew that car would be coming to find *him* that very evening, regardless of whether he was able to locate it or not. In truth, the whole thing had been an exercise in trying to do something—*anything*—that made him feel less impotent; anything to slow the inexorable movement of those ticking fingers toward their inevitable destination.

He would fight back, of course he would. He had his automatic in his pocket, and he was handy with his fists. He would try to take Reece down with him. That much he *had* decided. But he knew that in the end, that, too, would prove futile. A gesture born out of desperation. Even if he managed it—even if he put a bullet in the vile bastard—there were fifty, a hundred more men like him, just waiting for their chance to step up and take his place. That was the nature of the mob. He knew that it wouldn't end, not until the rotten core had been exposed and flushed out, the wound cauterized. They needed to find the Roman himself. But they were a long way from that. At that moment, Donovan was having difficulty even proving the man existed.

In his frustration, in the small hours of the morning, he had briefly entertained the notion of accepting the bribe. He'd dreamed up a whole scenario in which he managed to get inside the Roman's organization, becoming a trusted advisor, worming his way insidiously into the heart of the operation, and then, when the opportunity presented itself, taking out the men who mattered. But he knew how ridiculous that really was. He was no killer, no duplicitous agent, and he didn't have the stomach or the patience to see such an operation through to the end. He'd never win their trust, never do what was necessary. He'd be dead within a fortnight, and he'd die with a sour taste in his mouth and a stain on his hands. His colleagues—his *friends*—would look on his grave with disdain. No, he wouldn't take their blood money. Not tonight, not ever.

The clock chimed as it reached the hour. Nine o'clock. *Enough.* He'd wallowed for long enough.

Donovan got to his feet, abandoning the file he'd been pretending to read and reaching for his overcoat. It was a clear night, and he would walk home with a cigarette, maybe two. After all, he wasn't in any particular hurry.

His heart pounding in his chest, palms sweaty in anticipation of the meeting to come, he flicked the light off in his office and took his leave.

* * *

The Ghost, wrapped in his trench coat and clinging to a perch about thirty feet above street level, watched the policeman depart from the precinct building. A bone-deep cold chilled him to the core, and his breath fogged in the still air. The sky was clear: a thick black canopy above the city, peppered with shimmering pinpricks of light.

Far below, people were still milling about on the busy thoroughfare, hailing cabs, waiting for buses; going about their busy lives in search of distraction or entertainment. Going home to eat, drink, and fuck.

The Ghost watched as Donovan joined the flow of bodies, keeping his head down, his collar pulled up around his neck against the chill. The end of the policeman's cigarette was like a firefly in the gloom, bobbing and dancing erratically as he strode along the sidewalk. Other pedestrians danced out of his way, a symptom, the Ghost suspected, of a hard stare and a purposeful stride. The Ghost wondered what was bothering the man.

Stirring from his position on the ledge of the building, the Ghost tracked Donovan as he crossed the street and disappeared around the corner of an adjacent block, watching through the red filter of his goggles. He scrambled up onto the roof, securing his hat against a sudden gust and reaching inside his jacket to find the cord that would fire his rocket propellants. He gave it a sharp tug and the canisters ignited with a roaring flame. He felt himself lifting slowly off the rooftop and angled his body so that he could drift across to the roof of the department store across the street. From there he'd be able to hop along the buildings, tracking the other man along the street, at least until he changed direction again.

It hadn't been difficult to locate the policeman. The Ghost had found him emerging from the ruins of the Sensation Club a few hours earlier and had tracked him back to the precinct building, keeping to the rooftops and alleyways to avoid being seen. He'd taken the risk of venturing out in the mid-afternoon twilight, anxious to get on the trail of the man he hoped would lead him to the Roman. Donovan—that was the name he'd overheard one of the other detectives call him—had then holed himself up in the precinct and had remained there whilst a steady parade of junior officers quit the building, drifting away into the night. The Ghost had considered trying to find a way inside, or else a means to discover what the policeman was up to inside his office, but had given it up as a bad idea when he'd noted the police dirigible drifting ponderously above the precinct building, its searchlight sweeping languidly back and forth across the rooftop. So, instead, he had waited it out, and it looked as if his patience was about to pay off.

Donovan was up to something. That much was evident from the manner in which he carried himself: the nervous gestures with his cigarette, the fact he was chain-smoking, the speed at which he was charging along the street, as if he was running late for something important or wanted to get something over with. He kept glancing over his shoulder at the road behind him, looking at the cars as they hissed past him on the cold tarmac.

The Ghost wondered if someone was putting the squeeze on the detective. Either that, or his furtive behavior was down to something else, something less salubrious. He didn't think that was likely; Donovan was a detective through and through.

He would die that way, the Ghost knew, unable to separate himself from the job. He was wedded to it. It was so fundamentally a part of him that there was little else left, little of the man he had once been before the hunger consumed him, before he accepted the burden of the city and took it upon himself to put things right. The Ghost had seen it before, seen other men perish in the same way, and he'd recognized the look in Donovan's eyes that night on the rooftop in Suffolk Street. Obsession. Hunger. The desire for justice. He recognized it because he felt it too. Because the same desire burned behind his own eyes, stared back at him from the mirror each and every morning.

He wondered what had happened to the policeman to engender such a spirit, and what had happened in the intervening hours since their last encounter to dampen it. The Ghost still carried the scars of war, of what he had seen out there in the cold, muddy desolation of Europe. Old things. Ancient things. Things that made his skin crawl. Things that had changed him beyond repair, altered everything he held dear. Now he saw the world through different eyes. But what of Donovan?

The Ghost leapt across another chasm-like alleyway, light flaring briefly and brightly behind him as he sailed toward another nearby roof. He padded down gently, turning to watch the policeman as the man crossed a small park, emerging seconds later on the opposite side, glancing both ways and then darting across the street. He turned down another cross street. The Ghost followed, maintaining a respectful distance.

Soon after, Donovan reached his destination. He hovered outside the glass door of the apartment building; a modern construction, built in the last decade, with stepped tiers, tall windows, and sweeping curves.

The Ghost observed the policeman as he took a long, deep draw on his most recent cigarette, flicked the stub away into the gutter, and then checked the pocket of his overcoat, probably feeling for a weapon. Then the man glanced up and down the street before disappearing into the lobby, leaving the door swinging wildly on its hinges.

A row of stationary cars lined the curb at the front of the building; squat, black humps in the darkness. The Ghost trained his sights on them, altering the zoom on his lenses, dialing in on the four or five motionless vehicles.

Then he stopped dead, almost breathless. One of the cars had three exhaust funnels. It was unmistakably the vehicle he had seen the other night, purring away from the scene of Henry Sinclair's murder. Gideon Reece's car.

The Ghost sat on his haunches, flicking the lenses of his goggles back and staring up at the clear sky. One of two things was about to happen. Either Donovan was walking into a terrible trap, or the Ghost was about to discover that the policeman was working for the Roman.

Either way, he knew it wasn't going to be pretty.

Donovan flicked a glance at the elevator as he entered the lobby, and then marched on toward the stairs. If they were lying in wait for him, the sound of the creaking elevator echoing through the building would be a dead giveaway. This way, he could retain at least some element of surprise. He wasn't about to make it easy for them, and besides, he could do with the exercise. He grinned to himself at the thought. Now really wasn't the most practical time to be considering his waistline.

Mounting the stone steps, Donovan rested his hand in his pocket, feeling for the butt of his automatic. It was a comfort to him, a reassurance. He hated that, the fact that he relied upon his weapon to imbue him with confidence. But right now, on the stairwell of his apartment building, approaching what would almost certainly prove to be the fight of his life, he would take every bit of confidence he could find.

He took the six stories slowly, listening carefully for any signs of movement. The building seemed unnaturally quiet, and all he could hear was the rasping of his own lungs as he dragged at the air, the thudding of his heart in his rib cage. He'd seen the car parked out front; knew beyond a shadow of a doubt that Reece and his cronies were waiting for him inside. Part of him just wanted to get it over with, wanted to rush up that last flight of steps to his floor, charge along the hallway to his apartment, and burst in with a hail of bullets, mowing down as many of the crooks as he could before he was riddled with lead. But he knew that would be foolish. If he kept his cool, there was still a small chance that he could walk away from this alive. He clung on to that thought, no matter how small that chance might actually be.

His nerves jangling, Donovan crept up the last flight of steps to the seventh floor and peered around the corner. The corridor was empty. He allowed himself to exhale. No guards. That must mean they were already inside his apartment. He glanced back down the stairwell and fought the urge to flee. It wouldn't do him any good. It might buy him a few hours, at most. Better to get it over with.

Donovan moved softly along the corridor toward his apartment and stopped a few feet from the door. It was standing ajar, but he couldn't see much through the narrow gap. He edged nearer, listening intently for any sounds from within. Nothing. He could feel the tension in his shoulders, taste the bitter adrenaline on the back of his tongue.

One hand in his pocket, clasping the trigger of his gun, Donovan eased the door a little wider. The hinges were almost silent as the door swung inward, revealing more of the hallway beyond. Empty. He hadn't expected that. Perhaps Reece had come alone? He didn't think that was likely.

Donovan stepped over the threshold, carefully swinging the door shut behind him. The hallway was filled with the scent of fresh, sodden earth. Wrinkling his nose, he glanced around. Everything was as he'd left it: the holotube terminal on the small side table; a vase of flowers; a large mirror on the wall; a shoe stand just behind the door. A pile of mail was heaped tidily on the sideboard where he usually left his keys. It was the perfect picture of homeliness. Clearly, they weren't interested in his belongings.

Three doors led off from the hallway, and all were pulled shut. One opened into the kitchen, another to the drawing room, the last to the bedroom. The bedroom he shared with Flora. His grip tightened on the butt of his gun as he thought about Reece and his cronies violating the sanctuary of that room. Leaving that strange, earthy smell about the place. He wouldn't bear that, couldn't stand the thought of them rifling through Flora's things, making a mockery of his marriage. That would be too much.

Donovan continued stealthily along the hallway, stopping to listen at each of the doors in turn. Still nothing. No sign, other than the apartment door hanging open, that anyone else had even visited the place. Unsure what else he could do, Donovan picked a door—the drawing room—and turned the handle, allowing it to swing open. The hinges groaned alarmingly. Almost immediately, he realized his mistake.

They were waiting for him, just as he'd feared.

The room was cast in a gloomy half-light, lit only by the dim glow of a table lamp. Shapes huddled in the shadows around the edges of the room; the outlines of men, crowding in the semi-darkness. Donovan had the sense that there were at least five or six of them in there, skulking, waiting. The room was rich with the scent of fresh earth. And on the sofa, one leg crossed over his knee, his spindly fingers steepled before his chest, sat Gideon Reece. He was dressed in an immaculate black evening suit, just as he had been when Donovan had met him before. His eyes seemed to flash in the dim light, and his lips curled in a sarcastic smile. "Inspector Donovan. So glad you could join us."

Donovan didn't speak. His heart was hammering against his ribs. His palm felt sweaty against the butt of his gun.

Reece motioned to one of the men in the shadows and the main light blinked on, a sharp white glare that caused the policeman to squint. Reece laughed. "Nice place you have here. Homely. I like what you've done with it. I'm sure you and Flora could do with someplace bigger, though?"

Donovan bristled at the sound of his wife's name. "You leave my wife out of this, Reece."

Reece shrugged genially. "How is Flora? I understand she's away visiting Maud? A shame. I should like to have met her. I've heard she's terribly pretty." He flashed another grin, and it was all Donovan could do to restrain himself from pulling his weapon, then and there. But he knew that was what Reece was goading him to do, what he wanted. He knew that as soon as he whipped the automatic out of his pocket the five or six other weapons around the room would all bark, and it would be over. He suppressed his mounting rage. How did they know about Flora?

Donovan tried to size up what he was facing. Six of them, plus Reece. Two giants, standing at the back in long trench coats and hats, their faces hidden from view. Four others, all training their tommy guns in his direction. And Reece. He couldn't underestimate Reece. He met the other man's amused gaze. "I thought I had until midnight?"

Reece laughed. He glanced at his watch. "We can wait. We're not in a hurry, Inspector."

Donovan gave an almost imperceptible shake of his head. "No need. I have my answer."

Reece shifted slightly in his seat. He reached behind him, producing the large brown packet of notes he'd first offered Donovan in the car. Casually, he tossed it over to the inspector. Donovan didn't move, didn't make any attempt to catch it. The paper envelope struck his chest with a dull thud and fell to the floor, scattering banknotes over the carpet in a flurry. Donovan watched the notes settle on the deep red pile. There were hundreds of dollars in there, if not thousands. He lifted his head to face the crook. "There's my answer for you, Mr. Reece. You can tell the Roman that his offer is not welcome. I've given over my life to protect the city from men like him—like *you*— and I'm not about to throw that all away for... for *this*." He waved his left hand to indicate the pile of cash on the ground, careful to keep his right hand in his pocket, firmly gripping his automatic. He could hear the ire in his own voice; knew that he had only moments before the whole place descended into chaos.

Reece smiled, feigning resignation. He shook his head. "Such a waste. You could have been so useful to us, Inspector. And Flora could have been so happy." He motioned with his hand and two of the goons rushed toward the motionless policeman.

For Donovan, everything that followed happened in a blur, over in a matter of seconds. He pulled the automatic from his pocket and loosed three shots into the chest of one of the oncoming crooks. The man bucked as the bullets slammed home, spraying gobbets of blood into the air, spattering the wall behind him as he went down, his arms flailing wildly in the throes of death. Donovan whirled around toward the other man, but the on-comer was already too close. He had no time to bring the gun round to get a shot. Instead, he flicked his wrist out and slammed the butt of the weapon into the man's forehead as he charged in, stepping backward to avoid being taken down as the goon collapsed, unconscious, at his feet.

Donovan barely had time to breathe before the report of a second gun followed and his arm was punched backward, his fingers releasing their grip on the automatic as he staggered in shock. The gun clattered against the doorjamb, skittering away down the hall. Donovan realized he'd taken a bullet in his shoulder. The pain was like a hot poker being pushed through his flesh, the blood warm and wet and sticky. He suppressed a howl of agony, biting down hard, clenching his teeth in an attempt to allay the pain. The room was filled with the stench of cordite and spilled blood.

Donovan looked up through watery eyes to see Reece clapping his hands, slowly and sarcastically. A small silver pistol was lying on the arm of the sofa beside him. So, the bastard *wasn't* beyond doing his own dirty work. Donovan knew he'd been right not to underestimate the man.

He sensed movement by his feet. The man he'd struck with the gun was beginning to stir. The other was lying facedown in a growing puddle of dark blood. At least he'd taken one of them out for good.

Donovan stood there for a moment, breathing heavily, waiting to see what would happen next. The pain was like a foggy cloud all around him, muffling his senses, wrapping him in its terrible embrace. Then Reece was speaking once again. His thin, reedy voice cut through Donovan's pain like a knife. "A valiant attempt, Inspector. You're to be congratulated for your courage." A pause. "But you really should have taken the money..."

Reece stood, uncurling languorously like a cat stretching its limbs, and beckoned to the two big men who were still standing, motionless, at the back of the room beside the bookcase. The giants lumbered forward, and Donovan didn't struggle as they took his arms in their strange, claw-like grips and pinned them behind his back. He couldn't suppress a short cry of pain as his shoulder was twisted awkwardly in the process. He felt more blood seeping out of the wound, soaking his shirtsleeve.

He looked up at the face of the giant on his left, and was shocked to find it was blank and green beneath the brim of the hat. So that was why the place stank of damp earth. These men—these *creatures*—were constructed out of clay and moss. He wondered what appalling technology had granted them life; realized he would likely go to his death without knowing.

Donovan's shoulders slumped as the two moss men took his weight. Reece crossed the room to stand before him, a Roman governor before a crucified prisoner. The man's pale face gleamed in the bright light. He spoke to the two golems: "Take him to the roof," and then to Donovan: "You're going to have a nasty fall, Inspector. Flora will be told it was suicide. She'll wonder why. She might even blame herself. But you needn't worry." His face cracked into a toothy grin. "One of the boys will be sure to… comfort her."

Donovan thrashed against the moss men's grip. His shoulder felt like it was on fire, but he still tried to kick out at Reece, tried ineffectually to do something—anything—to hurt this terrible man. They could do what they wanted with him. But Flora…

His mind raced as they dragged him from the room, pulling him along the hallway, his feet sliding on the wooden floor, unable to gain a footing. He had no idea how he was going to find his way out of this. There were simply too many of them to fight back. But he had to. He had to find a way. He couldn't let them get to Flora. Somehow, he had to find the strength to protect her.

The mobsters followed behind the moss men in a black troupe as they heaved their prisoner up the stone steps toward the eighth floor, and then to the roof. The door slammed open onto a howling wind, a terrace shrouded in nightmare shadows and bristling clusters of holotube receivers. The two moss men dragged Donovan toward the rear of the building, where only a small lip separated him from a long fall. Beneath, the hard concrete beckoned. He was feeling woozy now, the pain and the blood loss causing his strength to seep away. The cold wind buffeted his face. He blinked. Was he falling already?

He heard Reece's voice shouting over the howl of the wind, and realized he was not. "It's not too late to change your mind, Inspector. One more chance. Think of what we can offer you. Working for us... you'll finally be able to make a difference."

Donovan spat. It was his only response.

Reece laughed. "Flora won't thank you for it, Inspector."

Donovan looked down at the dark abyss beneath him. He made one final attempt to tug his arms free, but it was no use. They were too strong. He sucked at the chill air, preparing himself for the inevitable.

And then one of the moss men's heads exploded.

SIXTEEN

The Ghost watched as Donovan crumpled to the ground, suddenly free of the lumbering moss golems. The mobsters were in disarray, waving their weapons around in the darkness as they tried desperately to spot their attacker. The remaining golem was stomping ponderously across the rooftop toward him, as if somehow drawn to him, as if it instinctively knew where he was concealed behind a farm of holotube aerials. Most likely, it had calculated the trajectory of the fléchette that had destroyed its partner. The Ghost smiled to himself. Perhaps the moss men were more intelligent than the mobsters, after all.

He swung his arm out, brandishing the long brass barrel of his fléchette gun in the direction of the oncoming golem. He squeezed the trigger, releasing a shower of silvery blades. They zipped through the night air, twinkling in the starlight, embedding themselves in the moss man with a series of tiny, dull thuds. The moss man continued to lurch toward him. The Ghost counted the seconds; three, two, one…

The golem detonated in a flash of light, scattering mud, clay, and brass over the surrounding rooftop. Tiny cogs and clockwork components tinkled in a shower over the nearby mobsters, pattering down on them like obscene rain. As one they raised their voices in alarm. One of them let loose with his tommy gun, spraying a nearby chimneystack with bullets, more out of sheer desperation than any real sense that the brickwork concealed his invisible assailant.

The Ghost allowed himself a wide grin. The explosive rounds had delivered exactly the result he'd hoped for.

He peered between the metal struts of the transmitters and caught sight of Gideon Reece, standing over the policeman, a tiny silver pistol held aloft. He couldn't get a bead from his position behind the aerial cluster. Nor did he want to finish Reece, at least not before he'd had chance to question him. Reece was his ticket to the Roman, his only lead.

He needed a distraction.

The Ghost leapt out from behind the forest of wires, loosing a spray of fléchettes into the air. They scattered on the ground in a wide semicircle around Reece and Donovan, and seconds later went up in a pyrotechnic display, flashing brilliantly in the darkness, the pattering boom echoing away across the adjoining rooftops. Reece, panicked, glanced from side to side, spotting the Ghost in the stuttering light. He squeezed the trigger of his pistol, but his aim was wide in the smoky aftermath of the explosions. The distraction was exactly what Donovan had been waiting for, however. The policeman, finally coming to his senses, leapt to his feet and charged Reece, bowling him over and sending them both careening across the flagstones. The Ghost moved just in time to miss a storm of lead, spat from the mouth of a tommy gun. The goons had likely spotted the red glow of his goggles bobbing in the darkness.

The Ghost rushed to where Donovan was lying on his back, nursing his wounded shoulder. The man looked pale. He needed to get him out of there. Injured, he was a liability, and the Ghost wanted him alive. "Donovan. On your feet! Out of here, now!"

The policeman looked up, his eyes darting from side to side as he tried to focus on the vigilante. The Ghost grabbed him by the collar and hauled him to his feet. He pointed to the open door that led down into the apartment building. "There! Go. NOW!" He shoved Donovan in the direction of the stairs.

The policeman nodded once and then set off at a run, his damaged arm trailing behind him as he pelted for cover. One of the mobsters moved to go after him, but Reece was back on his feet, dusting himself down. "Leave him! We can deal with him later. I want this one dead."

The Ghost swept the barrel of his fléchette gun in a wide arc that would encompass two of the mobsters. He needed Reece alive, but the others...

A handful of shimmering fléchettes spat from the end of the gun, but to his dismay, the Ghost watched as the silver spray stuttered and petered out. He squeezed the trigger again. Nothing. He must have used up all of his explosive rounds on the moss men and the pyrotechnic display he'd put on for Reece.

The remainder of the tiny blades struck the ground and detonated ineffectually, allowing the goons to duck easily out of the way. They swung their weapons around and took aim. The Ghost was out of time, a sitting target, and there were three submachine guns pointing in his direction.

He had to think quickly.

He ran to the edge of the building and leapt into the air, tugging the cord inside his jacket as he fell into a graceful dive. The darkness swam up to meet him as he rushed toward the street below. His heart was thudding wildly. What if it didn't work?

Then, all of a sudden, the rocket canisters tied to his boots ignited with a roar and he was kicked sideways by the force. He spiraled, keeping his hands clasped tightly by his sides to avoid slamming into the nearby building. For a moment he spun out of control, thought he was going to break his neck as he smashed into the sidewalk. Then, fighting the urge to panic, he arched his back, swinging his feet down low so that his body was now angled upward, back toward the lip of the building's roof. The rocket boosters caught his fall and he soared through the air, feeling the cold wind whistling past him as he rose once again into the night sky. His hat came loose, gusting away into the street below, but he plowed on through the darkness, riding on a plume of orange light.

By now the mobsters were at the lip of the building and had realized what had happened. They let loose with their tommy guns, bullets chattering into the sky as they tried to pick out the soaring vigilante. The Ghost didn't give them the chance. He weaved and twisted, turning gracefully as he dodged the oncoming streams of bullets. One tore through the skirts of his trench coat; another pinged off the brass barrel of his fléchette gun. But miraculously, the Ghost himself never felt the expected thud of hot lead burrowing into his flesh.

The gap between Donovan's apartment building and the next building on the block was only a matter of a few feet. The Ghost swept up through the top of the narrow alleyway, bursting out over the roof of the adjacent structure and cutting the rockets dead. He slammed painfully into the roof terrace, sliding along on his belly, his arms outstretched, sending clouds of gravel pluming into the air. He rolled quickly onto his back and scrambled to his feet. The three goons had not been dissuaded by his momentary escape, and whilst he had temporarily put himself out of the range of their bullets, he knew it would not be for long. He watched, dismayed, as one by one they leapt across the gap between the two buildings, each of them still carrying their black snub-nosed guns. Reece, it seemed, had made other plans, for he was nowhere to be seen.

The Ghost cursed himself for letting the man get away. He needed Reece. But first he had to deal with the imminent threat of those guns. He glanced around, weighing options and risks. He could fight, or he could run. Running most likely meant another leap off the side of the building, and that was risky. But so was standing his ground. He'd need to get close enough to the goons to fight back, and that wasn't likely, given the weapons they were sporting.

He backed up, glancing over his shoulder to judge where he had landed. Behind him, three biplanes sat on tall ramps, stark silhouettes in the moonlight, their noses pointing to the sky. The Ghost smiled. There was his answer.

He turned and made a dash for the second of the three flying machines. One of the goons called out, and then his tommy gun barked, but he was still too far away to hit his mark. The Ghost heard their boots crunching on the gravel as they gave chase.

The Ghost dashed up the steps alongside the old biplane, his lungs burning from the exertion. He glanced at the aircraft in its launch housing. It was modified from an original design: an older vehicle that had been retroactively fitted with a modern rocket launcher. The rocket booster was bolted into a sub-frame at the rear of the aircraft; a long, thin canister containing enough rocket fuel to power the vehicle up off the ramp and across the rooftops until the main propeller kicked in. It dispensed with the need for a runway for takeoff, but landing on the confined space of the rooftop again was a real skill, and most pilots found themselves ditching on a nearby airfield and having the biplanes lifted back in situ by airship.

The aircraft wasn't in great shape, but it would have to do. The green paint was peeling and the whole thing stank of oil. The propeller was a smooth blade of polished wood, and the four wings were flimsy and thin, formed from sheets of pressed steel. There were two pits in the body of the plane: one at the rear for the pilot, another at the front for a passenger.

Grasping hold of the side of the aircraft with his gloved hands, the Ghost vaulted over the edge of the steps, landing smoothly in the pilot's pit. He glanced back over his shoulder. The goons were closing in. Two of them split off, left and right, and he realized they were heading for the other aircraft. The third was standing at the foot of the steps, just behind the Ghost, readying his weapon.

The Ghost ran his hands over the familiar controls. He was momentarily overcome by a vision of being back in the war, of sitting behind the controls of a similar plane, spiraling out of control as he came in over the treetops to crash-land in a field full of bodies and blood and sticky mud. Of facing death. Of strange things that no man should ever have to see.

He shook his head, trying to lose the memory. Now was not the time. His fingers danced over the dials as he readied the controls, hardly noticing the *rat-a-tat-tat* of the bullets that were riddling the steel panels at his back. He pulled the ignition lever and the rocket engine flamed to life. He turned to see the mobster at the foot of the steps drop his weapon and scream, staggering away from the launch platform as his face melted in the backwash of the rocket engine. His suit went up in flames, and he stumbled and collapsed in a fiery heap, scorched to the bone.

The Ghost felt the biplane straining against its moorings and pulled a second lever, launching the vehicle up the ramp and away over the rooftops. He banked wildly, swinging the aircraft round to double back on himself, twisting knobs and pulling the starter cord that would give life to the main propeller. It choked angrily, as if reluctant to start, and then buzzed to life.

Behind him, the other two aircraft slipped their housings and shot into the air, illuminating the street below with the red glow of their rocket engines.

The Ghost searched the area around the cockpit, looking for anything he could use as a weapon. Nothing. This was a civilian craft. Unlike the vehicles he had flown in the war, this decrepit old thing didn't boast any machine-gun mounts or pneumatic cannons. It was down to his piloting skills, then. And luck.

The Ghost sent the aircraft into a steep climb, trying to get above the mobsters, who had both managed to start their propellers and were now cruising behind him, side by side. He expected they would try to fan out and flank him, but if he could get high enough, he'd be able to swing out of the way.

He leaned over the side of the cockpit. Far below, he could

see the glow of the city as he banked again, the twinkling lights of modern America. It was a beautiful sight, a sight to be proud of. A sight he intended to protect.

He started in his seat at the sound of bullets hammering into the fuselage below him. One of the goons had broken formation and was climbing beneath him, one hand clutching the control stick, the other spraying the undercarriage of the Ghost's aircraft with hot lead. The Ghost didn't fancy his chances, especially if the metal plates under his feet were as thin as the wings. He pulled back on the control stick, causing the nose of the craft to tip skyward, and jammed his legs under the control panels as tightly as possible as the biplane looped backward, turning full circle, the engine protesting with a howling whine.

The Ghost steadied the aircraft just above and behind that of the mobster who'd been shooting at him. He dipped the nose, driving the plane down toward the other aircraft. The mobster howled as he fought furiously with the controls, trying to swing to the left to avoid a collision.

At the last moment the Ghost flung his craft to the right, swerving away from the goon, with the result that the other plane banked sharply to the left and swerved in the other direction, leaving it out of the picture for a short while, at least until the mobster was able to bring it under control again.

The dive had brought him perilously close to the rooftops, but now the Ghost had to contend with the second mobster, who was cruising along just above him, blocking any hopes he had of heading skyward. In the distance he could see the upper half of the towering Atlas, shimmering hazy blue against the backdrop of stars. Above him, he saw the second mobster lining up his tommy gun over the side of the cockpit.

Waiting until the last possible moment, the Ghost shoved the control lever forward, dipping the biplane down and right, swinging around into Broadway. He leveled the craft about five stories up from street level, following the channel formed by the tall buildings as he buzzed uptown toward Times Square. Below, pedestrians were pointing and calling to one another as he raced over their heads. Above him, the mobster had to correct his turn, swinging wide as he tried to stay on the Ghost's tail. To his credit, the goon managed to wrestle the controls to his will, quickly coming up behind the Ghost, settling just a little higher to avoid dashing his wings on the fronts of the buildings. The Ghost caught sight of the second plane, too, sweeping back in from the east, heading straight for him.

He had to shake them. He needed to lead them in a dance.

The Ghost thought back to the evasive maneuvers he'd practiced during the war, patterns of movement that were still lodged in his brain. He grasped the control stick in both hands, rolling the aircraft through ninety degrees, the left wingtip only a hundred feet from the ground, the right pointing up at the heavens. Then, rotating the stick, he swept the nose around, bringing the wings up to forty-five degrees and shooting up and over the shopping mall on his left. The mobsters banked, following his movements. Just as he'd hoped.

The Ghost switched direction again, arcing the plane to the right. Once again, the mobsters followed suit, one of them pulling closer and offering another spray of lead from his tommy gun. The bullets drummed into the fuselage at the rear of the aircraft. The Ghost glanced back to see one of the panels, so damaged by the storm of bullets, shake loose and flit away behind him. He didn't have time to worry about what harm it might do to the pedestrians below.

He pulled the biplane around in a tight circle, watching to ensure that the others were behind him. Then he dipped the nose again, diving low into Fifth Avenue. This time, one of them followed him down.

The two biplanes *vipped* along, their engines roaring. The Ghost rocked the control stick gently from side to side, weaving the aircraft back and forth as they shot along the narrow channel, following the sweep of the road above the hissing cars and crowds of tiny people. Then, with only seconds to spare, he spun the biplane onto its side and changed direction, shooting down a narrow alleyway between two large office buildings. The undercarriage was only inches from the brickwork. The alleyway was soot black, but the Ghost was able to see by virtue of his glowing red goggles, able to make out the hazards that loomed in the shadows.

Avoiding an iron fire escape that clung to the side of one of the buildings, the Ghost tweaked his trajectory and shot out of the top of the alleyway, twisting the plane around in a loop to regain some height. The mobster who'd followed him into the tight space wasn't so lucky, however. Unable to see in the pitch darkness, and lacking the Ghost's years of flying experience, he was nevertheless carried away by the adrenaline of the chase. The goon had managed to swing his aircraft into the tight mouth of the alley in pursuit of the vigilante. But he didn't anticipate the iron staircase.

His biplane smashed into the unforgiving metal structure at full speed, shattering the nose of the stolen aircraft and driving the still-spinning propeller back and up into the pilot's pit. He most likely didn't have time to register the loss of his legs to the whirling blade, however, as moments later the fuel tank ignited, causing the entire aircraft to erupt in a ball of fire that spat burning debris out into the street in a waterfall of dripping flames.

The Ghost circled the wreckage once, and then prepared to climb before the remaining mobster had time to react. He felt exhilarated by the chase, by the heat of the combat. He spiraled the plane upward, higher and higher, until he penetrated the thin layer of gray clouds that hung in wispy streaks over the city. He could hear the buzzing propeller of the other plane beneath him as the mobster searched for him in the misty banks of gray. He circled, waiting.

Then, taking his chance, the Ghost dipped the nose of the biplane and banked low, dipping out of the cloud cover. The engine growled in protest. Almost too late, he realized the other plane was on top of him. He'd dropped too low. The tommy gun chattered. The Ghost veered, first left, then right, then dipped again. He looped, trying to repeat his earlier trick, trying to get above the other plane once more. But this time the goon was wise to him and put his own plane into a climb, causing the Ghost to veer hard to the right simply to avoid a collision. His fingers danced over the control panel. He cursed himself, once again wishing that the old contraption were more like the aircraft he had flown in the war.

He dipped again, hearing the wings creak under the strain

of his constant maneuvers. He wasn't sure how he was going to shake the other plane. He glanced back over his shoulder. The other aircraft was hovering near, holding steady, the pilot watching him, waiting for him to make the next move. It was now or never.

The Ghost yanked back on the control stick, causing the biplane to rear suddenly, driving it up into the path of the enemy plane. He heard the mobster scream as, unable to pull himself away in time, the front end of his biplane mowed into the tail of the Ghost's. The spinning propeller ate hungrily into the thin metal fuselage of the Ghost's plane, chewing the steel, mashing the two aircraft together and causing them both to veer drastically out of control. The Ghost was nearly jolted out of the pilot's pit and had to clutch desperately at the rim of the aircraft as he was tipped sideways, the entire thing shaking as the other plane embedded itself deeper and deeper into the fuselage.

The mobster was fighting furiously with his control stick, forcing it wildly to the left and right, doing everything in his power to separate the two planes as they spun out of control. The nose of the Ghost's plane dipped, and together the two biplanes fixed on a collision course with the sidewalk far below.

The Ghost could smell fuel, realized it was likely bleeding out of a split tank. He glanced at his control panel. The dial was in the red. He swallowed. The two mangled aircraft were about to become one huge fireball above Manhattan. From behind him came the sound of rending metal as the substructure that housed the rocket exhaust finally gave way, the iron struts creaking and snapping one by one under the weight of the other plane. He glanced back. The mobster was pale with fear.

The two aircraft were slowly separating in midair, the stress of their descent prizing them apart again as they tumbled through the sky.

The Ghost pulled back on the control stick, trying to force the nose of his damaged biplane up. The propeller screamed, the engine unable to bear the combined weight of the two aircraft. They were perilously low now, only a couple of hundred feet above Madison Avenue. The grinding continued as the Ghost fought with the controls and then, suddenly, the other plane broke loose, and he was spinning away, climbing, wavering crazily as he tried to bring the remnants of the biplane under control.

Beneath him, the other plane, no longer dragged along by the momentum of the Ghost's aircraft, plummeted toward the ground like a dropped stone. The Ghost thought he could hear the mobster's screams as the ruined biplane collided with the sidewalk, nose first, the tip of the left wing puncturing the window of a nearby store. The Ghost held his breath, expectant... and then the crashed biplane detonated with a boom that rebounded off the tall white office buildings lining the avenue, a sound that was likely heard all over Manhattan. Flames licked hungrily at the wreckage.

The Ghost had little time to celebrate, however, as without its tail and losing fuel, his own biplane was quickly losing altitude. He wrestled with the controls, trying to level the wings, trying desperately to keep the nose from pointing toward the ground as he swept along, narrowly missing the buildings on either side, unable to steer, unable to climb any higher. He was going to have to ditch it. He was going to have to try to land the thing on the road, on Madison Avenue.

The engine spat and hissed angrily, and then the propeller finally gave up, seizing as the motors that drove it locked up. No fuel. No controls. Only his momentum carrying him forward, carrying him inevitably down toward the slick tarmac below.

The Ghost glanced over the side of the plane. There were people milling about everywhere; running toward the crash site, dashing for cover, stopping to point and scream as they heard and then saw this second plane, out of control, diving out of the sky toward them. He considered bailing out, but he knew that the fall would kill him. At this speed, at this height, his body would be dashed across the street like a watermelon. He closed his eyes, tried to breathe, tried to fight the sense of rising panic, the tightening in his chest. He'd been here before, in France. He'd been through this and lived. He couldn't help wondering what the chances were that he would do so again.

He peeled open his eyes and calmly reached forward for the control stick. *He had no choice.*

The plane was listing to the right, so he threw his weight to the left, leaning out of the pit in an attempt to level the aircraft. It bobbed, buffeted by the sharp wind, and began to level out, but he realized he was still coming in too steep. With no propeller, gravity was drawing him inexorably toward the ground. He rocked back, shifting his weight again, throwing everything he had behind the movement in the hope that, this time, he'd be able to keep the shattered tail end of the aircraft down, preventing him from nosediving directly into the tarmac.

It was this decision, this moment, which he later reflected had saved his life.

The biplane finally came down, slamming into the road, its wing smashing through the windshield of a parked car, the impact ripping the roof clean off the vehicle, but also rending rivets loose in the main fuselage of the biplane so that the wing was whipped away, clattering off down the street. The undercarriage scraped and skidded along the tarmac, bouncing and hopping along the road and raising an enormous spray of bright sparks in the crashing aircraft's wake.

It spun wildly. Pedestrians dived out of the way to avoid flying fragments of shrapnel as it lurched along the road. Another car swerved desperately, mounting the sidewalk and narrowly missing the oncoming wreckage.

And then, finally, it shuddered to a halt.

The Ghost peeled open his eyes, realized he'd been holding his breath. He shuddered. His hand was still clutching the control stick, squeezing it for all he was worth. He became aware of the sound of screaming: shrill, terrified screaming. He saw a man running toward him, concern etched on his gleaming face.

He had to get out of there.

Grasping the edges of the pilot pit, he heaved himself free of the wreckage and dropped to the ground. He must have gashed his knee during the impact as his pants were torn and blood was running freely down his calf. He gritted his teeth, resting his hand against the remaining, shattered wing of the biplane.

"Hey! Mister, are you okay?" And then, "That was some—"

The Ghost turned away from the man, glancing back up the road. In the far distance he could still see the flames of the other aircraft as it burned, a steel tomb for one of the Roman's men.

Testing his injured leg gingerly, he established it would still support his weight. And then, without waiting any longer, without acknowledging the small crowd of people who were gathering around the wreckage, he turned and ran.

SEVENTEEN

Donovan knew his apartment was no longer safe, but his first instinct upon leaving the rooftop was to head there, not for the purpose of holing himself up, but with the aim of recovering his gun, the automatic he had lost in the hallway during his encounter with Reece and his men.

He was weak, terribly faint. He could feel the energy ebbing out of him like the warm blood that was still trickling down his arm, seeping into his clothes, as he pushed his way through the door and staggered down the hallway.

He found the weapon easily enough, even managed to reload it with a second clip, but the swirling darkness that limned his vision kept closing in on him and he swooned, dropping in and out of consciousness, unable to think straight. It felt a little like drowning, like being swallowed by something warm and dark and safe, and he knew that if he didn't fight it, that coziness, that sense of warmth and tiredness would overcome him, and he would never wake up again. He forced himself to keep moving.

He had no sense of how long it took him to stagger back along the corridor outside of his apartment to the stairwell. It felt like hours, but it must have only been minutes, for as he hung for a moment in the doorway, rasping for breath, he caught sight of Gideon Reece, bouncing off the walls as he flung himself down the stairs from the roof. He charged down the stone steps, his footsteps ringing out in the confined space. Clearly, the man wasn't so confident when he wasn't surrounded by a clutch of the Roman's goons.

Unable to use his right arm, Donovan hefted his automatic in his left hand, and from a slumped position against the wall let loose a series of potshots, trying to catch Reece as he fled the scene. The bullets ricocheted off the iron fretwork of the railings, left dusty pockmarks in the plasterwork, but Donovan was unable to hold himself steady and Reece rushed on, down and down the stairwell, toward safety, freedom, ducking as the bullets pinged around him.

Donovan staggered after him, firing until his magazine was empty, finally flinging the gun in frustration at the back of the disappearing figure. Reece hadn't even turned to acknowledge him, so intent was he on making good his escape. Donovan practically fell down the final flight of stairs, collapsing on the bottom step as he watched, through the tall glass-paneled doors of the apartment building, the three-funneled car roar away into the night, its tires hissing on the damp tarmac.

He felt the blackness closing in on him again.

When he came round, Donovan was on the sidewalk. He had no recollection of how he'd got there. The cold wind buffeted him, and he felt himself sway unsteadily on his feet. Above, he heard the roar of rocket engines firing as biplanes launched from the roof of a nearby building, riding away on bright spikes of flame.

He glanced in both directions along the street. His first instinct was to follow Reece, to head in the direction that his car had taken, but he knew his judgment was clouded; he was on foot, and wounded, and he didn't know how long it had been since Reece had left. What, then? The hospital? The precinct? Mullins?

Yes, that was it. Mullins. Mullins was reliable. Mullins was always reliable.

Donovan staggered toward his parked car. It was an old thing, and he didn't drive it often, but he was glad of it now. He leaned against the roof as he unlocked the driver's side door. His vision was blurring. He'd lost a lot of blood. He cursed himself. He should have done more. He should have taken out Reece when he'd had the chance.

Donovan swung the car door open and practically fell into the seat. He rested his good hand against the wheel. A cigarette. He needed a cigarette. He fought inside his jacket, struggling to prize the packet out from inside the pocket. Then, finally, he worked it free, flipped open the lid, and with his lips withdrew one of the white cigarettes. He pulled the tab, watched the tip flare. He sighed as the thick nicotine flooded his lungs. Donovan laid his head back against the headrest, allowing the smoke to plume out of his nostrils. His shoulder was throbbing. He was tired. So tired. The blackness was calling to him, offering sweet oblivion. He felt his eyelids closing. The cigarette tumbled from his fingers. Everything went dark.

He woke with a start. Someone was calling his name. Tired, weak, bleary-eyed, he peered at the face of the man who was leaning over him. The features bobbed. He could smell nicotine on the other man's breath. The man had two red pinpricks for eyes. *Who did he know who had red eyes...?*

Donovan's mind suddenly engaged. The Ghost! The Ghost had saved him from the Roman's men. The Ghost was here, now, leaning into his car.

"Donovan! Donovan!" A sharp pain as a gloved hand slapped him across the face. "Donovan!"

"Yes..." he croaked, his cheek smarting, "yes..." He couldn't think of what else to say.

"Donovan. I'm going to move you now. You're coming with me." The Ghost was leaning over him, wrapping his hands around Donovan's chest. The Ghost heaved him across the cab, groaning at the exertion, and Donovan felt a sharp spike of pain in his shoulder as he was lifted over to the passenger seat. The Ghost slid in beside him, coughing, and took the controls. Donovan noted that the other man's leg was bleeding heavily, his pants torn. Had the Roman's men done that to him? How had he managed to see off so many of them?

Donovan tried to ask the Ghost these questions but his voice was barely a whisper, and before he'd had chance to properly frame his words, the Ghost had fired up the engine and the questions were lost in the hissing of steam as the paddles engaged and the vehicle slid away from the curb. Donovan slumped in the seat. He had no idea where the Ghost was taking him. But he hoped, wherever it was, he'd be able to get some rest. The swirling darkness was waiting for him.

* * *

Time passed. He didn't know how long. He had a stuttering awareness of being driven at high speed through the city, slamming around corners, dodging the oncoming traffic as the Ghost rushed him toward their destination. But everything seemed to pass in a haze of slow motion, as if it wasn't real, as if he was seeing everything through a hazy filter of smoke or water.

And he was shivering. The cold, logical part of his brain knew this was because of the blood loss. But the part of his brain that was keeping him alive, the part that was forcing him to stay awake, to cling on to consciousness for all he was worth—that part of his brain didn't want to consider the logical truth, to acknowledge it or give it credence. That part of his brain was hoping that the Ghost was taking him somewhere safe and quiet, with doctors and surgeons and life-saving medicine.

The car juddered to a halt. Donovan looked out of the window. They'd stopped outside of an ordinary tenement building. No hospital then. He wondered what the Ghost had in mind for him. Was he going to leave him here to die? Donovan thought not. Not after what had happened on the rooftop.

He closed his eyes, heard the Ghost climbing out of the driver's seat, footsteps around the back of the car. Then the cold wash of the night air as the door was wrenched open, rushing into the cab, caressing his face. He drank in the fresh air. Moments later he felt the Ghost's hands underneath him, scooping him out of the seat and hoisting his supine body in a fireman's lift. His shoulder screamed in pain at every footstep, as the Ghost kicked the car door shut and staggered toward the building.

What came next was nothing but a series of vague impressions: climbing steps, his head and arms lolling like a rag doll's; passing through a door; being dropped roughly into a soft chair; the Ghost's voice, commanding, gritty: "Stay with me, Donovan." And then: "Here, drink this." A glass tumbler was pushed into his hand, hard beneath his fingers. He didn't want to lift it. It felt heavy, cumbersome. He wondered for a moment where he'd left his gun, and then remembered throwing it after the retreating mobster. It felt as if days had passed.

The Ghost was standing over him again, lifting his hand, bringing the glass to his lips so he could drink. He sipped at it, grateful for the long fingers of warmth that it spread through his body. Whisky. Bourbon. He swallowed again. And again, draining the glass. Warmth. He needed that warmth.

The Ghost took the empty glass and disappeared again. When he hovered back into view, Donovan had regained some sense of himself and his surroundings. They were in an apartment. To his left, a series of large panoramic windows looked out over the dark cityscape, the moon a bright bauble in the sky. It wasn't a homely place, more functional; a few chairs, a table, doors leading to a handful of other rooms. There was nothing personal here. No one *lived* here. Appropriate, then, that it should be inhabited by a ghost.

Donovan blinked, studying the man who stood over him. The vigilante's jaw was set, grim. He was holding a small brass tool: tongs, with vicious-looking tips. "This is going to hurt, Inspector." His voice was low and serious.

The Ghost stooped over him, roughly pulling open Donovan's jacket, tearing his damp, sticky shirt to expose the puckered wound in his shoulder. Donovan couldn't believe the amount of blood. He looked away, gritting his teeth. He knew what was coming. The Ghost used his thumbs to probe the wound and Donovan fought back a cry of pain. The Ghost pulled him forward, roughly, studying his naked back. After a moment, he allowed Donovan to rock back in the chair.

"It's as I thought—no exit wound. We're going to have to get that bullet out." Donovan gave a sharp nod. He didn't like the sound of that. The Ghost reached for the surgical tongs he had left on the arm of the chair. Then, glancing at Donovan's face, he pulled off one of his leather gloves, rolled it into a bundle, and passed it to the inspector. "Here, bite down on this."

Donovan took it, wedged it between his teeth. There was a sharp, stinging pain in his right shoulder. He bit down hard. The glove tasted of old leather and sweat. The Ghost wormed the tongs around in the wound, trying to locate the bullet, trying to get a grip on the small piece of lead that had punctured Donovan's flesh and would poison his bloodstream if it wasn't quickly removed.

"Got it!" The Ghost's exclamation was almost triumphant. There was a pause, and then fire, excruciating fire, as the bullet was ripped from the wound. The Ghost dropped the tongs and the bullet to the floor. "Now, apply pressure here, hard." Donovan did as he was told. More blood was oozing from the wound. He clamped his left hand on it, squeezing hard despite the pain.

The Ghost was fishing for something in a small room just off of the main living space. A bathroom. He returned brandishing a white strip of bandage, which he laid out on the arm of the chair. Grabbing for the bottle of bourbon, he prised Donovan's fingers away from the wound and sloshed a measure of the liquid over the shoulder. Donovan howled in pain as the alcohol burned his raw and bloody flesh.

Next, the Ghost proceeded to loop the bandage around Donovan's shoulder, tightly strapping his arm. Then, standing back to admire his handiwork, he poured Donovan another whisky and collapsed back into the chair opposite the inspector. "Drink that, then sleep."

Donovan sipped at his whisky, tried to focus on the other man. "Who are you?" His voice was a dry croak.

The Ghost shook his head. "Tomorrow."

Donovan drained the whisky. He allowed the darkness to seep in again, closing in around him as if the room were getting suddenly smaller. Yes, tomorrow.

Now, at least, he felt as if tomorrow might actually come.

Light streamed in through the window, bright and golden, picking out the dust motes that drifted lazily in the air above his head. The light stung his eyes. Donovan licked his lips. His mouth was dry. He must have slept for hours. He moved to sit up, but feeling the painful pull of his wounded shoulder, instead he allowed himself to fall back into the soft embrace of the chair.

He was in a terrible state. His clothes were torn, his chest exposed, dried blood matted in his hair. The bandage around his shoulder was soaked with a dark crimson stain—but he felt alive, more alive than he had in days. His head was clear; the foggy darkness that had plagued him since the rooftop had been banished, and he knew his own mind, knew that he was glad to have made it out of there in one piece, albeit damaged. All policemen were damaged, he reminded himself, some in more ways than others.

Donovan glanced around the room, trying to remember where he was. The Ghost! The Ghost's apartment. The other man was asleep in the opposite chair, his head lolled back, his goggles pushed up onto his forehead, still fully clothed. The vigilante had obviously stayed up, watching him, keeping vigil, ensuring that Donovan didn't slip away during the night.

Donovan studied the Ghost's face, wracking his memory. Who was he? Did he recognize that face? The rugged, square-cut jaw, the sandy hair; it was familiar, but he couldn't place it. Beyond the Ghost, the door to the bathroom was still hanging open. Donovan would try to muster the strength to clean himself up in there, soon enough.

At the other end of the living space another door was propped open, bright sheets of light spilling out from the room beyond. From where he was sitting, Donovan could just make out a row of weapons—guns; blades; other, more outlandish devices—mounted on a rack on one wall, and the corner of a desk, piled high with all manner of strange components and empty bullet casings. An armory. The man was serious, then.

Deciding not to put it off any longer, Donovan levered himself out of the chair. He was steadier on his feet than he'd expected. He flexed his neck and shoulder muscles. The bandage was tight and the wound pulled painfully. He made a fist with his right hand and almost yelped, but then tried again and felt the discomfort ease a little. He'd live, at least for now. He thought of Flora, of her pretty smile, her beautiful smell, and the thought alarmed him. Reece had mentioned her the previous night, said he knew her whereabouts. He needed to get to her, to warn her somehow. Or he needed to get to Reece.

Donovan glanced at the sleeping figure of the Ghost. He would help. He knew it now, without any shadow of a doubt. The Commissioner had been wrong about the man. His methods, well—perhaps they were a bit overzealous. But his spirit, his courage... they were unparalleled. Donovan only wished he could say the same about himself. The Ghost was clearly an ally, and at that moment, Donovan needed all the help he could get.

When he emerged from the bathroom a short while later, the Ghost was no longer asleep in his chair. Tentatively, Donovan made his way to the small kitchen area of the apartment to fix himself a drink. He set the tap running, turned as he heard sounds from behind him. A man emerged from the bedroom, dressed in a fine black suit, a crisp, clean collar that was open at the throat, and shiny black brogues. His hair was combed in a smart side parting. Donovan almost did a double take. The man was a picture of sophistication; he had the air about him of the very rich.

"So, this is the real you?"

The Ghost smiled, a wan smile. "No, I wouldn't say that, Inspector."

Donovan took in the apartment with an expansive gesture. "Where are we?"

"My apartment. Yours isn't safe, not at the moment. Neither

are the hospitals. If the Roman wants you dead, he'll be looking for you. Reece knows you were shot; he'll have people watching the emergency rooms."

Donovan nodded. "So... Reece got away?"

"Yes. For now."

Donovan drained the glass of water in his hand, gave a spluttering cough. "He'll come after me. I have to find him before he finds Flora."

"Flora?"

"My wife."

The Ghost nodded. "Rest here. You need to recover your strength. Fix yourself something to eat."

"Where are you going?" Donovan asked.

"There's someone I need to see." He smiled. "I'll be back later. I've laid out a clean suit for you, on the bed. I think it should be about your size."

Donovan shrugged. "Thanks." He caught the Ghost's arm as the vigilante turned to leave. "You said you'd tell me who you are."

"You know who I am, Inspector. What you saw... *that's* who I am. The rest is just window dressing."

Donovan nodded. He didn't need to know any more. "How can I contact you?"

The Ghost shook his head. "No need. I'll be back in a few hours. Wait here."

"Very well." Donovan watched the Ghost turn and leave, and then set about fixing himself some eggs.

* * *

After he'd eaten and dressed, Donovan searched out the holotube unit in the Ghost's apartment. He'd decided to call Mullins. The sergeant deserved to know where he was, or at least what had happened to him. He'd arranged for Mullins to call for him that morning, fearing the worst, and now, he realized, the poor bastard was probably panicking, running about the place trying to deal with the dead mobster he'd found on his boss's carpet. And besides, there was always the slim chance that Mullins had managed to get a lead on Reece. Donovan knew that was probably desperation talking.

The transmitter buzzed; a moment later, the blue light flickered to life and an image resolved in the display cavity. It was Richards, the precinct's administrator.

Donovan cleared his throat. "Richards. Donovan."

The man sounded immediately relieved. "Inspector Donovan? We've been trying to reach you all morning."

"Ah, right. Yes. I ran into a few complications last night. Can you put me through to Mullins?"

The administrator gave an exaggerated shrug. "That's just it, sir. Sergeant Mullins isn't here."

"What do you mean, Mullins isn't there?"

The other man sounded unsure. "There's been another murder, sir. Like the others. Sergeant Mullins is attending the scene."

Donovan ran his hand through his hair, flinched at the stab of pain in his shoulder. *Another murder?* He stared at the flickering blue image. "Right, man. Give me the address."

"Yes, sir. It's uptown. Five-two-two, Eighty-eighth, between Second and Third. Home of a Mr. Williamson, a banker."

Donovan nodded. "Right, I'll get over there straight away. If Mullins calls, tell him I'll be there within the next thirty minutes."

"Yes, sir."

Donovan flicked the switch, ending the transmission. The blue light blinked out, the picture fading from view. Another murder. The Roman had been busy.

He stood, looking for a scrap of paper on which to scrawl a note for the Ghost. Unable to find anything suitable, he threw his hands up in despair and decided to leave anyway. He'd take the Ghost's advice, to a point; he'd return here later to meet the vigilante. Clearly, Donovan's own apartment was unsafe. But he couldn't sit around and do nothing, not when there was a potential lead on the Roman, a fresh corpse, and a worried sergeant, out of his depth and unsure what had become of his superior officer. He couldn't sit and hide himself away knowing that, no matter how much pain he was in.

The Ghost had left a key dangling from the lock. Donovan seized it in his fist and set out. He'd be back soon enough. And together he and the Ghost could consider how they were going to find Reece.

The taxi hissed up to the sidewalk, slotting in behind the row of police vehicles that crowded the street like a mouthful of gleaming white teeth. Donovan had considered driving—his car was still parked outside the Ghost's apartment, after all—but he couldn't face it yet. The pain in his shoulder was still too intense, and he knew the seats would still be sticky with congealed blood.

He climbed out of the cab and paid the driver. Then, crossing the sidewalk, he mounted the steps that led up to the front of the large house, the home of Mr. Williamson, the dead banker. He rapped on the door. A uniformed man cracked the lock and held it open, peering out at him suspiciously through a slight gap between the door and the doorjamb. When he realized it was Donovan his demeanor changed entirely and he opened the door wider, beckoning the inspector in over the threshold. "Morning, sir."

Donovan bowed his head in acknowledgement. "Morning."

"They're in the back, sir."

Donovan made his way into the bowels of the house. It was spacious and richly furnished: plush, deep carpets, expensive-looking works of art plastered over every wall, furniture in the modern style. The banker had clearly carved out quite a career for himself.

Donovan followed the sound of voices to the dining room. There he saw Mullins and three other men standing around the oval dining table, regarding the naked white corpse of the banker. The man had been obese—grossly obese—and balding, with a stark, pale complexion. But now his face was blue, bloated, the blood vessels broken to form a cracked network of lines across his face. His thick, stubby fingers were spread out upon the table, his hands palm down on the glassy surface, adorned with innumerable gold and platinum rings. Banknotes—huge sheaves of yellowed banknotes—had been stuffed into his mouth, choking him, suffocating him with their papery promise.

His body had been positioned over the table, stripped naked

and posed so that his behind was jutting rudely into the air, his feet spread apart, his tree-trunk-like legs on either side of a carved wooden dining chair. More banknotes had been forced brutally into his asshole.

Bizarrely, the room smelled of freshly cut flowers. Donovan gave a polite cough. Mullins looked up. "Inspector! We've been trying to reach you."

"I heard. I ran into a spot of trouble." He looked at the sergeant expectantly.

Mullins looked concerned. "Is that a new suit, sir?"

Donovan waved a hand. No mention of the dead goon in his apartment? "Not now, Mullins. Is this…?"

"Yes, sir."

"What about the coins?" Donovan looked at the man's eyes. They were bulging from the sockets like glassy orbs. He looked away again.

"They're here, sir. One under each palm. It's definitely the work of the Roman."

Donovan nodded. If it was Reece, he'd been busy. He glanced back at the corpse, trying to hide his disgust. The banknotes were too much of a coincidence: Reece was sending him a message. He grimaced.

Mullins crossed the room, coming to stand beside him in the doorway. Together, the two men regarded the bloated corpse in all its macabre glory. "Do we have any idea what time?" Donovan said wearily.

Mullins shrugged. "Late." He was looking sideways at the inspector, as though sizing him up, as though he felt he needed to ask Donovan if everything was alright.

Donovan nodded. "I'm alright, Mullins." He paused, considering his next words. He didn't want to make matters worse by spilling the whole thing to his sergeant. Didn't want to admit he was working with the Ghost, a wanted vigilante. It would complicate things. And he didn't want Mullins getting wrapped up in Reece's games, either. "Did you stop off at my apartment this morning?"

Mullins nodded. "Yes. I knocked but you didn't answer, so I assumed you'd changed your mind and made your own way to the office. When I got there you weren't around. Then the call came in and we headed up here without waiting."

Donovan nodded. "I had a run-in with a few of the Roman's men. Roughed me up a bit."

The portly man wiped a hand across his brow. He looked concerned, had clearly noticed the way Donovan was carrying himself to ease the discomfort in his wounded shoulder. "What happened, sir?"

Donovan sighed. "Later. It can wait." He scratched around in his jacket pocket for a cigarette, realized with dismay that this was not *his* jacket pocket as his fingers closed on empty space. "Mullins, have you got a cigarette?"

"No, sir."

"Goddammit!"

The sergeant looked shaken. He quickly changed the subject. "Reports from the neighbors suggest the incident took place between two and three this morning."

Distracted, Donovan stared at the dead man's milky-white back. Two or three a.m. Well, it could have been Reece. That was long after he and the mobster had parted company.

"Do you need anything, sir?" Mullins's voice cut into his reverie.

"Just a cigarette, Mullins. If you can find me a cigarette." He swallowed. "Then I need to catch the bastard responsible for this."

The two men stood together in silence for a moment. Then, suddenly, Donovan turned to face the other man. "Mullins. Any luck finding that link you were talking about, the thing that connects the victims?"

Mullins looked solemn. "No, sir, not yet. But I know it's there. I will find it, given time."

Donovan sighed. "Time, Mullins, is the one thing we don't have." He stared at the floor for a few moments, a ponderous expression on his face. Then he reached into his pocket, retrieved a small folded envelope, and turned it over in his fingers. "You know, there is something you can do for me, Sergeant."

"Yes, sir?"

"You can see that this gets to my wife. She's staying with her sister in Brooklyn. I've written the address on the envelope." He paused, adding: "It's important, Mullins."

Mullins accepted the note. "Of course, sir," he said. "I'll have one of the men run it over directly."

"Thank you, Mullins." He smiled at the other man. "I'll leave you to make the necessary arrangements here."

"Can I ask where you're going, sir?"

"I'm going to find a cigarette, Mullins. And something illegal to drink."

The sergeant frowned as Donovan turned, left the room, and went off in search of cigarettes.

EIGHTEEN

There was no party that day at Gabriel Cross's capacious home on Long Island. Celeste had canceled it, shooed away all of the guests, tired of their presumption, their preening, and their constant, relentless need for validation. Tired also of being alone, of being trapped there, away from her life, from the city, with nothing to occupy her time, save for the execrable company of Gabriel's perpetual houseguests.

At least, that's how she described it to Gabriel as they drank coffee in the drawing room around eleven o'clock that morning. She was dressed in an immaculate blue dress that pooled around her knees like a splash of azure water, and she had kicked off her shoes, folding her legs up beneath her in the chair. Her painted toenails peeked out, matching the color of her hair.

Gabriel himself was slouched in his chair, twirling a cigarette in his fingers as he pondered her words. "But, Celeste, what is it with this anxiety to get back to the city? It's hardly as if you're desperate to reinsert yourself into society life." He gave a slight cough and smiled at her, a gleam in his eye. "It's no wonder you're feeling abandoned, anyway—you've frightened away all of the guests."

"Gabriel..."

He continued, unabashed. "Besides, I thought we'd decided

the city was too dangerous at the moment, anyway. All that business at Joe's." He blew cigarette smoke at the ceiling, glancing nonchalantly out of the window.

Celeste looked somewhat perturbed by this apparent indifference to her plight. "That was *days* ago. I miss the city. I miss... you." She paused, weighing her words. "You're never here, always off gallivanting—"

"Gallivanting!" Gabriel snorted. "Taking care of business, you mean. Looking after my interests in the city."

"Interests indeed!" She sounded indignant.

Gabriel gave her a sidelong glance. What was she thinking? What was the root of this sudden change in demeanor? "I'm trying to protect you. That's all, Celeste."

Celeste sighed. She offered him a weary smile. "I know. And you're a dear, dear man. But, Gabriel, I do not need your protection."

Gabriel stubbed his half-smoked cigarette into the ashtray, frustrated. "Then what about the other night? Car chases and gunshots? What of those?"

Celeste looked at the floor. The timbre of her voice changed. "There's... there's things about me you don't know, Gabriel. Important things. Dangerous things."

"Things that Gideon Reece is interested in, you mean?" Gabriel chewed his lips. He could see the worry that was etched onto her face; felt the need to somehow console her. Yet he was also aware of the emergence of a hollow feeling, a feeling that seemed to start in the pit of his belly and spread up through his torso, overwhelming him, making it difficult to breathe. He cared for this woman more than he cared for anything else in the world; more, even, than he cared for himself. He loved that he did not know everything about her. That was part of her allure, part of the frisson of their attraction. But this? This was troubling.

She did not answer him.

He leaned forward in his chair, bringing himself closer to her. "Talk to me, Celeste."

She was gazing out of the window. He wondered what she was thinking, what she was seeing behind those shining eyes. He could see the wintry colors of the garden reflected in them. After a moment, she turned to him. "I can't. I can't talk to you, not while you're like this."

Gabriel frowned. "Like what?" He didn't know what he could have done wrong.

"Oh, Gabriel. Haven't you worked it out yet? Haven't you realized? I know who you are. I know who you *really* are, beneath that ridiculous veneer." Her voice was barely a whisper. "Even if you don't know it yet yourself."

Gabriel slumped back in his armchair, wishing now that he'd asked Henry for something far stronger than coffee. Could she mean...? Did she know? Did she really *know*? How the hell had she worked it out?

He stared at her, unable to form any words.

"We all have secrets, Gabriel. All of us. Some of them are better left unshared." She brushed her hair back from her face. Her lips were parted. She looked more serious now than he had ever seen her before. "I needed you last night."

The moment stretched.

"I... I was needed elsewhere." He couldn't offer her any more than that.

Celeste smiled. "Yes, I rather think you were," she said. She flipped over the folded newspaper that was lying beside her on the coffee table. Gabriel could see the headline: DISASTER ON MADISON AVENUE, and beneath it: BIPLANES CRASH, TWO DEAD. WITNESSES REPORT VIGILANTE SEEN IN WRECKAGE.

Gabriel's heart was thudding in his chest. So she did know. Everything. But what did that mean? And what was she keeping from him?

He sipped at his coffee, and for a dreadful moment he wished for the party, wished that he was surrounded by those indolent, carefree specters that haunted his double life, dripping compliments and holding vacuous conversations in the doorways, fucking each other in the guest rooms and falling drunk into the duck pond. For a minute he wanted that, wanted to lose himself in its counterfeit embrace, to escape from the reality of this awful moment. *She knew.*

Gabriel swallowed. "Alright, Celeste. Alright. But this doesn't change anything."

Celeste shook her head. "It changes *everything*, Gabriel, can't you see that? Everything." He couldn't read her expression. "It was all a perfect lie, anyway, wasn't it? The parties, the jazz, the girls."

Gabriel shook his head emphatically. "Not you, Celeste. Never you. You were never that." He could see her bottom lip was quivering. He got out of his chair, crossed to her, wrapped his arm around her shoulders. "I had never loved, until I loved you."

She looked into his eyes. He could see the tears brimming, waiting to tumble down her cheeks.

"Look, once we're done here, once this is over with, we'll get away, we'll go somewhere new, together. Somewhere we can forget about it all." He kissed her forehead. "You choose. Anywhere."

Celeste shook her head. The tears were now streaming down her face. "Don't you see, Gabriel, that's just it! We can't. You don't understand."

The statement cut him to the core. "No. I don't understand."

She wiped her eyes with the back of her hand. "There's more to this than guns and nightclubs, mobsters and crashed airplanes. Much more."

"What do you mean? What do you know?"

But all she could do was sob, and all he could do in return was clutch her to him, holding her head to his chest and stroking her hair as she succumbed to her emotions.

Gabriel's head was full of questions. Questions that he did not know how to ask, that he couldn't even begin to phrase to the tortured, beautiful woman who lay beside him. How had she figured it out? How long had she known? What did it mean, for them? Did anyone else know? And what was it that was troubling her? Something else, something that she was clearly afraid to discuss. He thought he would go insane with the uncertainty. So many questions.

He lay on the bed beside her, fully dressed, his arms wrapped around her body. She was fast asleep. He watched her chest rise and fall with a regular rhythm. He'd wanted to spare her this, to save her. But then he thought of Donovan, holed up in the Ghost's apartment in Manhattan, concerned for his wife, hiding from the mob. Gabriel and the inspector were not so different, after all. He'd have to get back to the man soon. But...

He glanced at Celeste. How could he leave her?

Gabriel leaned his head back against the wooden headboard in frustration. He considered taking Celeste back to Manhattan with him, and then rejected the idea. It was too dangerous, and she'd be too much of a distraction for him. Here, he knew she was safe. He couldn't risk it. He wouldn't be able to focus. And if Reece's men got to her... he didn't even want to think about that. What did they want with her?

He used the side of his palm to smooth the hair back from her face. Her flesh was pale, like pure alabaster. He followed the line of her jaw with his finger. He'd do anything for this woman. Anything. Except let her go.

She stirred beneath his touch. Opened her eyes, smiled. Their eyes met. "How long have I been sleeping?"

"A few hours," Gabriel said. "Not too long."

Celeste propped herself on one elbow. He still had his arms around her. He didn't want to let go. "They need you, Gabriel."

"Who?" he said, but he knew what she meant.

"I can see it in your eyes. You're worried." Her voice was like silk. He wanted to wrap himself in it and hide away. But he nodded, just once.

"They need you more than I do right now. Go to them. The people you help... what you do... it's wonderful."

He felt the sense of hollowness returning. He wasn't that altruistic.

Celeste sat up, stretching leisurely. "I'll be here when you come back."

"You will? Really?" Gabriel was unsure.

"Of course I will."

"Celeste—"

"Shhh." She put her finger to his lips. "What do you always say? You have someone that you need to see." She kissed him then, and he drank her in: her scent, her taste, the touch of her soft skin through the delicate fabric of her dress. He knew he could drown in that heady wash of sense and emotion.

"I lo—"

"Shhh. Later."

Gabriel allowed himself to be shushed. He stared into her eyes.

"You can trust me, Gabriel," she said. "I'll do whatever's best."

"Alright. I'll go. There's a wounded policeman who needs my help." He climbed off the bed, brushing himself down. He had the horrible sense that he was walking away from something, that somehow he was abandoning her to the lions. He suppressed the urge to stay. She'd be safe here, at his Long Island home. No one would think to look for her here. "Later, then."

"Yes. Later."

He gave her one last lingering look, and then left the room.

Celeste waited until she'd heard the sputter of his motorcar, churning the gravel of the driveway as it hissed off into the wintery afternoon. She climbed down from the bed, straightening her dress. She glanced at the mirror, fixed her hair. She could barely look at herself, couldn't meet her own gaze. She wanted to break down and weep, wanted to call after Gabriel and tell him to come back, tell him to throw away his silly costume and run away with her like he'd said, somewhere safe and far away from Long Island and Manhattan and all the terrible things to come. But she steeled herself instead. She had a job to do, and the time was coming. Soon, she would need to act.

She swallowed. Her mouth was dry. She looked at herself again in the mirror. Then, as if adopting another persona, slipping it on like a new dress, a new mood, she sauntered out of the bedroom and wandered off in search of Henry.

Celeste found the valet in the dining room, polishing the silverware. He looked up as she entered, a kindly smile on his face. "Hello, Miss Parker. Is there anything I can do for you?"

She almost broke then. She could hear the tremble in her voice. "Thank you, Henry. I was wondering if you could bring one of Mr. Cross's motorcars around for me? I need to get some air. I'm feeling terribly cooped up in this big old house. I thought a little spin might do me good."

Henry nodded, carefully placing the candelabra he was polishing on the dining table, dropping the dirty rag beside it. "Quite so, Miss Parker. An excellent idea. If you'd like to make any final preparations I'll go and fetch one directly."

She stepped out of the doorway to allow him to pass, watched his back as he disappeared along the hallway.

Soon, she would be on her way. Soon, she would be facing the biggest challenge of her life.

She, too, was needed in the city.

NINETEEN

The Ghost bustled into his Manhattan apartment around seven o'clock that evening. The drive from Long Island had proved monstrous; there were too many other vehicles on the road, and he hadn't been able to keep his attention on the driving. Too many things were spiraling through his head. Thoughts about Celeste, Reece, the Roman, Donovan. They crowded his mind, jostling for attention.

He was still wearing his day suit, and wondered how much longer he would need to keep up the charade. Since everybody seemed to know already... In truth, though, he knew that there was no escaping it. He could rely on Donovan, of course, but declaring his true identity to the world would be tantamount to signing his own death warrant. Donovan was only a lone voice amongst the many, and the Commissioner wouldn't stand for it, wouldn't sanction a known vigilante on his streets, no matter how rich or influential he was. The Ghost needed to protect himself, needed to focus. Discovering that Celeste knew the truth—it had thrown him. But he had to shake the feeling, and quickly. Nothing had changed; the city still needed the Ghost... and the Ghost still needed the city.

He glanced around. Donovan was nowhere to be seen. Frowning, the Ghost strolled into the living room, looking for any sign of the policeman. He caught sight of him then, silhouetted in the open doorway of the workshop. He couldn't see Donovan's expression.

"It's quite an armory you've got here."

The Ghost crossed the room to stand before the other man. "Yes, it is rather."

Donovan stepped out from under the glow of the shining arc lamp, and his features resolved. He looked tired. He was still wearing the suit that the Ghost had given him earlier. "You took your time."

The Ghost shrugged. "I was busy."

Donovan pursed his lips. "There's been another murder." The Ghost raised an eyebrow, and Donovan continued, "A banker by the name of Mr. Williamson. Seen off by the Roman's men, same as before."

"Do you think it was Reece?"

"Yes, Reece or his cronies. I think he was trying to send us a message. I think he was trying to show us that he won't be stopped, that things carry on regardless. That perhaps we'll end up the same way, too." There was a tremor in Donovan's voice.

The Ghost grinned. "I think Reece says a lot of things."

Donovan brushed past him, heading for the kitchen, placing an empty glass on the counter with a gentle *clink*. "So what now? How are we going to find him?"

The Ghost smiled. So they were working together now, it seemed. "The three-funneled car—that's all we've got to go on. But I have a feeling that Reece will prove too impatient to wait for us to find him. Perhaps we should let him come to us."

"A trap, you mean?"

The Ghost grinned. "Something like that." He noticed that Donovan was still holding himself in an awkward posture. "How's your shoulder?"

"Bearable." Donovan's response was curt and clipped. He was clearly still in pain. It would be weeks before the wound would heal.

"I can find you something for the pain."

Donovan shook his head. "Not if it will dull my senses."

"Very well." He understood that impulse, that need the policeman had to keep his head clear. He also understood the need to take the edge off, too, to dull the sharpness of the real world, and felt it now as he considered pouring himself a fat finger of whisky. He looked at the stack of unwashed plates piled in the kitchen sink. "Have you eaten?"

"Yes."

"Right. Well, get in there and choose yourself a weapon. Preferably two." He indicated the door to his workshop. "I have to change out of this dreadful suit."

Donovan laughed. The Ghost stepped into the bedroom and pulled the door shut behind him.

Ten minutes later, as he was strapping the shaft of his fléchette gun along the length of his forearm, the Ghost heard the shrill chime of the holotube receiver. He opened the bedroom door, stepped out to see Donovan standing over the holotube unit. He looked up when he heard the Ghost enter the room, a concerned expression on his face.

"He rang off, didn't even give me a chance to speak. Must have thought I was you in the confusion."

"Who was it?"

"A man, asking for someone named Gabriel. A guy called Arthur. He had a plum in his mouth—British, I think. Something like that. Said he needed your help, that there was something going down at the museum. Said he was calling like you'd told him to if anything happened."

The Ghost stared at the policeman. "This is it. *This* is our lead. We need to get to the Met, fast."

Donovan frowned, running a hand through his ruffle of dark hair. "The Metropolitan Museum of Art?"

The Ghost swept up his trench coat from the back of a chair. "Trust me, Inspector. The Roman is making a move. This is the chance we've been waiting for."

Together, the two men hurried out into the cold Manhattan evening.

The Metropolitan Museum of Art was shrouded in darkness. High above, the moon was wrapped in a wintery wreath, the sky a leaden canopy of thick cloud. Tiny freckles of snow were falling, shimmering in the radial glow of the streetlamps. The snowflakes dusted their coats with fine, powdery blankets, each one existing for only the slightest moment before winking out of existence like a series of miniature dying stars.

The Ghost put a hand on Donovan's arm, holding him back, keeping him hidden in the long shadows thrown down by the tenement buildings across the street from the museum. He scanned the steps at the front of the main entrance with the enhanced vision extended to him by the goggles. His breath fogged in the chill air. He felt cold to the core of his being.

The two men had raced uptown in the Ghost's car, hissing along Fifth Avenue in the driving snow, the windshield wipers pelting back and forth, back and forth as they shot toward their destination. The Ghost had swung the car into a side road just opposite the main entrance to the museum, and now they stood, surveying the front of the building, looking for any signs of the trouble that had been reported as occurring within.

The Ghost noted three soft mounds on the steps at the front of the building: the carcasses of more dead birds, mangled, abandoned, and now being slowly covered by the falling snow. He looked at Donovan. "Nothing. No sign of anything untoward. Shall we try round the back?"

Donovan gave a brisk nod. Together, the two men stole away from their hiding place, moving swiftly through the thick curtain of snow. They hugged the walls where they could, prowling in the shadows. The Ghost was nervous, taut. He could see that Donovan was squeezing the butt of his handgun in the pocket of his borrowed coat as they passed along the side of the monolithic building. The place was deserted, the silence punctuated only by the occasional hiss of a car passing along Fifth Avenue behind them.

At the rear of the building, the Ghost once again caught hold of Donovan's sleeve, motioning for him to remain still. In the distance the dark shadows of Central Park stood ominous, the silhouettes of the leafless trees jagged, their branches pointing haphazardly at the sky like so many impish fingers. To the left of the two men a large truck was parked on the path, close to the building, its back doors pinned open, the rear end of the vehicle facing them so that they could see into the cavernous space inside. It was empty, yet to receive its load.

Beyond the truck, further along the path, the Ghost could see four cars, parked in a neat row. None of them had three funnels. He frowned. Perhaps he'd been wrong, after all. Perhaps this was just another heist by just another gang of mobsters, trying it on for size. But it seemed unlikely, too much of a coincidence. It *had* to be connected to the Roman.

A fire escape at the back of the building stood open, dim light leaching out onto the sidewalk. This was the door that Arthur had used to admit him the other night. He was sure he'd be able to find his way around inside from there again. Absently, he hoped that Arthur himself had found an opportunity to slip away.

The Ghost edged along the side of the building, keeping his back to the wall. Donovan followed, remaining close behind him. He guessed there would be a driver in the cab of the truck, perhaps also in the four cars, and decided that it wouldn't do to alert them. Not yet. The ensuing fracas would only draw the attention of those inside, and the Ghost wanted to maintain the element of surprise.

Seconds later the two men stepped up to the open doorway like moving shadows, checked briefly to ensure that the entrance was not guarded, and then slipped inside. Almost immediately, the Ghost had to stifle an exclamation of disgust.

One of the museum's night wardens lay on the floor just inside the doorway, a glossy red hole where his face had once been. The congealed blood glistened in the wan light. The man's lower face had entirely gone from the nose down. All that was left was a gaping wound, punched through the jaw and out the back of the skull. He'd been shot at point-blank range, left where he'd dropped. Brain matter had spattered one of the glass-fronted display cabinets behind him, and puddles of dark arterial blood had formed around the base of a wooden Native American idol. The Ghost glanced at Donovan, who was able only to shake his head in disgust.

The Ghost stepped over the corpse, grimacing, careful that his footsteps didn't ring out too loudly on the marble floor. Donovan had drawn the handgun and was glancing from side to side, trying to cover all of the exits. The Ghost could see the man was still wracked with pain, but he admired the way the policeman was gritting his teeth and forcing himself to carry on. The likelihood was that Donovan would be severely reprimanded for taking matters into his own hands, for allying himself with a known criminal. Perhaps he would even be kicked off the force. But he didn't seem to care. All that mattered to him was bringing Reece and the Roman to justice, and protecting his family. The Ghost could understand values like that, could empathize with that need for justice. Sometimes the ends *did* justify the means. Sometimes you had to fight on the enemy's terms. Sometimes the law just didn't come into it.

Cautiously they crept on, both men listening intently for any sounds that might give away the crooks' location. They passed through a large display of medieval art, an exhibition housing the ornate Gothic wonders of Old Europe. The Ghost found the place sinister, macabre. Faces stared down at him from the browning portraits that lined the walls, seeming to watch his progress as he made his way across the hall. He could hear Donovan's ragged breath behind him. They moved on, entering a long gallery filled with Byzantine splendor: gold idols, glittering jewels and riches, ancient artifacts and relics, each of them created in the name of human gods. The Ghost couldn't vouch for the existence of such gods, but he knew of gods that did exist, gods that didn't demand such worship, or require anything so parochial as golden idols.

Donovan moved forward and the Ghost shot to his side, only then realizing that another security guard lay heaped in the gallery up ahead, his uniform crisp and smart, save for where his chest had been punctured in three places, blood still oozing from the wounds. The shots had been made in rapid succession, ensuring the man's absolute, unequivocal death. His pale face stared up at them, now frozen stiff with terror.

The Ghost realized he was clenching his fists. He could feel the rage building inside him. He would make these men pay for their actions. He would harness that anger, and they would quake as he unleashed it upon them, a spinning whirlwind of vengeance and death.

He followed behind Donovan for the moment. Waiting for his chance.

They reached the great hall. It was a vast, cavernous space, which, during the day, would be filled with the chatter of voices and the press of bodies; the excitement of children brought along by their parents to gaze in awe through a window into the past. Now it was deserted, as silent as the rest of the empty museum.

Donovan paused, leaning closer to the Ghost. His voice was barely audible, but the Ghost could hear the exasperation apparent in his words. "They could be anywhere in this place!"

The Ghost shook his head. He had a notion of where they might be. "No. Come with me. This way."

Taking precautions to ensure they were not being watched from the balcony above, the Ghost led Donovan across the great hall toward the Greek and Roman wing, to the right of the main entrance. That was where they would find the mobsters. He was sure of it.

Mere moments later he was proved right. He saw Donovan start, holding out a warning hand, and took the cue, sliding sideways toward the shadows, keeping himself out of view. He became aware of the sound of voices from somewhere up ahead. Donovan dropped back, covering the entrance to the Greek and Roman exhibition with the hovering aim of his handgun. The Ghost gestured for the policeman to remain where he was. Then, gesturing to show that he was going to take a look, he crept forward, walking on the balls of his feet to ensure his shoes didn't scuff on the marble floor.

The entrance to the exhibition was a large square archway. The Ghost went right, keeping behind the wall, peering around the edge of the opening to take a look at what was happening beyond.

The scale of the operation was astounding. There must have been fifteen, twenty men in there. Moss men, too, at least five of them, possibly more, lumbering about between the exhibits. The mobsters themselves were standing around, laughing and conversing, whilst two of the moss men were slowly maneuvering the large marble wheel—the artifact that Arthur had shown him just a couple of days before—across the floor. They turned it slowly, almost reverently, as they guided it toward the archway where the Ghost was hiding. He heard a footstep to his left, turned to see Donovan approaching. The Ghost shook his head, waved the inspector across to the other side of the entrance. He saw Donovan's eyes open wide as he took in the scene of industry beyond.

So he'd been right. Gardici and the Roman were connected. Maybe *more* than connected. And since the museum—since Arthur—had refused to sell him the artifact he so desired, the Roman had now decided to take it by force. The Ghost found it hard to fathom the scene before him; the amount of planning it must have taken to prepare for such a bold heist. More than that, though, the Ghost was appalled by the sheer gall of the man; the sheer audacity required to have his men waltz in to the Metropolitan Museum of Art with the aim of stealing a two-thousand-year-old artifact, simply to satisfy his whims. He watched the mobsters as they milled about, allowing the moss men to carry out the work whilst they smoked and caroused, fearless of any reprisals. They'd killed all the guards, after all; what more did they have to concern themselves with?

The Ghost sensed movement out of the corner of his eye. Donovan was trying to get his attention. He met the other man's gaze, saw he was pointing toward the prone bodies of two further museum guards. Both of them had been shot, one in the belly, one in the throat. Blood still gurgled from the latter wound, but the man's chest had long since ceased to rise and fall with life.

Donovan raised his gun. "Do that exploding thing," he hissed beneath his breath, just loud enough for the Ghost to hear. The Ghost offered him a stern look in reply. But Donovan was right.

It would certainly give them something to think about...

He surveyed the scene once more. Where the hell would he start? Slowly, cautiously, trying desperately not to make a sound, he reached down beneath his right arm and eased the barrel of the fléchette gun around on its ratcheting gears, wincing as they groaned in quiet protest. It locked into place.

The two mobsters nearest to them were standing beside a glass case, lost in conversation. They seemed in a jocular mood, discussing their latest conquests, the club they had visited, the men they had killed. The Ghost had no qualms about ending their miserable lives. The city would be a better place because of it. But he could not kill in cold blood. He would take the moss men first; eliminate the most dangerous elements. That would give the goons a chance to fight back, too; a chance to be the first to aim their guns at him, to show their hands. That was the way it had to be, the salve he needed for his conscience.

He straightened his arm, leveling the barrel. Donovan was watching him from across the hall. The policeman was holding his body taut, ready to respond to whatever came next. The Ghost breathed deeply. He could sense the adrenaline as it coursed into his veins. His pulse began to race, harder, faster. He was coiled like a spring, ready for the inevitable battle to come.

The Ghost squeezed the trigger, feeling the soft rubber give in the palm of his hand. A spray of tiny glittering fléchettes sighed from the end of his gun, whistling through the air, embedding themselves indiscriminately in the torso of one of the two moss men handling the marble wheel. For a second, nothing happened. The Ghost could see the sweat standing out on Donovan's forehead.

And then chaos erupted.

The moss man detonated in a spray of brass and clay, the top half of it disappearing entirely, leaving just the stumps of its legs, still shambling awkwardly, bereft of any controlling apparatus. The marble wheel lurched dangerously, the remaining moss man struggling to keep it upright. The mobsters raised their voices in confusion, trying to work out from where this terrible, sudden threat had originated. And then Donovan opened fire, answering the question. The two men nearest to them dropped heavily, their bodies crumpling to the floor, one of them falling against the glass cabinet, his face and hands slapping the reinforced panels as he slid to the ground, a deadweight. Others replied with the chatter of their tommy guns. A glass case shattered, bursting in a spray of shimmering fragments.

The Ghost waved his arm in a wide arc, spraying a hail of the tiny metal explosives into the air. Howls of pain followed, and then worse, as four of the men exploded. One lost his head in a splash of crimson mist, another his heart and lungs as his rib cage cracked open, a third his left leg, causing him to collapse to the floor, shuddering in a fit as the shock took hold. The other the Ghost didn't see, save for the shadow of red gore he left on the white wall behind him, and on the white marble statues close to where he had been standing. Donovan and the Ghost rushed forward, fanning out, Donovan left, the Ghost right. He slid behind an ornate marble coffin just in time to hear bullets ricocheting off its surface, sending plumes of dust into the air, chunks of the ancient stone crumbling to the floor. Arthur was going to kill him.

The Ghost glanced around, trying to get a sense of what was

happening. Another of the moss men had moved in to replace the one he had destroyed, helping the first with its large burden. They had resumed the slow, steady march toward the exit with the marble wheel. One of the mobsters, the man who appeared to be in charge, was shouting to the others to protect the artifact at all costs, to prevent it from getting damaged. Perhaps that was something the Ghost could play for? Get himself near enough to the marble relic that they had to stop shooting at him or risk destroying it. But he would have to wait until the moss men were closer to the exit before he could make that move. At the moment there was a field of statues between him and them, and an army of gunmen behind him, waiting for him to show himself.

He could see Donovan, partly obscured behind a glass case containing a display of ancient weaponry. The policeman had given up shooting with his left arm, switching the gun to his preferred right. He was grimacing in agony with every shot, but it was clear he intended to stick with the fight, and his aim was true; he had felled a number of the goons.

As if to prove the point another man dropped, one of Donovan's bullets buried between his eyes. More of them rushed forward to fill the ranks of the dead, however, in a seemingly endless onslaught. Their weapons barked furiously, bullets filling the air as they tried to weed out the two interlopers who had so suddenly introduced such chaos and death into their lives. The goons showed a blatant disregard for the ancient exhibits, hammering them indiscriminately with their ammunition, much as they showed a similar disregard for the deaths of their own compatriots. The Ghost couldn't believe they could be so cold. Perhaps they had learned to save their mourning for a more appropriate time, for the small hours of the night when they were alone with their thoughts? Or perhaps he was crediting them with too much humanity. It mattered little. It made them easier to kill.

Peering around the edge of the coffin, the Ghost could see one of the moss men lumbering through the forest of statues, knocking them aside like bowling pins, fragile marble arms, heads, and other appendages sent skittering away into the corners of the room as the sculptures shattered on the hard floor. The moss man continued on, crushing the tumbledown sculptures beneath his heavy mechanical feet.

The Ghost heard Donovan cry out as the glass case beside him shattered, showering him with fragments. The Ghost needed to get to him. He leapt up, loosing another spray of fléchettes, catching a man in the arm, taking down the other moss man, and inadvertently blowing the head clean off a statue of Nero in the process. Bullets hailed around him in reply and he dove sideways, cartwheeling across the marble floor, his trench coat billowing with the sudden motion. He heard a bullet whistle past his head, inches from his skull; felt another narrowly miss his chest, opening a rent in the fabric of his black suit and scorching the flesh beneath. Pain bloomed, but he fought it down, sliding across the slick marble toward his friend, his nostrils filled with the cloying scent of cordite.

Donovan had shaken off the majority of the glass, and save for a small shard that had buried itself in his thigh and a few scratches across his right cheek, he seemed relatively unharmed. Together, the two men returned fire tit-for-tat with the mobsters. The Ghost was painfully aware that all the while, the two moss men were rolling the marble relic away toward the exit. If he wanted to stop them, he'd have to make a move soon. He glanced back. They were nowhere to be seen. Hell! They'd already made it to the great hall. He'd have to go after them while Donovan held their position, take them down, and then get back to help the policeman with the mopping up. He stood and turned quickly, directly into the swinging fist of another of the moss men. The blow caught him hard across the jaw, snapping his head back and lifting him three feet into the air, sending him sprawling backward, careening into another glass display case that shattered beneath the impact.

The Ghost fell to the floor amongst a shower of shimmering fragments. Bleeding and almost senseless from the blow, he spat blood, shook his head to try to clear the fogginess. The huge golem was looming over him again, raising its fist. He rolled, just in time, as the fist slammed down against the marble floor, narrowly missing his head. Three inches closer and his face would have been a bloody pulp, spread across the floor.

The Ghost kicked out his legs, flicking himself up onto his feet. The other fist came around, lower this time, catching him in the guts, causing him to double over. Blood and vomit spewed involuntarily from his lips. He couldn't breathe, but was aware of the sound of bullets *vipping* all around him as the firefight continued unabated. He toppled sideways. Stars were dancing before his eyes. No. *No!* He couldn't stop now. He wouldn't give in. It wouldn't end here. He gasped for air, steadied himself.

More gunfire. He looked up. Donovan was standing beside him, his arms fully outstretched, firing shot after shot into the moss man's blank green face. The only effect was to momentarily distract the lumbering monster, but it was long enough for the Ghost to raise his arm and squeeze the trigger of his fléchette gun.

The moss man barely seemed to register the tiny, dull thuds of the explosive shots as they buried themselves in its waist. The Ghost didn't have time to get out of the way, but he called out to Donovan: "Get down!"

The golem exploded in close proximity to the Ghost, its midriff blowing open, scattering its mechanical innards all around him, pattering down on him as he covered his face in the crook of his arm. The massive body fell backward, crunching the last remains of the glass cabinet as it collapsed to the floor, a heap of damp clay and mangled skeletal frame.

The Ghost didn't have time to breathe a sigh of relief. The remaining mobsters were circling closer, readying their guns. Donovan was still taking potshots at them, causing them to duck behind the nearby cover. But they both knew they were running out of time.

The Ghost looked up. High above, the plaster ceiling was molded into thick, white ribs of architrave. He took a measure of the remaining mobsters: four of them, one to the left, three in a huddle behind the ruins of a display case. He hefted the barrel of his fléchette gun, pointing it toward the ceiling. Then he squeezed the trigger, closing his eyes, hoping beyond hope that he was within range. He waited for the sound of the tiny blades striking home in the plasterwork, but it never came, lost beneath the sounds of tommy guns chattering and bullets clanging off the walls. He rolled, throwing himself out of the way of the mobsters' deadly projectiles.

Seconds later, just as the goons were preparing to take another shot at him and Donovan, there was a huge explosion from above. The Ghost watched, awestruck, as a massive chunk of ceiling plaster broke loose, surrounded by dark clouds of plaster dust and smoke. His aim had been precise. Particles of the stuff rained down from above, but the boulder-sized lump dropped like a stone, turning over and over in midair, landing squarely atop the cluster of three men with a sickening crunch. All he could see from where he was crouched was a shattered leg, protruding from behind the remains of the broken glass case.

Shocked, the remaining mobster lowered the barrel of his gun, his mouth agape in mute horror, and it was only a moment's work for Donovan to put a bullet in his temple before the man regained his senses and started shooting at them again. The man dropped where he stood, his dead finger nervously depressing the trigger of his gun as he fell, scattering hot lead over the marble floor for a handful of seconds. Then silence. Nothing but death, dust, and silence.

The Ghost peered around. There was no further movement, except the settling plaster dust and the slow swinging of a damaged chandelier. The hall had taken on the aspect of a grim charnel house, filled with exploded body parts, dark smears of stinky blood and spilt viscera, and the passive, blank faces of the funereal statues, mourning for their lost kin.

He got to his feet. "Donovan?" He looked at the policeman, who was on his knees, staring wide-eyed at the scene of devastation. "Can you walk?"

Donovan nodded. "Yes. I can walk. I'm fine." But it was clear that he wasn't.

The Ghost crossed the floor, his feet crunching on the debris, and hooked a hand beneath the policeman's arm, hauling him to his feet. "Come on! We're not finished yet." They didn't have time now for Donovan to revel in his shock.

The Ghost left the exhibition hall at a run, his coattails flapping behind him, Donovan at his heels as he crossed the great hall in pursuit of the two moss men and their heavy burden.

There was no sign of them. He pressed on, retracing his steps from earlier, not caring now whether he brought attention to himself, whether anyone would hear him coming. He ran along the imperious Byzantine corridor, across the medieval hall, but still there was no sign of the lumbering golems. Unconcerned as they were with subtlety, the moss men had clearly made good progress in their escape whilst the Ghost and Donovan had been fighting for their lives in the other hall.

The Ghost reached the fire escape in the American wing and ducked out of the door, sliding on the slick snow, just in time to see the large truck swerve away from the building. One of the rear doors was clanging open as it weaved away down the path toward the road, its wheels leaving a spray of watery slush in its wake. Through the sliver of the open door, the Ghost could see the two moss men propping the marble wheel against the inside of the truck. He raised his arm, let off a hail of shots, but to no avail. The driver was too quick, and the Ghost was too late. The fléchettes skipped harmlessly across the surface of the road, fizzing and popping in the pale snow.

Donovan appeared in the doorway behind him, gasping for breath. "We lost them?"

It was a rhetorical question, but the Ghost nodded and

answered regardless, his voice grim. "Yes. We lost them."

The roar of another engine sounded as one of the four parked cars up ahead suddenly screamed to life, peeling away from the museum and shooting off toward the road in the wake of the truck. Black smoke curled from its exhaust funnels. The Ghost thought about going after it, but then, as if the thought had entered his mind unbidden, he remembered his friend. He looked at Donovan. "Arthur! He's still in there, somewhere."

He charged back into the museum, nearly bowling the policeman over in the process. He leapt over the remains of the dead guard, nearly missing his footing and sliding in a puddle of greasy blood. He tried not to think about it as he ran on through the great hall, up the flight of steps and along corridors until finally, out of breath, he came to the door to Arthur's office. He seized the handle and flung the door open. Inside it was dark. All the lights had been extinguished.

"Arthur?" No response. "Arthur, are you there?" He heard whimpering from over by the desk. He crossed the room and found the curator cowering there, curled up, fetal, beneath the desk, his knees drawn up under his chin. The Ghost dropped into a squat. "Arthur, it's me. Gabriel."

Arthur turned his head to look at him, and for a moment there was no sign of recognition in his terrified eyes. The man was visibly shaking, frightened out of his wits. But something seemed to register in his brain: the sound of the Ghost's voice, or the appearance of the vigilante's disheveled face. He focused, and his eyes regained their usual luster. "Gabriel?" he whispered. "You came."

"Of course I came."

"They… they're here for the marble wheel."

"Yes, Arthur." The Ghost's voice was low and soft, calming. "I'm afraid they got away with it, too. There were too many of them."

Arthur looked pained. "Was it Mr. Gardici?"

The Ghost smiled sadly. "I don't think your Mr. Gardici was quite who he claimed to be, Arthur. I suspect the man you were really dealing with was the person I know as the Roman."

Arthur's shoulders fell. "I wish I'd known, Gabriel. I would have *done* something. I would have tried to stop him." He was crestfallen, accepting the burden without question. As if he could somehow have prevented it all. This was the greater tragedy, the Ghost reflected, not the lost antiquities or the money it would take to repair the damage to the museum, but the impact it would have on Arthur. He would never forgive himself for failing to predict what had happened that night. He would blame himself for the deaths of the museum guards. He would be irrevocably altered by it. The Ghost knew this without question; he had seen it in fellow soldiers during the war, seen it even in himself. That perpetual, haunting question: *What if? What if I had done something different?*

The Ghost reached under the desk and clasped Arthur by the wrist. "I know, Arthur. I know." He pulled the curator out from the small, confined space into which he had forced himself. "Come on, Arthur. We need to get you home."

Arthur looked unsure. "What about the exhibits, the collection? Did they touch anything else?"

The Ghost hardly knew how to break the news to his old friend, especially given his fragile mental condition. "It's a bit of a mess down there, Arthur. Probably best if you leave it for the morning. We'll get it cleaned up. I have a policeman with me."

Arthur nodded. "Very well." He leaned on the Ghost, and then, as if seeing him properly for the first time, he looked the vigilante up and down appraisingly. "You're a mess, Gabriel."

The Ghost couldn't hold back his laughter as, together, the two men set off in search of Donovan, and home.

TWENTY

The next morning, the Ghost woke feeling already tired. He was in his apartment on Fifth Avenue. He'd given Donovan the bed, deferring to the wounded man, and consequently he'd slept only fitfully in an armchair, waking almost hourly to find himself staring out of the window at the sleeping city below.

His thoughts were filled with Celeste. He kept replaying their conversation of the previous day over and over in his mind. He didn't know how he'd left things between them, didn't know how he'd be able to put things right. And in the small hours of the morning, sloshing bourbon into a glass tumbler and staring out at the distant stars, he admitted to himself how much she had hurt him by clinging on to her secrets, by not opening up to him with her concerns. He knew then, too, what he had done to her, and wondered if she was punishing him for that misdemeanor, causing him to feel that same sense of helplessness, of abandonment, a sickness in the very pit of his stomach. It had started at the very moment he'd discovered she would not confide in him, and it had not yet abated. He closed his eyes and breathed out slowly, fighting the nausea. All he had wanted to do was keep her safe.

He stirred again, glancing at the clock on the wall. It was nearly seven. He stood, stretching his weary limbs, and crossed to the bathroom, where he bathed, shaved, and otherwise tried to busy himself with inane activities for as long as possible. His body ached all over from the exertions of the last few days. The combat had put a strain on him, but he knew it was not yet over. He needed to discover exactly what the Roman wanted with the stone wheel, with Celeste. And he needed to find Reece and the three-funneled car. He had very little to go on.

When he emerged from the bathroom an hour later, dressed in an immaculate black morning suit, he found Donovan was up, fixing breakfast. He felt drawn to the steaming pot of coffee, which he knew would imbue him with more energy, banishing the lethargy of his sleepless night. Banishing too, he hoped, the gnawing sense of hollowness in his gut. He sat down, drinking deeply from a mug of the hot oily liquid. Donovan was eating eggs from a plate balanced precariously on his knee. If his appetite was anything to go on, the man was starting to get his strength back. "Did you sleep well, Donovan?"

The policeman shrugged. "No. Not really."

It was an honest reply, and the Ghost wouldn't have expected anything less. "How's your shoulder?"

"Painful. I think I must have opened the wound last night at the museum." He spoke around a mouthful of food.

The Ghost nodded. "I'll help you strap it again in a while. I need to make a call first."

Donovan nodded, taking his cue. He quickly finished his breakfast, and then disappeared with his coffee into the bedroom, leaving the Ghost alone with the holotube transmitter.

The Ghost flicked the switch and dialed up a number in Long Island. He leaned back in his chair, grateful for the warmth of the coffee. The holotube unit hummed as it came to life, but no picture resolved in the mirrored cavity, and the only sound was the frustrating pips of a tone that told him the other unit was engaged. Someone was already on the line. He knocked the switch to the "off" position, quitting the transmission, and rocked back in his chair, staring forlornly at the silent unit. Five minutes passed. He tried again, and this time the device chimed with its familiar tone, ringing out on the other end.

Someone flicked the receiver in Long Island. There was a crackle of static, and then a face emerged from the blue haze. It was a man in his fifties, balding, with a neat, clipped moustache. Henry. The Ghost smiled. "Morning, Henry."

"Morning, sir." The valet was hesitant.

"Is Miss Parker available to take a call?"

"Ah, that's just it, sir. I've only just got off the line with the police. Miss Parker isn't here."

The Ghost glowered at the flickering image. "What do you mean she isn't there? And what have the police got to do with it?" He felt a dawning sense of terror. Surely they hadn't found her, not there?

"Miss Parker borrowed one of your cars yesterday, sir, said she was going for a short spin to get some air. I expected her back within the hour. Only she didn't return."

"What?" The Ghost rubbed a hand across his smooth chin. Had she left him? Was that it? Had she run out at the first opportunity, disgusted with him, taking her secrets and her condescension with her?

"I fear there's more, sir. The Manhattan Police Department—they found the car abandoned in Times Square in the early hours of this morning. They assumed you had been driving, of course, and called to arrange for the vehicle's collection. There's also an accompanying fine to be paid – the car was parked illegally. Evidently, there was no sign of Miss Parker."

The Ghost felt panic welling up inside him. No sign of her? "And she didn't give you any indication of what she was planning, Henry? Where she might have been headed?"

Henry looked rueful. "No, sir. No indication whatsoever. Miss Parker simply requested that I prepare a vehicle for her and explained that she was going for a little spin. I thought nothing of it, sir, until she failed to return."

"Very well, Henry." There was no point admonishing the man. He was clearly concerned, and he couldn't have been expected to see through her ruse. "Times Square, you say?"

"Yes, sir. That's what the police indicated when they called. I told them I would endeavor to get in touch with you this morning." The valet stared out at him from the cavity in the holotube unit, his image unwavering. "What can I do to aid you, sir? I feel responsible. I feel—"

"Henry." The Ghost cut him off. "Henry, this is not your fault, and not your responsibility. I will find Miss Parker, and I will bring her home. You are not to trouble yourself over the details."

Henry sighed. "Very good, sir." But the Ghost could tell that the man considered it far from very good. Beneath his calm exterior he was evidently riddled with anxiety.

"Now, if you could make the necessary preparations for Miss Parker's return, I'll be sure to let you know when I have any news." The Ghost kept his voice level, although he felt less than calm himself. It was best to keep the valet busy.

"Thank you, sir." Henry cut the connection. The Ghost watched the pale blue light of the hologram fade to nothing, like descending twilight, and then flicked the switch at his own end, powering off the unit. The humming ceased. He stared at the mute box, turning things over in his mind. He wouldn't allow himself to consider the worst; couldn't give credence to it, couldn't even acknowledge it as a possibility. He convinced himself she had abandoned the vehicle to teach him a lesson, that she was somewhere now, sleeping off a heavy night in a quiet hotel room, and that later, when she'd come to her senses, she would find him and shower him with playful kisses. But at the back of his mind he knew that there was a more likely explanation, and it gnawed at him, chewing him up inside.

What could she have been up to? She'd said she wanted to come to the city, and she'd found a way to do just that. Was it really boredom, that city-sickness that afflicts so many, dragging them toward the metropolis like so many moths to a flame? Or was it to do with her secret, that thing so terrible that she was reluctant even to discuss it with him? He knew then that he would have it out of her, one way or another.

He thought of her beautiful, pale face, framed by tumbling red waves. Imagined her bringing a cigarette luxuriously to her lips, drawing smoke into her lungs, letting it play out of her half-open mouth in long riffles. Saw her on the stage at Joe's, her voice the only thing that kept the world turning, the axis around which all of life revolved.

He would find her, and he would fix things. He would stop Gideon Reece. The Ghost had thought the man's absence from the museum the previous night was significant. What if he'd been busy in other ways? He couldn't bear the implication.

The Ghost got to his feet, reached for the suit jacket he had draped over the back of his chair. He didn't have time to change. He called to Donovan as he strolled purposefully toward the door. "Donovan? I'll be back in an hour. Don't go anywhere."

He didn't wait for a response.

The snow of the previous evening had begun to melt, reducing into a miserable gray slush that sloshed around the Ghost's ankles as he walked. Cars hissed by, spraying gobbets of the stuff into the air, their wheels splashing in the newly formed rivers that ran along the gutters in glistening rivulets.

He set a brisk pace for the walk to Times Square, but the Ghost was unable to stop his mind from wandering, imagining a hundred and one different scenarios of what he might find when he reached his destination. Had she left him a note in the car? Could she have been back to collect it in the intervening hours since the police had found it? Where had she stayed last night?

As he made his way along 48th Street he passed a stall selling fresh rolls and his stomach growled hungrily at the comforting smell. He kept walking. There would be time to eat later.

Entering Times Square was like walking into a brightly lit circus of towering billboards and gaudy theater fronts, alive with splashes of the brightest colors and lit with thousands of electric bulbs of the most brilliant yellow. Cars flew by; people negotiated the press of the crowds, even at this hour; theater owners plied their wares to the passersby. Here was Broadway in all its glittering glory. The Ghost couldn't stand it. To him it was redolent of fakery, of pretense and showmanship. It was the opposite of Celeste's soulful music; it was loud, obnoxious, and not at all for him.

He found the vehicle easily, pulled up to the curb at a jaunty angle, apparently abandoned in a no parking zone. It was black, like each of his other cars, with long sweeping curves, two tall exhaust funnels, and a cream leather interior. The coal hopper on the back was pristine, almost as new. The vehicle had hardly been driven since he'd bought it.

The Ghost looked around. There were a few people milling about nearby, but none of them were paying him or the car any attention. Good. He fished in his pocket for his ring of spare keys, and then reached over and opened the driver's side door. He bowed his head and peered inside, searching for any clue Celeste might have left him as to her whereabouts. He felt his heart lurch. There was a message there, certainly; a message of the type he had feared. Two perfect, shining Roman coins rested on the driver's seat, catching the streaming sunlight that was pouring in through the windshield.

The Ghost stepped back from the car. He could feel the panic, which until now had remained buried in his gut like a lead weight, beginning to take hold, flooding into his chest; a cold compress that made it difficult to breathe. The icy wind whipped his sandy hair into his face, stinging his eyes, as he stood on the sidewalk trying desperately not to visualize what Reece and his goons might have done to the woman he loved. He could only hope that it was not too late. He would rather die than see her defiled in a similar way to Landsworth or Williamson.

The Ghost had to remind himself that this was not personal for Reece or the Roman; they did not know of his affair with Celeste, so her abduction could in no way be construed as an attempt to strike a blow at the vigilante who had already foiled so many of their plans. He couldn't believe they had worked it out. He'd been too careful, covered all of his tracks. No, there was something else at play here, something about the woman that the Ghost did not know. Something to do with whatever it was she was so afraid of. He had no idea what to do next, not even how to respond, but he knew he had to find a way to get to her.

He ran his hands over his face, then reached inside his pocket and withdrew a cigarette. He pulled the tab, watched it flare, sucked the nicotine deep down into his lungs. He felt it bite. How the hell was he going to get her back? He shuddered to think of the head start that Reece already had on him. If she'd been taken during the night, then it was what—ten, twelve hours?

And then it hit him, like a sharp slap in the face: Jimmy the Greek. Jimmy might know where they'd taken her. It was an outside chance, but it was all he had.

He flung his half-smoked cigarette toward the gutter, where it fizzed out in the melting snow. He didn't have his weapons with him, hadn't even brought his service revolver. But there was no time to lose.

The Ghost opened the car door again. He slid into the driver's seat, fired up the engine. It choked, and then sputtered, failing to take. It was cold and unwilling to cooperate.

He leapt out again, ran around to the trunk, and extracted a shovel. He proceeded to scoop shovelfuls of dusty black coal from the hopper, throwing it into the furnace, fanning the fire with a small pair of bellows. Once the engine was running again the hopper would feed the hungry flames as needed, but abandoned, the fire had been left to die down to a faint yellow wisp.

A few minutes later, sweat dripping from his brow, the Ghost slid back into the driver's seat. The front of his suit was filthy and his hands were black claws, but now the engine was stoked and it fired with a familiar growl. He grabbed the wheel and swung the car away from the curb, forcing his way into the flow of traffic.

He hurtled along the roads, the tires sliding on the slushy ice as he careened dangerously around each corner, but he was determined to make up for lost time. He counted the minutes as he rushed toward Jimmy the Greek's run-down apartment block in Greenwich Village.

The Ghost slung the car toward the sidewalk at speed, mounting the curb and sliding six or seven feet along the street before he managed to bring the vehicle under some semblance of control, and then, finally, to a stop. Black smoke belched from the abused engine funnels. The Ghost climbed out. He left the door open and the engine running, not caring as he bounded to the main entrance of the tenement building, crossed the lobby, and then flung himself up the stairs.

He'd stand for no evasiveness from Jimmy the Greek. If the snitch showed any sign that he knew where the Roman's men might be holding Celeste—even the slightest hint of information—then the Ghost would know it, through whatever means were necessary. If that meant a beating, then so be it. He was resigned to that already. Nothing could get in the way.

He was panting for breath when he came to the old brown door of Jimmy's apartment. He took a moment to compose himself. Then, hearing no sounds from within, he rapped loudly, five times, with his bare knuckles, and waited. The sound echoed out around the empty building. Nothing. There was no answer, and no sounds from within. No familiar cursing, no scrabbling around inside to hide his embarrassing photographs. No sounds at all. He knocked again. "Jimmy? Answer the door, Jimmy!"

Still nothing. He tested the handle. The door was locked. Was he out? The Ghost glanced at his watch. More likely the snitch was asleep in bed; he'd have no reason to be out at this early hour of the day, and the Ghost knew from experience that Jimmy was nocturnal, a creature of habit. He tried knocking once more, hoping to rouse the lazy bastard from his bunk. "Jimmy? I'm coming in there, Jimmy, whether you answer the door or not!" There was still no response, no sounds from within the apartment. No sounds from anywhere else in the whole tenement building.

The Ghost looked from side to side. The stinking heap of garbage across the hall lay undisturbed. He backed up, raised his foot, and kicked out hard at the lock. The impact jarred his ankle, and he remembered he was only wearing a pair of brogues and not his usual reinforced boots. Nevertheless, he tried again. The door rattled in its frame, but the lock held. He backed up a little further, gritted his teeth, and charged forward, presenting his shoulder to the door. This time the frame burst with a loud, splintering crack, and the Ghost stumbled into the room, carried forward by his momentum. The door bounced back against the wall with a loud bang. He looked up, and then paused in horrified awe at the grotesque sight before him.

Jimmy the Greek was dead. His body had been strung up, his arms outstretched, pulled taut and bound with thin, silken ropes, which had been suspended on hooks from the ceiling, each one in the far corner of the room. The result was that Jimmy had been posed like a crucified Christ, his head hanging to his chest, his feet bound and pointing toward the floor. He'd been suspended about three feet off the ground, facing the door. His eyes were open, fixed in a terrified stare that caused the Ghost to shudder from across the room. The poor bastard had been aware of what was happening to him.

The Ghost stepped closer. He couldn't tear his eyes away from the appalling sight. Jimmy had been stripped to the waist and the word "SNITCH" had been crudely carved into his chest with a sharp blade. Blood had run from the wounds, pooling on the floor beneath his feet. The blood loss had caused his skin to take on a pale, waxy complexion. His hair was lank and sweaty and hung loosely around his neck.

But most disturbing of all, Jimmy's lips had been crudely stitched shut with coarse black twine. Clearly, someone hadn't liked what Jimmy had had to say.

The Ghost shook his head in abject dismay. It smelled like the man had shit himself, too. Not surprising, really. The Ghost looked around, trying to get a sense of what had happened there, in that room, of who had done this to Jimmy. He had his suspicions, of course, and they proved well founded; on the kitchen counter he found a pile of Jimmy's photographs heaped upon the envelope that had once contained them, and on top of those, two perfect Roman coins.

He looked back at Jimmy, at those terrible bruised lips, wired painfully shut. He wouldn't be spilling any more secrets, that was for sure. And if he had known what had become of Celeste, well—someone had gone to a great deal of trouble to keep him from sharing that secret.

The Ghost put his hands on either side of the grimy sink and leaned over, spewing forth a stream of gaudy vomit, his body wracking as he coughed up the remains of yesterday's meal. He felt giddy and light-headed. He stood there for a moment, forcing himself to breathe. Then, after it was over, he ran the tap, washing the coal dust off his hands and wiping his mouth on his sleeve. He noticed he was shaking.

There was little he could do for Jimmy now. The man had made his own bed, and now, alas, he was lying in it. But there was one thing, one small gesture. The Ghost took the bundle of glossy photographs and threw them into the sink. Jimmy had wanted to keep his private life a secret. He could oblige that much, at least. When the police came later the whole place would be turned over. There was no need for them to find these. He wouldn't have people laughing at the dead snitch. Not for this. Not for a few dirty photographs of clockwork women.

He reached into his pocket for a cigarette. He lit it and dropped it into the sink. The flames soon caught the crisp paper, and a few moments later, all that was left was a pile of smoldering ash.

With a heavy heart, the Ghost quit the apartment, pulling

the door shut behind him. Donovan could send his men down later, clean up the whole sorry mess. For now, though, he needed to focus, needed to concentrate on finding a way to help Celeste. She was in grave danger, and he intended to wreak vengeance on the men who had put her there.

TWENTY ONE

Donovan was growing impatient. The Ghost had been gone for hours—three, at least—and while the other man had asked him to wait for his return, Donovan thought that there were better things he could be doing with his time than lounging around, staring out of the window at the hazy Manhattan morning. He'd already washed and bathed, eaten a small breakfast, and checked over his wounds.

The fragment of glass embedded in his thigh had been a trifling matter, and he'd extracted it the previous evening upon their return to the Ghost's apartment. Now the leg was sore, but the pain was nothing in comparison to his shoulder, which still throbbed with a dull ache, pulling painfully when he moved it. He supposed it was remarkable really that they had managed to get out of the museum alive, both of them relatively unscathed.

But what had they learned? That was the question plaguing the inspector. Perhaps nothing that would help them in their quest to bring down the Roman. Yes, of course, it was damning evidence—the Roman's men had stormed the Met, a national institution, wreaked havoc, and destroyed hundreds, if not thousands, of priceless relics in their efforts to steal one of them. But to what end, what purpose? What did the Roman want with an ancient marble wheel? The Ghost didn't seem to know, and nor did the curator, who Donovan had questioned quietly and firmly in the back of the Ghost's car as they drove him home.

Donovan cursed himself. If only he'd been fit, perhaps they wouldn't have gotten away. Perhaps now they would have a lead. As it was, he was left stewing in the vigilante's apartment, wondering what was in store for them next. Donovan didn't like that thought much. He could hardly believe how things had changed in the course of the last few days; how his life had been so easily disrupted, threatened, knocked out of sync. He only hoped that Mullins had managed to get the message to Flora, telling her to take an extended break, to go somewhere with Maud, to visit another state. He'd promised to tell her more when it was over. He hoped she would trust him. She needed to trust him, at least until he could bring this whole matter to an end, once and for all. After that... after that they could figure it all out together.

Donovan fingered the butt of the handgun in his jacket pocket. There was one thing he could be doing: he could check on Mullins. After all, it was likely Mullins would have been roped in that morning to clean up the mess at the museum, and Donovan felt he owed the man an explanation. The Commissioner would have to wait. But Mullins deserved to know what was going on.

He fixed his resolve. That was what he would do. He would leave a message for the Ghost at the apartment, then head to the precinct and search out the sergeant. He was unsure why the other man had left in such a hurry that morning—something relating to the call he had made—but he guessed the Ghost would return later with news.

Heaving himself up out of the chair, he scratched a note on a piece of old card and propped it on the table beside the half-drunk bottle of bourbon before taking his leave.

He knew the Ghost would find it there.

The precinct building was a hive of industry as Donovan entered through the revolving doors. He wondered if the Commissioner had seconded more hands from the other nearby precincts to cope with the mess his inspector had been leaving in his wake. Men in blue uniforms milled about with apparent purpose; people he didn't recognize, unfamiliar and, therefore, somehow suspicious. But Donovan was oddly comforted by the sight of Richards, the precinct administrator, who stood behind an oak desk in the lobby, coolly regarding the inspector over the top of the shifting rabble.

Donovan approached the desk, realizing for the first time since leaving the apartment that he was still wearing the suit from the day before, now torn and bloody, and slept in. God, he was losing his edge.

Richards seemed to recognize his discomfort and gave him an appraising look, as if weighing up how to approach the impending conversation. "Good morning, sir," he said hesitantly. "Is… everything alright?"

Donovan sighed. "Yes, Richards, everything is quite alright."

"Very good, sir." The man sounded unsure.

"Is Mullins here?"

"Yes, sir. Upstairs."

Donovan grinned. "Thank you, Richards." He was relieved that the man hadn't deemed it appropriate to ask any penetrating questions. He wasn't yet sure how he would go about answering them.

He left Richards at the desk and crossed the hall, avoiding a gaggle of busy officers who appeared to be bustling around with no apparent purpose other than to create further bustle. He climbed the steps to the second floor, shaking his head. At the top, he pushed his way through the double doors with his good shoulder. They creaked as they swung open, but none of the men inside the large, open-plan office looked up to see who had entered. To a man they were hunched over their desks, wrinkles of concentration etched on their brows. Donovan scanned the faces: Jansen, Green, Hatton, Mullins. He frowned. So who had been sent to the museum?

He crossed to where the sergeant was standing over another man, a brooding expression on his face. Mullins looked up as he heard Donovan's footsteps on the linoleum. "Inspector." He seemed startled. "How are you? Have you heard about the museum?"

Donovan gave a brief nod of acknowledgement. "Yes. I was there. It seems I'm having difficulty keeping myself out of trouble at the moment."

Mullins grinned. "I think it's a sure sign you're getting closer, sir." He stepped away from the desk, and together the two men moved to one side so as not to be overheard. "What happened in there?"

Donovan shrugged. "I caught a tip-off. Went there, found them in the act. Bastards got away, though."

"Some of them did." Mullins grinned. It was clear the sergeant was impressed by his late-night exploits. "And the Ghost was there, too...? We found traces of his strange ammunition."

"Yes, he was there."

"Was he working with the Roman's men?"

Donovan had to stop himself from glowering at the sergeant. "Have you been down there, Mullins? Seen how many dead mobsters are strewn about the place? The man saved my life more than once. No, he was not working for the Roman. You don't have to trouble yourself about the Ghost."

Mullins looked at the floor, shamefaced. "The Commissioner sent Jefferson down there, sir. I haven't seen it. But I've heard reports, snatches of information from the other men. Sounds like it was carnage."

"It was," Donovan said, morosely. "It was most definitely that." He looked around. The other officers were studiously getting on with their work. "Did you manage to get my message to Flora?"

Mullins nodded. "Yes, sir. All taken care of."

Donovan breathed a sigh of relief. "Have you got any coffee, Mullins?"

"Yes, sir. But first, I have something for you." The sergeant was smiling.

Donovan raised an eyebrow. "Really?"

"Yes. I found it."

"Found what?"

"The link. I found the link between the Roman's victims." Mullins beamed up at him, his round face splitting into a wide grin.

Donovan's eyes widened. "Well, man! Spit it out!" He reached for a cigarette. It was the last one in his packet. Mullins frowned at the smell of the sweet smoke as the inspector lit it and sucked impatiently on the filter.

"A power station, sir."

"A what?"

Mullins coughed as Donovan blew smoke in his face. "A power station, down in the Battery. That's what links the victims. Well, some of them, anyway. It was Williamson who gave it away. I found paperwork in his office when I started looking through his affairs. I drew a link immediately to Landsworth. Both of them were heavily invested in the construction of a new power station. I checked back, found some of the others were involved in it, too. Their bank records were all the same. Considerable sums of money. Thousands."

Donovan could feel the excitement welling up inside him. A lead, at last! "And it's in the Battery, you say?"

"Yes, sir. It's only just become operational." Mullins was clearly pleased with himself.

"What's the holding company?"

"Well, that's just it, sir. I can't find one. At least, not a corporation. All of the payments and receipts were made out to the same person, transferred into a personal account in the name of Mr. Gideon Reece."

Donovan almost cried out in excitement. He rubbed a hand over the back of his neck, took a long, thoughtful pull on his cigarette. What did the Roman want with a power station? And why had the investors all been murdered now that the construction was complete? He had a feeling that the trail was suddenly growing warm once more. He needed to get hold of the Ghost. "Good work, Mullins. I think I need to pay this power station a visit." He looked up at the sergeant, his eyes shining. "Now, if you could just fetch that coffee I'll fill you in on the rest of it…"

The Ghost's car purred up outside the newly constructed power station in the Battery, stirring the gravel as it slid to a stop. The station itself was a large gray industrial building: squat and square, with three tall iron turrets erupting from its otherwise flat roof. In the midday light they were silhouetted, and looked to Donovan like three stubby fingers, pointing at the heavens.

Around the building itself, construction materials lay abandoned haphazardly: a pile of stone blocks; wooden batons of varying lengths, now damp from exposure to the sea air; coil after coil of thin wire. Further out, past the building, Donovan could see the harbor. Turquoise water lapped gently at the wooden jetties, parted by the prows of numerous ferries. In the distance, shrouded in hazy fog, was Liberty Island. The imposing statue dominated the landscape for miles around, standing guard over the city, watching.

Liberty. That was what he was fighting for. Liberty for himself, and for the people of New York. Liberty for Flora. Liberty for the Ghost.

Donovan had finally managed to get through to the Ghost on the holotube, after trying him five or six times at the apartment. The vigilante had picked him up around the back of the precinct, this time in full regalia, and had explained to him the situation with the jazz singer, Celeste Parker, and the snitch, Jimmy the Greek, as they drove at speed toward the Battery. Donovan understood the man's pain, understood his need to keep busy, to get to the woman before it was too late. He hoped it wasn't already too late. But he feared the worst. He wondered what it would do to the vigilante. He could hardly be described as sane at the best of times. Would this be enough to push him completely over the edge?

Donovan climbed out of the car. It was cold, and a stiff wind was gusting in off the harbor. He turned up the collar of his borrowed coat. As the Ghost climbed out of the driver's side, Donovan paced around the edge of the station, looking for any signs of life. To his surprise, he saw another vehicle was parked beneath a tree, carefully positioned so as to be out of sight from the main approach to the building. It was sleek and black, its rear end facing toward him as he moved closer. He could see that the back of the car had been modified: the coal hopper shortened and a third exhaust funnel extended out of the engine housing. There was no mistaking it. Gideon Reece was here.

Frantically, Donovan beckoned the Ghost over. The vigilante trudged across the gravel courtyard toward him, and when he saw what had caught Donovan's attention, a wide grin spread across his face. He flicked his arm, and the barrel of his strange gun ratcheted up into position along his forearm. Donovan mirrored the grin and slipped his handgun out of his pocket, cracking it open to ensure that it was fully loaded. Now was their chance. This was it.

He watched as the Ghost pulled a short blade from inside his left boot and approached the car. He walked around it once, glancing in through the windows, checking to ensure it wasn't alarmed or booby-trapped. Then, satisfied, he dropped to his knees and gashed the tires one by one, moving around the vehicle quickly. When he was done, he returned to Donovan's side. He lowered his voice to a whisper, barely audible above the howling wind. "That should stop the bastard slipping away again."

Both men clearly understood the need for subtlety. They didn't want to risk alerting Reece to their presence. Using hand gestures to signal their intentions, they parted. The Ghost went left, Donovan right, fanning out as they approached the main entrance to the power station, one on either side of the grand doorway.

As he stood with his back to the wall, his shoulder throbbing, watching for the Ghost to make the next move, Donovan wondered what he would do when he found himself facing the crook. Could he pull the trigger in cold blood? Surely that was the right thing to do, the quickest, easiest way to end all of this. The man deserved it, needed to pay for the things he had done. But Donovan was a police officer, and he bristled at the thought of murder. He believed in the judicial system. That was what separated him from men like the Ghost, and while he recognized the need for such men, he also recognized the need for order, a structure to society. There was a fundamental line between what was right and what was wrong, and Donovan had yet to cross it. Besides, they needed Reece alive. He was their ticket to the Roman.

The entrance to the power station was a large stone doorway that housed two white wooden doors. There was an inscription on the lintel above the doors, words chiseled out in neat Latin script, and for the life of him Donovan could not decipher what it said. He didn't suppose it mattered. It was probably some obscure Roman reference, like the coins left in the vicinity of the murder victims.

Donovan swallowed. He watched as the Ghost reached over and turned the handle, so slowly it was almost painful, swinging one of the double doors open. It folded inward, the new hinges squealing loudly. A tense moment passed, and then, hefting his weapon, Donovan stepped cautiously inside.

The interior of the power station had to be one of the most remarkable sights the inspector had ever seen. All around him, confronting him almost immediately as he stepped through the doors, were vast banks of Tesla coils: huge gray wire cages, spitting out millions of volts of electricity, each of them crackling with ribs of lightning, blue and white plasma that spat and snapped at the air in all conceivable directions. Donovan could feel the static charge tugging at his hair, permeating the atmosphere. There was a smell of fresh ozone, like the heady scent left behind by a storm. The entire setup was strangely, mystically beautiful.

The Ghost closed the door behind them, and then took a moment to drink in the view. There was no doubting it was an impressive sight, and Donovan could see how easy it must have been for the Roman, and for Reece, to enamor potential investors with its magic. The sight of even one of these strange machines would be enough to bring people flocking, handing over their cash in exchange for the dreams of the future it granted. This was real power, the ability to wield such amazing energy. He wondered once again what purpose it served for the Roman.

He tore his eyes away from the flickering banks of machines and focused on their immediate problems. Reece was nowhere to be seen. They were standing in a small open space that comprised a lobby. It was about the size of the Ghost's living room. The floor was a grid-work of iron struts, which continued on to form a short staircase leading up to a network of gangplanks and walkways that weaved like a spider's web amongst the crackling coils. There was a small desk, too, but it was not manned, covered in large heaps of paper: diagrammatic drawings and blueprints. The Ghost approached the desk, rifling through this ephemera. He looked up at Donovan and shrugged. "There's nothing untoward about this. Just building plans, architects' drawings, bills for materials."

Donovan nodded. That was how the mob worked. They kept everything above board, on paper at least. Their business dealings were impeccable. But behind those fronts, those regular-seeming establishments and corporations, they hid their true colors.

Donovan crossed to the short stairwell. There was only one other path to take from here, and that was into the forest of coils. Somewhere, he figured, there would be a control room, and that was where they would find Gideon Reece. His feet clanged on the iron steps, and he tried to lighten his step, to move with more grace and less noise. He felt jumpy, nervous, even, as he anticipated what was to come. The Ghost followed behind him in silence.

The proximity of the Tesla coils made Donovan's skin crawl. So much power. He didn't really understand how they worked;

had never been able to fathom the inner workings of machines. To him it was like magic—flick a switch and the light bulb blinked on. That was all he knew. That was all he *needed* to know.

Breathing hard, Donovan prowled along the gangway, constantly aware of what was going on around him, looking out for any sign of his nemesis. The walkways weaved and twisted like arteries connecting the flickering electrical organs of the power station; an all-powerful giant rendered from iron and given life. The two men navigated them like a maze, taking note of each junction so that they could retrace their steps when they happened upon a dead end. He thought of Reece like a deadly spider, lying in wait at the center of his web.

As it transpired, however, Reece was *not* waiting for them at the center of the web. When they finally found the control station, there was no one there. The room was bare, open to the gangway and consisting of only two stud walls and a glass partition, propped up against the iron framework that supported the walkway and the nearest bank of coils. Five large panels of winking diodes, white dials, and steel switches lined the furthest wall, whilst a large map of Manhattan was pinned on the other. There was a series of small colored pins dotted over the surface of the map, denoting—Donovan guessed—the locations of substations and relay towers, emanating out from the power station across the Battery in a long, curving line. The thin glass partition offered them a view of another nearby bank of coils, each of the incredible machines still spitting electricity into the air.

The Ghost crossed to the control panels, studied the readouts for a few moments, and then turned his attention to the map.

Donovan kept watch, his palm sweaty against the butt of his revolver. He didn't understand any of this, and wanted to make sure Reece wasn't about to sneak up behind them.

Four, five minutes passed. Finally, the Ghost called him over. "Donovan. Look here." His voice was urgent. Donovan abandoned his vigil on the gangway and approached the map, following the line traced by the Ghost's finger. "Relay stations."

Donovan nodded. "Yes, I gathered as much."

"But look." The Ghost followed the line of pins. "All of the power is being siphoned off to one location. Here." He tapped at the map. "The readouts tell the same story. Everything. All of the power being generated here in the plant. The whole station has been designed to feed electricity to this one point on the map."

Donovan nodded. "That explains it. I bet the investors didn't bank on this. They thought they were buying into a new power station that would feed all of Lower Manhattan. They were never going to make any money out of this. If Landsworth and Williamson and the others were getting nervous about their investments, it explains why Reece had to finish them off. The Roman wouldn't have wanted the authorities sniffing around." He couldn't believe the sheer gall of the man.

A shoe scuffed on the metal gangway behind them. "My, my. I *am* impressed." The sinister, silky voice spoke from somewhere over Donovan's shoulder. He whirled round to see Gideon Reece standing on the walkway, five or six feet away, clutching his small silver pistol. Its nose was hovering between Donovan and the Ghost. "Drop your weapon, Inspector."

Donovan hesitated, thinking about rushing the crook, but

then a quick wave of Reece's gun made him reconsider. He'd never make it, not without accepting another bullet. He didn't fancy those odds. He dropped into a crouch, keeping his eyes on Reece at all times, and placed his weapon on the iron platform before him.

"And you, too." Reece waved his gun at the Ghost. "Show me your hands."

Reluctantly, the Ghost lifted his arms above his head, releasing the trigger mechanism of his fléchette gun, a small rubber bulb that drooped from his sleeve on a snake of black piping. Donovan could see he was gritting his teeth. "Where is she, Reece?" the Ghost barked.

Reece looked momentarily confused, furrowing his brow. Then his face cracked into a wide grin. "The jazz singer?" His lips quivered as he suppressed a laugh. "Oh, now this really is beginning to get interesting—"

"What have you done with her?"

Reece shook his head, adopting a patronizing tone. It was as if he was goading the Ghost, challenging him to make a move. "Is that it? Is that why you followed me here? For a *woman*?"

Donovan thought the Ghost was about to start forward. He was pent up, his neck muscles twitching; a bull readying itself to charge. If he did, Reece would undoubtedly put a bullet through him. He hoped the vigilante could restrain himself long enough for them to get a proper chance to take down the crook.

"What does the Roman want with all this power?" Donovan gave Reece a hard stare, trying to distract him from baiting the Ghost. All the while he was keeping his eye on the hand that held the silver pistol.

Reece shrugged. "He has his reasons. He doesn't pay people to ask questions." The crook smiled again, but it was an empty gesture; he clearly didn't know the truth. He tapped his foot. "I must say, gentlemen, that I'm impressed with your persistence. Particularly you, Inspector. I thought you might have given up long ago. You should have taken the money."

Donovan almost laughed, ignoring the gibe. "I suppose you plan to take us to the Roman?"

Reece sneered. "You presume too much, Inspector. Why wouldn't I just kill you here and be done with it?"

Donovan smiled inwardly. If that had been the man's intention, he'd have done it by now. He was boasting, proud of himself for catching the two men who had persistently been causing him problems. Donovan peered over Reece's shoulder. The crook was alone, and there were two of them. He bided his time.

The Ghost was still seething, obviously waiting for an opportunity to pounce. That was good. If Reece thought the Ghost was the dangerous one, the one who would make a rash move, then that left things wide open for Donovan.

"If you've harmed her, Reece..." The Ghost's voice was solemn, full of menace.

Reece was nonchalant. He turned his body slightly toward the vigilante as he provoked him with more taunts. "You're too late to save her now, any—"

Donovan dove. He sailed through the air toward the crook, his arms outstretched, colliding with the thin man and sending them both tumbling along the gangway. Reece cried out in surprise, as if indignant that the policeman had even dared to attack him. But he was caught off guard. He squeezed the trigger of his gun as they went down. There was a sharp *crack*, and the bullet shot away harmlessly into the power station, clanging off a distant coil.

Donovan grabbed for Reece's wrist, slamming his gun hand back against the iron struts over and over again, whilst at the same time trying to pin the crook's shoulders down with his weight and his damaged shoulder. Reece was strong, far stronger than his figure suggested. He maintained his grip on the silver pistol and fought back, half getting himself into a sitting position. Donovan raised his right fist and struck the man hard across the jaw, but the blow lacked real power, tempered by the pain in his shoulder, the weakness caused by the bullet wound. It was enough, however, to distract Reece for a second, just long enough for Donovan to knock the weapon out of his hand. The silver pistol went sliding away across the gangway behind them, skittering to a stop in the crackling shadow of a Tesla coil.

The loss of his gun seemed to imbue Reece with new vitality, however, and he heaved Donovan off of him, throwing the inspector roughly to one side, rolling in the opposite direction and then coming up on one knee, his fists ready. He whipped out, striking Donovan hard with two jabs to the face. He felt his head snap back and his lip split, warm blood gushing down his chin. He had to think quickly.

Over Reece's shoulder, back in the control room, Donovan saw with dismay that the Ghost was facing a difficult situation of his own. A moss man had come lumbering out of the darkness, catching the vigilante by surprise, striking him hard across the face with its powerful fist. The Ghost was currently being thrown around like a rag doll, slamming against walls and the control desks or trying to pick himself up off the floor.

Reece was laughing as he rounded on Donovan with another blow. Donovan tried to get his arm up, and succeeded in partially deflecting the attack, although it still glanced painfully off his cheek. His blood was up now. He couldn't give up, not after all they had been through.

He returned the assault. A quick succession of jabs and hooks, learned in the schoolyard. He caught Reece in the face, felt the satisfying crunch of the man's nose under the impact. He drove another blow into the crook's gut, causing him to double over, spluttering with pain. That was more like it. He readied himself to follow through with another battering, but staggered back suddenly at the sound of an immense explosion in the confined space of the control room. Clearly the Ghost had managed to loose off some shots from his fléchette gun, shredding the moss golem. The boom echoed around the power station, causing the gangways to vibrate with shock. The Ghost had fared badly, however; whether from the moss man's final blows or the impact of the explosion, Donovan did not know, but he lay unconscious, drooped across one of the control panels, blood trickling from a wound in his head.

It was down to him now. Down to Donovan. One man against another. He willed his shoulder to hold out, flexing the muscles, trying to ease the pain. Reece had seen the sorry state of the Ghost too, had glanced back over his shoulder at the sound of the explosion. One on one, he likely thought the odds were in his favor, with Donovan wounded by the bullet he had put there himself only a few days before.

The two men faced each other. Reece now had his back to the control room. On either side, Tesla coils hummed and chattered in bizarre concert with one another, lances of plasma hissing in the air around them. Donovan punched out, but Reece was quick, dipping his head neatly out of the way. The crook jabbed at his wounded shoulder, his knuckles digging deep into the damaged flesh of the gunshot wound. Donovan screamed as pain wracked his upper torso. Reece struck again, aiming at the same spot and layering pain upon pain in sharp, stabbing waves. Donovan stumbled backward, trying to get his arms up in defense, but his right arm wouldn't respond, now weak with agony. He took another blow to the face and nearly went down. He couldn't believe the man's strength. Darkness swam at the edges of his vision, drawing him in.

But then he thought of Flora, of Landsworth, Sinclair, Williamson, of Celeste Parker. He grunted angrily. No. He would put this man down, and he would do it now.

Donovan closed the gap between them, thrashing out with both fists, not caring where his blows were landing, just content that they were connecting at all. He threw all of his power behind each attack, shredding his knuckles as he struck out blindly. All he could see was red fury, and it made him relentless as he punched again, and again, and again, not bothering to parry the blows that came back at him, forcing himself onward, burning through the hot pain in his shoulder. Again, and again, and again.

Blood spattered from Reece's face, but Donovan, consumed by hatred, did not stop until he was breathless, and Reece was cowering before him on his knees. Donovan stepped back, regarding the crook. The man's face was battered and bruised, his lips split, blood dribbling down his pale chin. He looked up at Donovan, an incredulous expression in his eyes, as if he couldn't believe what had happened to him, as if the mere thought that this wounded policeman could have reduced him to such a sorry state was utterly unbelievable.

Donovan backed away, not taking his eyes off the villain. His heel encountered something hard on the walkway beneath him. He glanced down. The silver pistol. He scooped it up, testing its weight in his hand. It was small and light, a dishonest weapon. This was the gun that had put the bullet in his shoulder. There was a delicious sense of irony in that. He cocked the gun and raised his arm, leveling the barrel in the direction of the other man's head. Reece was drawing ragged breaths, and Donovan wondered if he'd broken a rib, maybe more. But then, suddenly unsure, he realized that the mobster was actually laughing.

He watched Reece spit out a gobbet of dark blood and then climb to his feet, holding his head high. He wiped blood from his eyes with the back of his sleeve and then turned to face Donovan, adopting his usual air of superiority. But Donovan could see that his eyes were wild, insane. He wondered what the man intended to do.

Reece opened his arms wide, making a target of his chest. "Pull the trigger, then, Donovan. Do it!" He was grinning like a madman. "Come on! Finish it!"

Donovan eased his trigger finger back a fraction, but then hesitated. Reece was laughing out loud now. "You can't do it, can you? A policeman to the last. You won't put a bullet in an unarmed man."

Donovan tried to conjure up images of the men Reece had murdered, tried to summon back the red mist. He knew what he had to do. But still he couldn't bring himself to squeeze the trigger. He wouldn't cross that line.

Reece took a step forward. "You see, Inspector." He was sneering now, regaining his confidence. "This is why I'll always win. Men like you, they simply won't do what's necessary. Even when your own life is in the balance, you cannot bring yourself to kill in cold blood."

"But *I* can." The voice was deep, like boots crunching on gravel. The Ghost appeared on the gangway behind the maniacal crook. He grabbed Reece fiercely around the waist, lifting him into the air. Reece's face flickered, first with confusion, and then with panic, as he suddenly realized what was happening.

The Ghost staggered under the man's weight, took two steps toward the railing, and then hurled the crook over the edge of the gangway, into the waiting embrace of a Tesla coil. Reece screamed—a piercing, gut-wrenching scream—as he collided with the nearest machine. Fingers of plasma reached out, as if grabbing for him, and he howled in pain as the electricity jerked into his body. He hung for a moment, suspended by the energy that crackled through him, as if clutched by the hungry machine, his body twitching frantically as his nervous system was overloaded.

And then it was over, and his corpse dropped in a heap to the floor below. The stench of charred meat filled the air.

Donovan let the silver pistol fall from his grip, clattering to the ground. He stared at the dark figure of the Ghost on the gangway before him, his features stark in the stuttering light of the electrical discharge. Then, breathing hard, he crossed the gangway and leaned over the edge of the iron rail. Reece lay on the concrete floor below, slack-jawed and pale-faced, wisps of smoke still curling disturbingly from the back of his head. His eyes were fixed open in terrified shock. Above, the Tesla coil continued to spit out forks of flickering lightning, humming and buzzing with purple-blue energy.

Donovan couldn't reconcile the dead husk of the crook with his impressions of the man who had formerly inhabited the gangly body. Reece had loomed so large in his thoughts for the last few days, had threatened him, shot him; in his darkest hours represented even death itself. Now he was broken and dead, his body charred and ruined, the power gone out of him. He had been reduced to nothing more than another dead mobster.

He heard footsteps on the metal walkway beside him. "He was a stain. He needed to be purged." The Ghost's voice was grim, level. He was staring down at the steaming body, his lips pursed in disgust. Donovan couldn't tell if that disgust was inspired by the stench of the smoldering corpse, or by the realization of his own actions.

He was right, of course. Donovan knew that. Reece had been a plague upon the people of New York, a blight that needed to be stopped. He deserved what had happened to him here. But the methods... Donovan could not approve of those. He hoped the Ghost could live with himself; guessed that there were layers to the man that he had yet to peel away.

Donovan sighed. He was tired. He hung his head. "Our only lead died with him." His words were not a condemnation, merely a statement of fact.

The Ghost stood back from the railing, dusting off his gloved hands, as if finally brushing away the residue of Gideon Reece. "No. He told us everything we needed to know."

"How so?" Donovan frowned, perplexed.

"When you asked him what the Roman needed with all that power, he would only say that he had his reasons, or words to that effect," said the Ghost.

"How does that tell us anything?"

"It tells us *everything*! The power from this station is being channeled to a single location a few miles away from here. He confirmed that it *was* the Roman who needed the power. He might not have spilled the whole story, but you can follow the logic... If we follow the trail of energy, we get to the Roman."

"Yes, you're on to something there." Donovan pushed himself away from the railing, past the Ghost and along the gangway to the control room. The remains of the moss man were still scattered over the floor and surfaces and a black stain was smudged across the wall; a shadow of the explosion that had taken place in the small room. Donovan stepped over the heap of discarded earth, looking up at the map on the wall. He followed the line of pins with his finger.

The Ghost appeared behind him. "It's not far from here. We can be there in twenty minutes."

"Shouldn't we call for backup first? Or at least take a few minutes to formulate a plan?"

The Ghost shook his head. "The police will only get in our way." He glanced back up the gangway, a meaningful gleam in his eye. "Prevent us from doing what's necessary." He put a hand on Donovan's shoulder. "Besides, we don't *have* any time.

I need to get to Celeste. Reece said we were already too late, but I can't give up on her."

Donovan nodded. He could see the look in the other man's eyes; the need to keep moving, to keep fighting for the woman he had lost. Donovan searched the floor for his abandoned handgun, found it, and hefted it in his good hand. "You better lead the way, then."

TWENTY TWO

"Are you sure this is the place?" Donovan sounded decidedly unconvinced as the Ghost pulled the car to a stop before a set of ornate iron gates. Beyond the gates—which, when drawn together, depicted a scene of a man fighting a raging bull—a gravel driveway led up to a large, rather ostentatious mansion, set back from the surrounding buildings in its own private grounds. The Ghost had parked the car in the shadow of a large tree while they took a moment to reconnoitre the area.

The Ghost regarded Donovan coolly from the driver's seat. The muscles in his neck and shoulders were aching and he was dying for a cigarette. He tried not to sound too weary as he framed his response. "Yes. This is the place. Look at the row of armored cars parked out front, and the wire frame on the roof. That's where the electricity is being pumped in."

He watched Donovan strain in his seat, trying to get a better look. The midday sun had given way to an overcast, gloomy afternoon. Brooding clouds hung overhead like oily thumbprints smeared across the sky.

The Ghost regarded the building at the end of the driveway. It had an ominous quality to it, dark and foreboding. It had been built in the classical style: a square central block approached through a portico and surrounded by towering

Corinthian columns. Two identical wings adjoined the main building to either side, tall sash windows looking out across the grounds in long, symmetrical rows. A wire tower erupted incongruously from the roof of the mansion, taller than its chimneys, reaching up toward the sky as if trying to scratch the underside of the clouds.

This was the Roman's lair, that unseen enemy whose shadow had stretched so far and wide over Manhattan these last few months, who presided over the actions of Gideon Reece and his small army of golems and goons.

The Ghost hoped they weren't hurtling headlong into a trap. Even if they were, it was his only hope to save Celeste. That was all that mattered to him, he realized, the thing that drove him on. Donovan could have the Roman, could deal with the mob boss in any way he chose, just as long as he allowed the Ghost to get Celeste to safety first. He felt his pulse quicken as he thought of her, imagined the terrible pain she might be in. If she'd suffered... if the Roman had harmed her in any way... well, that would change things. But for now he would concentrate on getting her back. He had to believe she was still alive, that Reece had been toying with him back at the power plant. Even to consider anything else was unbearable.

He turned to the inspector. "Are you ready?"

Donovan shrugged. "Will I ever be ready for something like this?"

The Ghost laughed. "Now there's a question. Come on. We have work to do."

The two men clambered out of the car. The Ghost was thankful there were no guards on the gates, but that didn't mean they wouldn't be seen. They had to tread very carefully.

The gates were too high to scramble over, so instead they took the wall, Donovan hoisting the Ghost up first and then allowing himself to be pulled up behind him. They dropped into a tree-lined bed of shrubbery, ducking into the shadows, watching the great house for any signs of movement. There were none. The gardens seemed to be deserted. The Ghost couldn't help feeling suspicious at the lack of guards. It was either a sign that they were, indeed, walking into a trap of some kind, or else that the Roman was so arrogant as to assume that he didn't need to post guards in the grounds of the mansion. He hoped it was the latter.

The Ghost beckoned to Donovan, and together they set out, clinging to the flower beds and the shadow of the redbrick wall, which appeared to run around the entire perimeter of the property.

As they drew nearer to the side of the house, Donovan pulled gently on the Ghost's sleeve, drawing his attention. He followed the line of Donovan's finger, seeing a man in a gray suit emerge from behind the big house, carrying a snub-nosed tommy gun under his arm. So he'd spoken too soon. There were guards, after all.

The Ghost considered his options. Too much trouble now would almost certainly get them caught. He didn't want to bring the Roman's whole household down on them, at least not until they were well inside and had a measure of where they might be holding Celeste. But if they didn't get rid of the guard, there was no way they were going to make it across the lawn to the house without being seen. The net effect was the same: either way, there would be trouble.

Carefully, the Ghost reached up and flicked the lenses of his goggles down over his eyes. Suddenly, everything was red. He twisted the dials, zooming in on his target. The man was heavy, overweight. He had one arm in a sling beneath his suit jacket and he was sweating profusely, out of breath from his walk around the gardens. The Ghost smiled to himself. It was the man from the bank, the mobster he had allowed to live, the one he had sent away with a message for the Roman. Well, here was his chance to take another message to his employer. The Ghost dropped to his knees, squelching in the soft loam. He raised his arm, sighting along the barrel of his fléchette gun. He grabbed the rubber bulb that served as a trigger and gave it one short, hard squeeze, opening his palm to let it fall away again. A single fléchette whistled away into the air. Seconds later, the fat man gave a short, stifled cry, dropping his gun and glancing down at his belly. Confused, he lifted his jacket, revealing a small tear in the white fabric of his shirt and a tiny sickle-shaped stain of blood. He looked as if he was about to cry out, but then the little blade exploded inside his belly, blowing a fist-sized hole right through him, scattering offal and blood over the gravel path with a sickening *squelch*. The man folded and collapsed into a heap.

The Ghost didn't bother to look over his shoulder at Donovan. He simply got to his feet and ran for the house, bursting from the cover of the trees and hurtling across the lawn toward the cover of the walls. He heard the thunder of Donovan's footsteps behind him. He tried not to look down at the body of the dead mobster as they rushed past, rounding the corner to the back of the building and finally coming to rest in the shadow of a large awning. Donovan was panting for breath. He looked as if he wanted to say something, to comment on the Ghost's actions in taking the guard's life in such a peremptory fashion, but the Ghost silenced him with a stare. Now was not the time for squeamishness or morals. Now was the time for action.

As the Ghost had anticipated, there was a rear entrance into the house, through a set of glass double doors that opened into a large solarium. Inside, the solarium was filled with exotic plants; large leafy specimens, covered in bright green foliage, along with lemon trees and colorful orchids, as well as a plethora of other flowers he could not identify.

That was their way in. That was their chance. They risked encountering more guards hidden behind the foliage inside, but if they did, he'd just have to deal with them at the time.

The Ghost crossed to the solarium doors, ducking beneath the sill of a tall window to avoid being glimpsed by anyone inside. Beyond the window the room seemed to be a refectory or dining room laid out for a large group of people; no doubt this was where the Roman's men—or at least the ones he kept closest to him—took their meals under his watchful gaze.

He tested the doors, was surprised to discover they were unlocked. Again, that cold sense of fear and doubt. It felt too easy.

The solarium was hot and humid, even now, in the midst of a freezing November. He felt prickles of sweat stand out on his forehead as he worked his way inside, snaking through the leafy avenues of plants and vines, the columns of fruit trees and beds of orchids. He kept the barrel of his weapon raised at all times, scanning the spaces between the flora, alert for any sign of danger.

The solarium opened out onto a dayroom with gleaming polished floorboards the color of amber, and thick Turkish rugs in myriad hues and patterns. Landscapes—of Europe, he supposed—lined the walls, and a walnut sideboard was covered with a plethora of antique items, from a golden carriage clock to a silver letter opener in the shape of a miniature sword. There was one door—currently closed—that would presumably take them deeper into the house. The room had a musty smell about it, of dust and neglect. The fireplace told the same story—it had not been used for months, perhaps longer. The room evidently now served only as a corridor to the solarium and gardens.

The Ghost turned to Donovan, who was still extracting himself from the maze of plant life. "Once we go through that door, we should split up. I'll look for Celeste, you look for the Roman."

Donovan frowned. "Are you sure that's a good idea? What if we run into trouble?"

The Ghost looked serious. "We've come here *looking* for trouble, Donovan." He let that hang for a moment, then continued, "I'll locate Celeste, get her out to the car, and come back. If you find yourself in a tight spot, try to hold them off until I can get to you. This way, at least one of us has a chance of success, even if the other gets caught. We'll end it, here, today. All of it."

Donovan didn't look happy with the arrangement. His face took on a dark and brooding expression, but he nodded in acknowledgement.

The Ghost crossed to the door, pressed his ear up against the panel. No sound from beyond. He guessed the door would open into a hallway connecting the refectory with the rest of the house. He waited for a moment, glanced up at Donovan to ensure he was ready, and then turned the handle and eased open the door. His heart was in his mouth as he readied himself for a shooting match.

But he was greeted by silence. The hall beyond the door was quiet and dimly lit by the watery afternoon sunlight that was streaming in through a glass dome in the ceiling. There was a grand staircase leading to the upper floor, with sweeping balustrades and a sumptuously carpeted tread. A small oak side table housed an old holotube unit, and a great, shimmering chandelier hung low over the marble floor, set with long strings of glassy stones. Five other doors radiated out from the large space: the main entrance, the door to the refectory, and three others leading to unknown destinations.

The Ghost would start with the upper floor, work his way back down. If Celeste was here, as he hoped, they'd most likely be holding her in one of the bedchambers. He'd leave the ground floor to Donovan for now. He looked at the policeman, who was glancing nervously out into the hallway, clutching his borrowed gun. Was it really fair for him to send this man into the lion's den alone? He knew it wasn't. But then... Celeste. Celeste was here, and she needed his help. At least the policeman could look after himself in a fight. He clapped a hand on Donovan's shoulder. His voice was low and soft. "I'll take the upper floor. When I find her, I'll get her out quick and come after you."

He slipped into the hallway, moving lightly so that his boots made hardly a sound as he crossed the marble floor. He reached the stairway and looked back to see Donovan inching across the hall toward one of the other doors, then ran on up the stairs, the soft maroon carpet muffling the sound of his passing.

The Ghost had no idea what he was going to find up there, but he hoped—beyond all reasonable hope—that he would find Celeste, and that she would still be alive and well.

Donovan was still aching from his fight at the power station, from the gunshot wound in his shoulder, and from two sleepless nights spent tossing and turning in a strange apartment, worrying about his wife. His entire life had been suddenly turned upside down, seemingly on the toss of a coin, and he was still trying to make sense of what had happened. The death of Gideon Reece had lifted a heavy weight from his shoulders— regardless of how it had happened—but he wasn't so naive as to assume the problem had gone away. Reece was simply the Roman's mouthpiece, the man who did the dirty work, and Donovan needed to tackle the problem at its core. He needed to take down the man at the center of the web.

The only thing was, when it came down to it, he didn't know if he'd be up to the job.

He supposed it didn't matter how he felt. He was there, with a gun in his hand, creeping around inside the mansion of a murderous mob boss. He had a job to do, and he needed to keep the mobsters busy while the Ghost got the girl away to safety.

He eyed the three doors on the other side of the hall. He had a suspicion that the door on the far left, behind the stairs, would lead to the kitchens. Of the other two he was unsure. One could be the drawing room. The other a library or study.

There was only one sure way to find out.

Donovan decided to try the middle of the three doors. He crossed the hall, glanced once at the stairs to discover the Ghost had already ascended out of sight, and then, drawing a deep breath, opened the door and stepped into the room beyond. It was dark, and he scrabbled for a light switch on the wall behind him. He found it, flicked it, and then stared in awe at the wondrous scene that stuttered to life before him.

He'd been wrong on all counts. The room beyond the door did not house a library or study, nor was it set out as a drawing room. Rather, it was a fantasia of bizarre artifacts and oddities from all over the world, a cornucopia of priceless artwork and treasures. Donovan tried to take it all in: a Michelangelo—the original—housed in a rough wooden frame; a Rembrandt, the same. A collection of ancient swords from all periods of history: a Saracen blade, a machete, a European broadsword—even a cavalry sword from the last war. Jewelry, pottery, papyrus scrolls. A set of leather-bound Latin tracts from old Europe. A statue of Isis from Ancient Egypt. The model of a small wooden boat, a stone tablet engraved in an ancient language, a marble statue of a Greek or Roman god slaying a bull. All of these things and more. And to top it all, a glass case containing a tailor's dummy dressed in the armor of a Roman centurion, carrying a long spear and a tall, curved shield.

It was a treasure vault, filled to the very brim with items of unimaginable value. The Roman must have been hoarding them for years. How long had his criminal network been in operation? How many priceless artifacts had he stolen from vaults or museums around the world? Donovan couldn't believe the gall of the man. He was clearly an egomaniac, a collector who had taken his obsessions to a ridiculous extreme.

He moved further into the room, awestruck by the scale of the hoard. He approached the glass case, leaned closer to examine the centurion's armor. It was probably the best-preserved example in the world. It was near immaculate. Scarred, yes, where the man who had originally worn it had been struck in battle, but it gleamed like burnished gold, its decals and detailing still vivid. The chest bore the engraved head of a lion, the mouth fixed open in a fierce roar. He examined the spear. Surely the wood must have been replaced? Its long, sturdy shaft was the height of a man, tipped with a razor-sharp head of iron. The shield was a beaten panel, dented from successive blows, but still ablaze with color: bright, fiery red, crossed with flashes of yellow lightning. From the helmet, a plume of jet-black hair erupted.

Donovan heard the sound of someone laughing softly in the doorway behind him. And then a voice: "Remarkable, isn't it? I come here every day to look at it, to remind myself of how far I've come. Sometimes it saddens me, to think of home. But mostly it gives me the resolve to carry on. I don't suppose you'll understand, Inspector Donovan, but I miss those days. I miss the urgency of it all, the danger. Rome was such a jewel, a bright, shining light of civilization in a barren, heathen world." The voice was warm and gentle, thickly accented with a somber Italian lilt.

Donovan whirled around, his handgun by his side, his finger already twitching on the trigger. The man in the doorway was of average build, middle-aged, with olive-green eyes and coarse black hair that was turning to gray around the temples. He was holding his hands out before him to show he was unarmed. He was dressed in a neat black suit with a black tie, and he had a stately air about him, the air of a man untroubled by something so mundane as an armed intruder in his home. He seemed to accept the situation with grace, as if he'd seen it all before and knew the incursion for what it was.

The Roman looked longingly at the armor in the case behind the inspector. "I remember when it was made for me, as if it were yesterday." He sighed. "It still fits, you know. Just as snug as it did all those many years ago."

Donovan just stared at him, clutching the grip of his gun.

The Roman seemed to shrug off the reverie. "I see Gideon failed me once again." He regarded Donovan through narrow eyes. "So be it. He's an impulsive fool, full of self-import and theatrics."

"He's also dead," Donovan replied laconically, trying to prevent his hand from shaking.

The Roman nodded slowly, accepting this information without even a flicker of emotion. "How interesting. Did you enjoy his death, Mr. Donovan? I hope very much that you did. It's important to take at least some satisfaction in the killing of another, don't you think? Otherwise it's such a waste of a life."

Donovan didn't know how to respond to such heinous logic. Instead, he indicated the glass case with the nose of his gun. "It's quite a collection you have here. But I don't see the marble wheel you stole from the museum the other night. Where is it?"

The Roman's expression changed. All of a sudden he looked

hard, serious, dangerous. His ire was up. Donovan repressed a shudder. The timbre of the man's voice had altered, too, becoming stern and commanding. "The item you refer to, the marble 'wheel,' belongs to me. It was stolen from my house in Pompeii over eighty years ago, taken by a cadre of amateur grave robbers. They sold it to your precious museum, and I decided it would serve me well to leave it there until I needed it. Circumstances have changed. Now I want it back."

Donovan offered the Roman an incredulous stare. Was he really claiming to have owned a house in Pompeii? That this armor—this *centurion's* armor—was originally his? Donovan nearly lost his composure. The Roman was clearly insane, so wrapped up in his fantasy that he'd begun to believe it himself, begun to adopt the personality and history that his assumed moniker implied. Only... the man's eyes were sharp and appraising, and he lacked the maniacal qualities of Gideon Reece. He didn't *look* insane. The artifacts in the room, too: none of them would have been easy to acquire, unless he'd been there at the time they were made...

But Donovan knew that was crazy talk. Nobody lived that long. Most likely he'd acquired the items through nefarious means, exploiting his criminal network to obtain the treasures he desired, and was now so addled by the power he'd attained that he'd been swept up in his own myth, convincing himself he was a reincarnated Roman foot soldier.

Donovan actually found himself feeling sorry for the man, right up until the moment he swept into the room, catching Donovan off guard, and twisted his wrist so sharply that he dropped the gun on the hardwood floor and fell to his knees, croaking in agony. Then he remembered just who he was dealing with. But by then it was too late, and the Roman was calling for guards, who appeared moments later in their droves, armed and ready to serve their insane master.

Upstairs, the Ghost was having trouble restraining himself. He'd been lurking around the corner at the top of the stairs for nearly five minutes, concealed behind a wall, patiently watching two goons as they paced back and forth along the landing, shooting the breeze in a relaxed fashion as they guarded one of any number of white bedroom doors.

He fought the urge to step out onto the landing and shoot them both dead. He much preferred the direct approach, but he needed to know which of the rooms they were watching over, and besides, he had his principles. When the time came, he would let them be the first to raise their guns in anger. Then he would kill them both and find Celeste.

Standing there deadly still was beginning to take its toll on him. As long as he kept on moving he was okay, but now his muscles were starting to protest and the aches and bruises of the previous few days were starting to light up his nerves with pain. The moss man at the power station had given him a severe beating—more severe than he'd let on to Donovan—and he was starting to fear that the blow to his head had left him concussed. He was tired and sick to his stomach. But he recognized that could also be to do with the fact that he hadn't eaten that day, or a symptom of his reticence to discover the truth about Celeste. He had to save her—of course he did—but just as powerful as his desire to do so was his fear over what he might find. And even then, there was the terrible secret she had kept from him. Was it connected to all this? Did she know something about the Roman that she hadn't been able to tell him?

The Ghost watched the two mobsters as they reached the far end of the landing, turned, and started back. As they did so, the one on the left flicked a quick glance at one of the bedroom doors, the same door he'd glanced at as he passed along the landing in the opposite direction. That was it, then. That was the door to Celeste. To his future. To whatever lay ahead.

The Ghost readied his fléchette gun and strode out casually into the passageway, facing the two goons as they strolled toward him. The one on the right saw him first and started, recognition flaring in his eyes. He scrambled for his gun. The other, who'd been talking, took a second longer to realize what was happening, and by the time he'd reached for his weapon he was already dead, an explosive round in his throat. The Ghost had seen him go for his gun. That was enough. He couldn't help it if the goons were slow to the draw.

The other opened his mouth to call out and just as quickly a flashing blade embedded itself in the back of his throat, passing between his teeth to pierce the soft tissue behind his tonsils. His head detonated on the count of three, spreading brain matter across the walls, just as the other body toppled to the floor beside him, a hole where its throat used to be. The sounds of the explosions echoed in the confined space, and the Ghost hoped they wouldn't be heard elsewhere in the house. He kept his weapon at the ready just in case.

The Ghost strode on down the hallway, his heart hammering

in his chest, his palms sweating inside his leather gloves. He faced the door, tried the handle. It was locked, of course. He glanced down at the pulpy mess of the two goons by his feet, had to look away in disgust. He backed up, careful to avoid tripping over the bodies, and then kicked out at the door, crunching the lock and bursting it open, the top hinge splintering away from the frame to come to rest at a jaunty angle. He pushed it to one side and rushed forward into the room.

Celeste Parker was sitting on the edge of the bed, staring up at him, her eyes wide with surprise. He didn't see anything else, didn't pay attention to the room around her. She looked immaculate, untouched. Her auburn hair fell in a perfect wave about her shoulders, framing her pretty, pale face. She was dressed in a short blue dress that revealed her shapely legs, and to the Ghost she was the most beautiful thing he had ever seen.

He ran to her side and she leapt up, flinging her arms around his neck. Then she pushed him away, grabbed his face in both hands, and kissed him deeply on the lips. "Oh, Gabriel. You brave, stupid fool. What are you doing here?"

The Ghost grabbed Celeste by the shoulders, holding her firmly, as though scared that he might somehow lose her again. "What do you think I'm doing here? I've come to rescue you. I have a car outside. We need to make a run for it."

She gave a minute shake of her head and pulled away from him. The look on her face was of someone grieving, distraught. "No, Gabriel. You don't understand. I can't go." A pause. "Haven't you worked it out yet?"

The Ghost grunted impatiently. "No, I haven't. I haven't worked anything out. What the hell is going on here? We need to *go*." Celeste was weeping now, and he clutched her to him, holding her head against his chest. "Celeste, we can talk later. Whatever it is, whatever you think you can't tell me, we'll work it out. We'll fix it, together. But right now we need to get out of this house before someone finds the bodies I've left in the hallway."

She beat her fists against his chest, as if trying to drive him away from her, as if trying to fight against some terrible enemy that only she could see. He grabbed her by the wrists. Her body was wracked by sobs as she poured out the emotion she had bottled up for so long. She looked up into his face, her mascara running in long tributaries down her cheeks; black rivers that coursed all the way from her heart. All he wanted to do was hold her, comfort her, but he needed to get her to safety. He felt his heart rending in two.

"Celeste..." His voice was a whisper now. "Celeste—"

"I love you, Gabriel, but you have to know something."

"Tell me. Anything."

She sucked at the air, trying to regain her composure. "Gabriel, I *can't* be with you. I'm going to die."

The words were like ice to him, causing him to stiffen in fear. He forced a smile, confused by her sudden outburst. "No, Celeste. You're safe now. I'm going to get you home."

She shook her head. "I only wish it were that simple. But the lives of thousands of people depend on it." She dropped to the bed and the Ghost glanced at the door, anxious that they didn't have very long before the alarm would be raised and they suddenly found themselves with unwanted company. Her words slowly registered through the haze.

"Celeste, you're confused. Look, come on. We can talk later."

"No!" She was suddenly furious with him, frustrated that he seemed not to be paying attention, hearing what she had to say. "This runs deeper than you think, Gabriel, deeper than the mob, deeper than the Roman and Gideon Reece. This is a story that spans centuries, and there's no other way of ending it."

The Ghost stared at her, dumbfounded. "What are you talking about?"

"The Roman. That's who I'm talking about. Do you know who he is? Who he *really* is?"

The Ghost shrugged. "He's a mob boss, a plague on the city. A madman. He needs to be eradicated."

Celeste was shaking her head. "He's all of those things, true, but he's something else, too. He's a Roman centurion from the first century. His name is Gaius Lucius Severnius."

The Ghost didn't know whether to laugh, or to break down. Her mind had snapped. The shock of her abduction, of the way that she'd been treated—it had taken its toll on her, and she was caught up in some terrible fantasy regarding her captor. He considered coshing her on the head and carrying her out to the car over his shoulder. But there was Donovan to think of, too; he needed her capable so she could drive the car.

He wondered if Celeste could see the disbelief in his eyes. When she spoke again, her voice was soft, measured. Disconsolate. "I knew you wouldn't understand." She looked up at him, her eyes pleading, and then continued, trying again. "There are more things in this universe, Gabriel, than you could possibly imagine. The Roman made a pact with one such thing. Now it's time for him to do so again. I have to be here to stop him."

Gabriel frowned. "I know more than you think, Celeste." He thought back to the farmhouse in France; shuddered at the unbidden memory. He knew about the things that lurked in the darkness. Could she be telling the truth? She clearly believed it herself. He felt as if he were trapped in some sort of terrible waking nightmare.

He reached out and put his hand on her arm, as much to ground himself as to comfort the woman before him. "So you're saying the Roman has walked this earth for nearly two thousand years, that he's mixed up in some sort of supernatural union that extended his life."

Celeste shrugged. "Not supernatural, no. These entities, they're all around us. They're here, now, in this very room, just out of step with us, inhabiting a different dimensional space. We cross paths with them all the time, but neither is aware of it happening. Do you understand?"

The Ghost shrugged. "Yes, I think I understand."

Celeste continued, "The Roman discovered a means to collapse those dimensions together, to give those creatures a physical presence in our own space and time. And they rewarded him for it. A hormone they secrete from a gland in their abdomens, it arrests the aging process in mammals. It slowed his aging for nearly two thousand years, kept his body repairing itself, over and over. But now he's started aging again, and he needs to bring another entity through if he wants to live."

It all made a terrible sort of sense to the Ghost. The things he'd seen in France, the monsters he'd encountered when he was alone and delirious following the crash. The sights that had made him the man he was. Could this be the explanation? The hair on the nape of his neck was prickling, standing on end. "How do you know all of this, Celeste? And what has it got to do with you? Why does it mean you're going to die?" He almost choked on the question.

She fixed him with an intense stare. "Because I'm the only one who can stop it. The Roman cares only for his own life. That much is obvious. He'll gladly sacrifice the city to the creature, give it up and move on. When you've lived for two thousand years, other people's lives, they must seem small and unimportant, flames that flicker briefly before going out. The creature is dangerous, Gabriel. It will hurt people. A lot of people. And I can stop it."

"If what you're saying is right, then we'll stop it together." He hefted his fléchette gun as if to underline his point. "There's no need for anyone to die."

Celeste sighed. "Your weapons won't stop it, Gabriel. But my blood is poison to it." She wiped away the remains of her tears with the edge of her palm. "I've always known this might come to pass. I come from a long bloodline, reaching all the way back to those first days, when the Roman Empire was at its height and the world's religions were being born. My ancestors stopped that first creature, back in Rome, sacrificed themselves for the greater good. And ever since, my family—a large, extended family, with branches all over the world—has kept watch on Severnius and others like him, patiently waiting, observing. It's just my damn bad luck he's chosen this place, and this time, to act." She reached out, took his hand in hers. They were damp with her tears. "I love you, Gabriel Cross. Never forget that." It sounded final.

The Ghost's heart was hammering in his chest. He felt dizzy, confused. He couldn't let her go through with it, whatever she was planning to do. He had to find a way to help her. And then a thought occurred to him. "So why does the Roman want you here, if he knows the truth about you, about the risk you pose to his plans? Why didn't he just kill you like the others?"

"I'm his insurance policy. If it goes wrong, if the entity won't cooperate with him, I'm his loaded gun. He traced me through the bloodline, through the Sisterhood."

"Then it's clear what I have to do." He spoke with a firm resolve, but inside he was dying, shaken to the core by this confession from the woman he loved, the woman he had vowed to protect with his life. "I have to kill the bastard before he gets anywhere near to summoning this creature."

Celeste stood then, clutching him to her, her face so close to his that he could smell the sweetness of her breath. "Then we'd better be quick. He's planning to do it today."

The Ghost kissed her again, long and hard, and then turned toward the door. "Stay here," he commanded, knowing full well that she would not. Then he ran for the hallway, her soft footsteps falling in behind him.

The Ghost could hear voices from the hallway down below. Waving for Celeste to keep back, he leaned cautiously over the banister, using the targeting zoom of his goggles to take a better look. Donovan was there, held by two moss golems who lumbered along behind a middle-aged man in a black suit, a man with jet-black hair and a tanned complexion. Mr. Gardici. The Roman.

The small group approached a posse of mobsters who were waiting near the foot of the stairs. The Roman had his back to the stairs. "Take him down to the Mithraeum. He's inquisitive, and I'd like him to see what we're doing here. Bind his hands so he can't get up to any mischief." The Ghost imagined the Roman grinning as he continued: "And besides, he'll make a rather interesting morsel for our visitor."

The Roman watched as the moss men dragged a subdued Donovan out of view. He dusted down the front of his immaculate black suit, apparently pleased with himself. Then, turning, he disappeared after the others, a wide grin splitting his face.

The Ghost flicked his lenses back into place and turned to Celeste, pushing himself away from the banister. "I'm going down there after them. Find somewhere safe and stay out of sight."

"The safest place I can think of right now is with you." Celeste stared defiantly into his eyes, then continued to follow him down the stairs, treading cautiously to avoid giving them away. Near the bottom, she caught his arm. "The Mithraeum is his temple. It's underground. We need to find the entrance. That's where everything will take place."

The Ghost gave a curt nod, still unsettled by her unusual knowledge of these things. He wondered what the hell they were walking into, what hideous things they would see. He swallowed, wiped his brow on the sleeve of his coat. He wouldn't let it come to that. He'd get there first, and finish the Roman before he had a chance to summon the creature, before Celeste had an opportunity to do anything stupid. He would damn himself to hell before he'd let her give her own life.

And it might yet come to that, he considered, as he padded silently across the hallway, searching for the door that would lead him to the subterranean temple.

Donovan allowed himself to be dragged along by the shambling monsters, seeing no benefit in trying to fight back at this point in the proceedings. If he did try anything, the moss men would likely rip him apart, each one tearing at a shoulder until his limbs were wrenched painfully from their sockets. Instead, he allowed himself to become floppy, a deadweight, and hoped that this ruse might buy him some time to consider his options. He hoped also that the Ghost was on his way back from the car by now, but he couldn't count on the vigilante arriving in time to help him. He'd already relied on the man too much in the course of the last few days; perhaps now was the moment for him to stand up for himself. He would be patient, wait for the opportunity to present itself. But at the back of his mind was a nagging doubt. He feared it was already too late.

As the moss men squeezed through a small doorway and into a brick-lined passageway that appeared to descend beneath the house and garden, he wondered what the Roman was planning. The tunnel had clearly been mined out beneath the foundations of the old house, probably sometime in the last few years, and electric lamps had been strung on long fat cables at regular intervals along the walls. The walls were slick with damp, and there was a rank, musty smell in the confined space; partly, he assumed, emanating from the two golems who were forcing him along, his boots scraping on the dirt floor of the sloping passage. His shoulder had begun to ache again, the gunshot wound open and oozing blood down the inside of his sleeve.

He saw a pair of tiny red eyes in the distance, wondered momentarily if it was the Ghost lying in wait, but then realized his perspective was shot in the darkness, and it was nothing but the hungry eyes of a rat, regarding him eerily in the gloom. It scuttled away as the moss men lumbered closer. They continued on.

Presently, after what felt like an age, the floor of the tunnel leveled out and the moss men came to an abrupt stop before a pair of wide double doors. They were roughly hewn, banded with iron fittings, and he wondered if they had been stolen, too; a relic from an old monastery or church, brought here for the Roman's deluded rituals, the doorway to his subterranean dungeons. Christ—the thought suddenly occurred to him that the lunatic might actually have built an arena down there, that the reference to him being an "interesting morsel" might mean he was about to find himself thrown to the lions, literally, like the Christians of old. That was no way to go.

A mobster from the leading party stepped forward and pushed one of the twin doors aside, offering Donovan a glimpse of the room beyond. It wasn't what he'd been expecting. It was a large, open space—a cave hollowed out from the bedrock—with two long, parallel stone benches lining the walls to either side. The floor was compacted dirt, and a row of wooden torches sputtered and guttered in iron brackets affixed to the walls. The cavernous space terminated in a high stone arch, about a hundred yards beyond the doors, above which an intricate and elaborate fresco of the celestial heavens was painted in startling blue and yellow. It looked like something from a history book, a painting in the ancient tradition, dedicated to the magnificence of a powerful, mythical god.

Beyond the arch was a large recess that housed two rare items. The first was a life-size marble sculpture of an armored man killing a bull, his cape flapping open behind him, capturing the movement so well that it looked almost as if the man had been frozen in glistening white marble, caught in the act. A snake and a dog were drinking from the wounds of the slain beast, and a large scorpion was attacking the man's testicles. Donovan had no idea of the tableau's significance.

The second item was the marble wheel that Donovan had witnessed being stolen from the museum. But now the wheel was suspended vertically in a large wooden frame, flanked on either side by two tall metal towers that fizzed and sparked with veins of dancing electricity: the channeled energy from the power station. The glow of the two towers lit the underground room with flickering, brilliant light.

The mobsters led the way into the room, filing through the door one by one, taking seats on the stone benches along either side of the chamber. The moss men heaved Donovan through behind them, handling him roughly, dropping him on the floor at the foot of the marble wheel so that he jarred his hands as he tried to prevent himself from landing on his face. They lumbered away, leaving it to one of the mobsters to bind Donovan's wrists behind his back with a silk tie and maneuver him to a space near the end of the bench. It seemed he was going to be awarded a good view.

He sat down heavily, testing the bonds by flexing his arms discreetly behind his back. They were firm, but he guessed he could free himself, given enough time. He set to work, angling his body away from the others so that they wouldn't see what he was up to. He scanned the faces of the mobsters on the opposite side of the chamber. There were five, no, six of them, and each of them wore an identical expression: a mix of awe and terror, their faces pale and frozen in rigid fright. He wondered how the Roman managed to hold such sway over these men, whether they were simply weak-willed, or whether he had some other means of keeping them in line. He supposed he might find out, if he could stay alive long enough to discover exactly what was going on.

It was only a matter of minutes before the Roman himself put in an appearance, striding across the center of the room, his head held high as he approached the recess at the far end of the chamber, just a few feet from where Donovan was seated. He turned to regard his audience. "Gentlemen. Welcome." He followed this with something in Latin, an elaborate litany that sounded very much like a religious verse, although Donovan had little experience of the language or its meaning. Then, more in English: "Today marks the culmination of all our efforts. Today great Mithras himself smiles down upon us from his place in the Heavens. Today we grant life to those who have known no life, and reward those deserving few amongst us who have given themselves over to the worship and instruction of the constant soul."

The Roman was breathing hard, barely containing himself as he drew out those last few words, and from where Donovan was sitting he could see the mad gleam in the man's eyes, the sweat standing out on his forehead, the spittle frothing from his lips. Donovan didn't doubt it at all—the man was utterly insane.

The Roman moved round to stand beside the electrical tower to the left of the marble wheel. Donovan noticed for the first time that there was a large lever there, wired up to the metal pylons, and was able only to sit and watch as the mob boss took this lever in both hands and cranked it toward himself. The mechanical contraption gave a long, grating moan, and then suddenly the room was flooded with light.

Reflexively, Donovan tried to shield his eyes, but as his hands were still tied securely behind his back he was able only to squint into the sudden pulse of bright energy, white and hot and painful. The massive electrical currents being drained from the power station had somehow been discharged into the marble wheel, and most bizarrely of all, the circular hole in the center of the wheel was now filled with a puddle of crackling blue energy. It looked to Donovan like the surface of an azure sea, rippling with waves of intense light. He felt himself being drawn into that light, being swallowed by its embracing depths, entranced by its hypnotic movements as it hummed and spat with the sheer intensity of the power involved.

Then the air was filled with the fetid stench of death, and something terrible burst forth from the surface of the light, something so exquisitely otherworldly that Donovan felt himself almost swoon with shock. Six vast translucent tentacles whipped out from the puddle of blue energy, each a full ten feet long, probing around the mouth of the portal inquisitively, patiently, as if searching for an anchor to pull the rest of the creature through the opening, or else searching for prey. Each glistening tentacle dripped with a thick, cloying mucus and terminated in a tiny mouth filled with needle-sharp teeth that snapped hungrily at the air.

Donovan was overwhelmed by a desire to run, to get as far away from the creature as humanly possible. But the mobsters each had the same idea, and they were scrabbling frantically for the door, fighting amongst themselves to be the first out of the cavern. He'd never be able to fight his way out, not with his arms still tied behind his back. He rose to his feet, backing away slowly from the hideous thing, attempting to keep out of the reach of its monstrous, questing mouths.

And all the while, the Roman stood beside the marble portal, his hands behind his back, laughing insanely to himself as he watched his people flee in abject fear.

TWENTY THREE

From the shadows at the back of the chamber, the Ghost watched the tentacles emerge from the puddle of light and was filled with an upwelling of panic, fear, and a sense of sudden loss. He'd failed. For a fleeting moment he was back in France, climbing out of the wreckage of his airplane, stumbling toward the nearby farmhouse, almost blinded by his own blood streaming down his face from a terrible wound in his scalp. He witnessed himself open the door and fall in, replayed that initial sense of dawning horror as he saw what was waiting for him there in the darkness.

This creature—this foul, hideous monster—was born of the same nightmares, molded from the same recalcitrant dreams. He fought the urge to turn and flee. To run now would be to turn his back on everything he'd fought for, everything that defined who he was. To run now would be to abandon Celeste, and he knew he would fight for her until the bitter end.

He watched as the tentacles snaked out, two of them snapping forward like forks of lightning, each one striking a fleeing mobster and burrowing expertly into their backs. He stood there transfixed, as he saw the creature draw the blood from their corpses, channeling it along the hollow, translucent flesh toward its waiting maw, still trapped, he presumed, on the other side of the portal. He watched the dark blood course along inside the tentacles, saw the pale, drawn bodies collapse to the floor, discarded, reduced to nothing but dry, empty husks.

Donovan was still backing away from the monster, ducking its probing appendages, trying desperately to free himself from his bonds. He sidestepped a sudden swipe from a tentacle, and then shifted too late to avoid another, which crashed into him with a sharp, jerking crack, sending him careening into the wall. He collapsed in a crumpled heap, and was still.

The Ghost had to act. He darted forward, showering the nearest tentacles with a sparkling spray of explosive fléchettes.

The monster reared as the rounds struck home, but the tiny blades failed to take, rebounding off the rubbery flesh and scattering to the ground, detonating like firecrackers amongst the dust. Chaos reigned as the remaining mobsters tried to get away, screaming as one after another, the creature stabbed at them with its darting tentacles, biting deep into their flesh, drawing the very lifeblood from them as it patiently, relentlessly sated itself.

He spotted the Roman, crouched to one side of the marble portal, clutching a tommy gun that had been discarded by one of his dead goons. He would have to wait. First, the Ghost had to deal with the monster.

He rushed forward, ducking beneath a flapping appendage, sprinting for the mouth of the portal, his long black trench coat billowing behind him as he ran. He heard Celeste scream from somewhere behind him as he dropped to one knee and raised his arm, firing deep into the portal itself, giving everything he had to the monster, willing the fléchettes to take, to bite into the strange translucent flesh and burn it up from within. But the creature's only response was to whip him hard across the face with one of its tentacles, sending him sprawling to the floor. He tried to roll, flipping himself out of the way of the snapping mouths, but he was too slow, and one of the thrashing tentacles buried itself in his left thigh, chewing its way into the muscle.

The Ghost screamed in agony as the sharp teeth gnashed at his leg, gulping blood and flesh alike. He saw the vital fluid flow away down the gullet of the strange organ and he grasped at it, trying desperately to wrench it free. It was no use; the tentacle was buried too deeply in his leg, and he couldn't gain a good purchase on its slippery, mucus-slick surface.

Gasping with pain, feeling the energy literally draining out of him, the Ghost reached down inside his jacket, pulling the cord and igniting the rocket propellants that were strapped to his boots. Bright spurts of flame licked out from the brass canisters, and he fought to angle himself so that they kissed the tentacle that was buried in his leg. But it was no use. The fire hardly seemed to touch the creature, provoking no response, doing no harm whatsoever to the thick, pellucid flesh.

He heard the chatter of gunfire, looked up to see Celeste charging toward him through the chaos. "Get back!" he screamed at the top of his lungs. "Get... back!"

But it was too late. Bullets from the Roman's gun had already punctured her thin, beautiful body, causing gobbets of blood to spatter the wall behind her as she ran. She stumbled as the bullets struck home, coughing and spluttering, blood streaming from multiple wounds in her chest. The Ghost screamed in horror and protest, refusing to believe what he was seeing unfold before his eyes. "No! No! No!"

Something inside of him broke.

The Roman stepped forward from the shadows, the tommy gun smoking from the hot discharge of bullets. He was still laughing.

But the last laugh would be Celeste's. As her body pitched forward toward the Ghost it was caught by a thrashing tentacle, which burst into her rib cage, grasping her in its terrible embrace and lifting her high into the air, swinging her above the writhing mass of drained corpses and tentacles below. The Ghost watched her bright red blood as it surged along the hollow appendage toward the cyclopean monster on the other side of the dimensional rift. Up there, she looked like a rag doll being tossed around by an errant child. Tears prickled his eyes. Blackness swam at the edge of his vision.

The creature gave a sudden, jerking shudder. The Ghost howled in pain as the tentacle buried in his leg began to thrash uncontrollably, tossing him back and forth with the motion. He jarred his elbow on the ground, felt a rib crack as he was lifted into the air and then dashed to the ground again in a single violent movement. Then the tentacle burst from his leg and withdrew, slapping the ground feebly as it crept back toward the portal. He realized the translucent flesh had begun to take on a grayish hue, and stared in astonishment as the tentacles gave one last sorry flutter of movement, and then dropped, motionless, to the ground. There was a strange, disturbing, keening sound—the dying gasp of a creature from another world—and then everything in the Mithraeum was silent, still.

Blinking, the Ghost pulled himself along the ground to where Celeste's broken body lay in a tangled heap. Tears were streaming freely now, coursing down his cheeks. He climbed to his knees, laid her out flat on the ground, gently cradling her head. She was pale and cold, and she was very much dead.

He heard footsteps behind him and he spun around to see the Roman approaching, brandishing the tommy gun before him, his face tired, unreadable. Behind him, the light of the portal still fizzed and crackled. The dead beast was sprawled across it, half in this world, half in the other.

The Roman waved the nose of the gun in the Ghost's face. "Get up."

The Ghost lowered Celeste's head gently to the ground and stood, shakily, flinching at the pain in his wounded leg. He felt woozy and light-headed from the loss of blood. But his anger burned deeply and fiercely. This was the man who had killed Celeste. This was the man who had taken everything dear to him and dashed it on the ground, who had murdered and taunted and wounded and worse.

The Ghost no longer cared if he lived or died; didn't know if he could continue without Celeste. He stared at the Roman with such a look of menace on his face that the mob boss actually took a step backward, before planting his feet firmly on the ground and stabbing the gun forward so that its barrel was pressing against the vigilante's stomach.

"What would be a fitting death, do you think, for a man as troublesome as you? The gallows? Poison? The guillotine? To tell you the truth, I haven't the patience left to decide. So I'll settle for a bullet in the gut, just like your little lady." The Roman sneered, glancing down at the dead woman by his feet.

The Ghost moved like lightning, striking whilst the other man was gloating. He swept his arm up and out, sending the gun clattering to the ground a few feet from where they were standing. Then he raised his fist and struck the man hard across the face, sending him spinning backward to the floor. Blinded by rage, the Ghost rushed forward, ignoring the screaming pain in his leg, intent only on one goal. He reached down, hauling the Roman up by his collar. He struck him again, then again, and then lost count of the number of times his fists pounded into the man's face, channeling all of his rage, all of his hurt, years' worth of pent-up anger and confusion and aggression into each blow. Tears streamed from his eyes as he beat the Roman's body to a bloody pulp, and then finally, his knuckles bleeding, he dropped the unconscious man to the ground and fell to his knees, weeping. The Roman's chest was still rising and falling with a bloody, rasping wheeze.

After a moment, the Ghost got to his feet and limped across to where Donovan was stirring. He knelt down beside the inspector and freed his hands, then coaxed him back to consciousness. Donovan had cracked his head against the wall when the tentacle had bowled him over and was sporting a bloody welt from the blow. The Ghost helped him to his feet. "The Roman's still alive. We've got him, Donovan. You should take him to the precinct, throw him in a cell. Today we do it your way."

Donovan nodded his assent, tentatively touching the wound on his head.

His breathing ragged, his chest burning, the Ghost hobbled

over to the mouth of the portal, staring into the bizarre miasma of that other place. It was strangely beautiful, alluring. But the Ghost couldn't see the attraction of living forever. He could barely see the attraction of living at all.

He crossed to the lever and shut off the power. The portal crackled and hissed for a moment and then stuttered out of existence, winking like a dying star. The remaining tentacles, now severed from the rest of the gargantuan body, slumped to the floor amongst the dead. The Ghost reached up and grasped hold of the lip of the marble wheel. Heaving, he shook it loose from its wooden housing and toppled it over, stepping to one side as it crashed to the ground, shattering into a series of jagged fragments.

The Ghost started suddenly at the sharp report of a gun going off. He made to duck, and turned around quickly, whipping his fléchette gun into place. But he saw it was Donovan, standing over the Roman's bloody corpse, a gaping hole in the side of the mobster's head.

"He went for the gun." Donovan met the Ghost's skeptical look with an unwavering gaze, as if challenging him to disagree. Then he shrugged. "Today, my friend, we do it your way."

The Ghost smiled, a sad, lonely smile. He crossed the floor to where he'd laid out Celeste's body on the dirt. He scooped her up, cradling her in his arms. He buried his face in her long auburn hair, drank in her smell for the very last time, kissed her forehead.

"I'm sorry. I know you tried so hard to save her."

The Ghost nodded. His voice cracked as he spoke. "And in the end, Donovan, she was the one who saved me." And he knew the other man could never understand how profoundly true that statement was.

He turned toward the exit, staggering under the extra burden of Celeste's corpse, his wounded leg trailing behind him. Then, at the door, he stopped and glanced back at the inspector, still standing in the middle of the ruination, looking lost and unsure of what he had to do next. "It's over, Donovan. Finished. Go back to your wife. Tell her you love her, get blindingly drunk, and make passionate love to her. Then go and get that shoulder checked out at the hospital. This never happened." He offered the inspector a meaningful look. "You understand? It could never happen."

Donovan nodded. "I suppose tomorrow the place will be mysteriously gutted by a fire?"

The Ghost looked sanguine. "Something like that. Perhaps after Arthur's had a chance to take a look at the contents of that room full of treasures. The Roman owes him that much." He reached up, brushing the hair from Celeste's pale face. "Come on. Time to go home."

Donovan dropped his gun beside the Roman's corpse and followed behind the vigilante. "Do you... would you like some help? With Celeste, I mean."

The Ghost shook his head. This was one burden he intended to carry alone.

TWENTY FOUR

From the drawing room, Gabriel Cross could hear the sounds of people carousing merrily in the garden; men and women engaging in that perpetual game of courting, daring each other to make a drunken pass, each of them wishing they only had the gumption to do it themselves. The Johnson & Arkwright Filament had been stoked and the swimming pool was steaming in the cold winter afternoon. Ariadne and her cohorts had congregated in the water, looking cold despite themselves, but steadfastly refusing to admit it.

The party went on. The party always went on. The party was life, in some abstract fashion; he needed the party like he needed air, and he could give it up only so much as he could give up breathing, even if both of them proved painful. The party was necessary. It reminded him of what he had, and what he had lost. It reminded him of who he was.

Gabriel looked up, watching the revelers through the window with a sad smile on his face. He knew what Celeste would have said. But Celeste wasn't there any longer, buried now in his family mausoleum. He'd tried to trace some of her family—that elusive, unusual family she had spoken of—but his search had proved fruitless, and so instead he had given her a space amongst his long-dead relatives in the grounds of the old house. He knew she would have enjoyed the irony of that.

He hoped her family would be proud of what she'd done; what she'd sacrificed. She'd been true to herself to the last, true to him, also. He loved her for that. Loved her for her tenacity, for her passion, for her sultry smile and her honesty. She'd known him for who he truly was, known him better even than he knew himself. He owed it to her now to live that life, to embrace what she had taught him about himself, to be done with pettiness and vengeance. He had a job to do, and he would do it. He would do it for her, and he would do it for the people of New York.

Gabriel realized he'd been toying with the controls of an electrical device on the windowsill as he stared out at the party. He looked down. It was the bastardized holotube terminal from his Manhattan apartment, the one he'd turned into a recording device in an attempt to capture Celeste.

He flicked the switch, waited for the unit to warm up. And there she was, perfect in her long, clinging dress, her hair pinned up to one side, swinging her hips gently as she caressed the microphone. She parted her lips to sing, and her voice echoed out around the room, drowning out the revelers' voices, drowning out the ache in his wounded leg, drowning out everything but the hole in his heart where Celeste used to be. He flicked the switch and she stuttered to a stop, fading out to nothing in the mirrored cavity of the small box. Tears were streaming down his cheeks.

He wiped his eyes with the back of his hand. Celeste wouldn't have wanted this. He leaned back in his day chair and steadied his breathing. Then, reaching for a cigarette, he pulled the tab and took a long pull of nicotine, feeling it flood into his lungs.

He heard someone calling his name from the garden and looked up. His people needed him. He pulled himself to his feet and straightened his rumpled suit.

He had an appointment in the city later. But for now, Gabriel Cross had a party to attend to, and that was exactly what he intended to do.

From the roof of the precinct building, the Ghost could see half of Manhattan, lit up like a fairy tale, doused in starlight and wonder. He looked out across the rooftops as if he were a lion surveying its territory. A police dirigible floated high overhead, its searchlights crisscrossing the sidewalks below.

Beside the Ghost, Felix Donovan stood in the gloaming, his shoulder now expertly strapped and healing, the wound on his head slowly beginning to mend. The man had been lauded as a hero for his role in bringing down the Roman, and while the Commissioner had not been pleased to hear that Donovan had taken to working on his own, leaving his sergeant behind to clean up his mess, he couldn't fault the man's results.

Of course, as far as the Commissioner was concerned, Donovan still had his work cut out; there was a vigilante loose in the city, and the inspector had been tasked with bringing him in. Somehow, the Ghost knew that Donovan wasn't about to repeat his recent success. At least, not any time soon.

"How are you, Gabriel?" The concern was evident in Donovan's voice.

The Ghost turned away from the view, regarding the

inspector from beneath the brim of his new hat. "Well enough, Donovan. Well enough. What about you? How's Flora?"

Donovan smiled. "I took your advice. Let's just say we're enjoying each other's company, more than we have in years."

They both laughed.

"It feels kind of empty, doesn't it?"

The Ghost ceased his laughing and met his friend's gaze. "Yes. I know what you mean. I've never been good at sitting by whilst the world keeps turning."

Donovan looked as if he was about to speak when he suddenly stopped and looked up. A dead bird was plummeting out of the sky, its broken, mangled wings fluttering aimlessly as it dropped onto the gravel rooftop nearby. Its body made hardly a sound as it landed.

Both men approached the bizarre corpse, stooping to take a look. It was just like the others the Ghost had seen all over Manhattan, and in his Long Island garden.

Donovan shrugged. "What is it with all these dead birds?"

The Ghost looked up. He caught a glimpse of a strange object in the sky, distant now, buzzing away over the rooftops. It glinted in the reflected light of the city; made of brass, about the size of a human being. He pointed it out to Donovan. "I have no idea. But judging by that, I think it's high time we found out."

Donovan grinned. He watched as the Ghost charged toward the lip of the building, launching himself into the air, his rocket boosters igniting as they fired him away on a bright plume of flame, his trench coat flapping open behind him like a shadowy pair of wings.

ABOUT THE AUTHOR

George **Mann** was born in Darlington and has written numerous books, short stories, novellas and original audio scripts. *The Affinity Bridge*, the first novel in his Newbury and Hobbes Victorian fantasy series, was published in 2008. Other titles in the series include *The Osiris Ritual*, *The Immorality Engine*, *The Executioner's Heart*, *The Casebook of Newbury & Hobbes* and the forthcoming *The Revenant Express*.

His other novels include *Ghosts of Manhattan*, *Ghosts of War*, and the forthcoming *Gods of Karnak* and *Ghosts of Empire*, mystery novels about a vigilante set against the backdrop of a post-steampunk 1920s New York, as well as the original Doctor Who novels, *Paradox Lost* and *Engines of War*, the latter featuring the War Doctor alongside his companion, Cinder.

He has edited a number of anthologies, including *Encounters of Sherlock Holmes*, *Further Encounters of Sherlock Holmes*, *The Solaris Book of New Science Fiction* and *The Solaris Book of New Fantasy*, and has written two Sherlock Holmes titles for Titan Books, *Sherlock Holmes: The Will of the Dead* and *Sherlock Holmes: The Spirit Box*.

Occasionally he finds time to breathe.

GHOSTS OF WAR

GEORGE MANN

New York City is being plagued by a pack of ferocious brass raptors, strange creations with bat-like wings that swoop out of the sky, carrying their victims away into the night. The originator of these skeleton-like creations is a deranged military scientist, who is also part of a plot to escalate the cold war with Britain into a full-blown conflict. He is building a weapon – a weapon that will fracture dimensional space and allow the monstrous creatures that live on the other side to spill through – and only the Ghost and his unlikely allies can stop him.

AVAILABLE MARCH 2015

GHOSTS OF KARNAK

GEORGE MANN

Things are quiet in New York. Unusually quiet. The Ghost knows that something's wrong. Something's going to give. When an expedition returns from Cairo to exhibit their finds at the Metropolitan Museum of Art, Gabriel takes a keen interest. Ginny, an old friend and lover, was part of the expedition, but something's not quite right with her. Something that's related to a strange cult known as The Circle of Thoth, a baboon with a clockwork eye, dust devils on Fifth Avenue, robed assassins, sacrificial rites, a 'resurrection machine' and a ghostly figure clad in trailing bandages, seen floating over the rooftops of the city...

AVAILABLE OCTOBER 2015

GHOSTS OF EMPIRE

GEORGE MANN

In the aftermath of the events surrounding the Circle of
Thoth, Gabriel takes Ginny to London by airship to
recuperate. But he isn't counting on coming face-to-face
with a man who claims to embody the spirit of Albion
itself, sinister forces gathering in the London Underground
and an old ally – the British spy, Peter Rutherford – who
could desperately use his help.

AVAILABLE OCTOBER 2016

THE CASEBOOK OF NEWBURY & HOBBES

GEORGE MANN

A collection of short stories detailing the supernatural steampunk adventures of detective duo, Sir Maurice Newbury and Miss Veronica Hobbes in dark and dangerous Victorian London. Along with Chief Inspector Bainbridge, Newbury & Hobbes will face plague revenants, murderous peers, mechanical beasts, tentacled leviathans, reanimated pygmies, and an encounter with Sherlock Holmes.

THE REVENANT EXPRESS
A NEWBURY & HOBBES INVESTIGATION

GEORGE MANN

Following their bloody encounter with the beautiful but deadly Executioner, Sir Maurice Newbury's assistant Veronica Hobbes is close to death, her heart removed and replaced with an unstable mechanism. Desperate to save her life, Newbury and Veronica's sister Amelia board the immense *L'Esprit du Paris*, a sleeper train bound for St. Petersburg, in the hope that the illustrious Gustav Faberge might have the answer. But Newbury's enemies are also on board. As they steam across Europe, Newbury and Amelia must do battle with an outbreak of vicious revenants, a cultist who is determined to reclaim a stolen item, and a figure from Veronica's past, a woman hell-bent on revenge...

AVAILABLE AUGUST 2015

SHERLOCK HOLMES
THE SPIRIT BOX

GEORGE MANN

Summer, 1915. As Zeppelins rain death upon the rooftops of London, eminent members of society begin to behave erratically: a Member of Parliament throws himself naked into the Thames after giving a pro-German speech to the House; a senior military advisor suggests surrender before feeding himself to a tiger at London Zoo; and a famed suffragette suddenly renounces the women's liberation movement and throws herself under a train. In desperation, an aged Mycroft Holmes sends to Sussex for the help of his brother, Sherlock.

DID YOU ENJOY THIS BOOK?
We love to hear from our readers. Please email us at:
readerfeedback@titanemail.com

To receive advance information, news, competitions, and exclusive offers
online, please sign up for the Titan newsletter on our website:

TITANBOOKS.COM

Follow us on Twitter:

@TITANBOOKS